KU-009-887

# BELLE
# ÉPOQUE

MERTHYR TYDFIL COLLEGE

32023

# BELLE ÉPOQUE

ELIZABETH ROSS

HOT
KEY
BOOKS

First published in Great Britain in 2013 by Hot Key Books
Northburgh House, 10 Northburgh Street, London EC1V 0AT

First published in the US in 2013 by Delacorte Press

Text copyright © Elizabeth Ross 2013

The moral rights of the author have been asserted.

All rights reserved.
No part of this publication may be reproduced, stored or transmitted in
any form by any means, electronic, mechanical, photocopying or otherwise,
without the prior written permission of the publisher.

All characters in this publication are fictitious and any resemblance to real
persons, living or dead, is purely coincidental.

A CIP catalogue record for this book is available from the British Library.

Paperback ISBN: 978-1-4714-0208-1


1


Typeset by Palimpsest Book Production Limited, Falkirk, Stirlingshire
This book is typeset in 10.5pt Berling LT Std

Printed and bound by Clays Ltd, St. Ives Plc

**FSC**

Hot Key Books supports the Forest Stewardship Council (FSC),
the leading international forest certification organisation, and is committed
to printing only on Greenpeace-approved FSC-certified paper.

www.hotkeybooks.com

Hot Key Books is part of the Bonnier Publishing Group
www.bonnierpublishing.com

There are two ways of spreading light:
to be the candle or the mirror that reflects it.
—*Edith Wharton*

# Chapter 1

"Perfect, just perfect," says the stout man.

He scrutinizes me, his suit pinching across his rotund torso, and I assume that this is Monsieur Durandeau, but he doesn't introduce himself. Instead he walks around me in a circle as I stand still and awkward in the middle of the sitting room. A faint perfume lingers in the air.

*Perfect*: no one has ever described me like that before.

I glance down at my grubby hem and scuffed boots. What I see is a stray, a runaway—just another waif on the streets of Paris.

A younger man, tall and handsome, with a square jaw and waves of brown hair, pops his head around the door.

"Laurent, come in." Durandeau beckons him over and nods toward me. "What do you think?"

The young man approaches and looks at me like he's sizing up a prize heifer. This is supposed to be an interview, but neither of them is asking me questions—am I a hard worker, can I cook or sew? They haven't even asked my name. I think back to the job notice, now crumpled in my pocket.

Young women wanted for undemanding work.
Propriety guaranteed.

1

I assumed the work would be like any other position offered to a young woman without connections—washing linens, starching collars, scouring pots and pans. But now a buzzing fly of doubt pesters me.

The younger man gives his appraisal. "Not spectacular." He pauses. "Perhaps for the Dubern contract?"

"Exactly!" Durandeau bellows. "Remember, the countess asked for a light ornamentation. You don't want to deck out a debutante like a society matron."

A countess? I look from one man's face to the other, trying to fathom what it is they think I'm perfect for, and decide that somewhere I must have lost the thread of conversation. My stomach growls and my eyes dart from theirs. I'm feeling woozy; no wonder I'm confused. I have started to skimp on food the last few days. It's only been a few weeks since I arrived in Paris and I've already spent most of my francs on a dingy garret room. Turns out running away was the easy part; it's struggling to get by day in, day out, that's hard. Maybe I should have stayed in the village and accepted the fate Papa arranged for me. I wouldn't be hungry, that's for sure, not as the butcher's wife. I salivate imagining the goose, pheasant and duck hanging in Monsieur Thierry's shop. But then I think of my supposed husband—not a day under forty, with hammy forearms and a dangerous smile.

"Yes, I think she'll do nicely," Durandeau says, bringing his hands together in a decisive clap, which causes his double chin to tremble. "We'll show her at noon. See what the countess says."

Standing silently, I can't help but take my own inventory of Monsieur Durandeau. I'm reminded of a pigeon: his short legs strain to hold that barrel of a body, and his fat chest puffs out of a pearly satin waistcoat.

After Laurent is dismissed, Durandeau finally finds his manners. "What is your name, young lady?"

"Maude Pichon." My voice is husky, I've been quiet so long.

"Pichon . . . what kind of name is that?" he asks. "Where are you from?"

"Poullan-sur-Mer." He looks doubtful, so I elaborate. "It's a village in Brittany."

"That would explain the accent, but we can work on that."

I can feel the hackles of my Breton pride quiver. "What's wrong with my accent?"

But he answers my question by posing another. "What age are you? Sixteen, seventeen?"

"Sixteen, monsieur."

He nods. "And your parents?"

"My parents are dead." A half lie; my father might as well be dead to me. I cannot go back home. Not only did I thwart his marriage plans for me, I stole all the money in the shop till. It seemed like a fortune at the time, but everything in Paris costs more than I could have imagined.

"How tragic," he says insincerely. "So you read one of our announcements. We haven't had much luck with them. More delicate phrasing was required, in retrospect."

3

The job notice was thin on information, but work is work—how flowery should a help wanted notice be?

"Now we have Laurent as a recruiter of sorts. He's charming and sympathetic. We've had much better results that way."

His ambiguous statements bother me, and I finally muster some courage. "Monsieur, what is the job exactly?" I ask.

"The pay is more than fair," he continues, ignoring me. "We'll provide you with an adequate wardrobe. I'll send you down the corridor to our seamstress, Madame Leroux. She should be able to get you something more appropriate to wear before the clients arrive." He wrestles a five-franc coin from his pocket and presses it into my hand. "Welcome to the agency," he says.

I forget my unanswered questions as I stare at the gold coin in my palm. My spirits lift. I have the job? I'm delighted and dumbfounded at the ease of this feat as Durandeau ushers me out of the salon and down the corridor at a march.

Madame Leroux is mumbling to herself as she picks stitches out of the sleeve of a dress. Piles of fabric and dresses in various stages of repair or creation hang around the room. Spools of different-colored thread are stacked precariously like tiers of wedding cake. She uses her teeth to bite at some unwieldy stitch.

"No way to run a business . . . making fine dresses out of cheap material." She tuts and glances up at me, as though the choice of material is my fault. Her hair is wild and unkempt; the strands falling into her eyes like my father's draft horse. Tutting again, she puts down her work and approaches me.

"Let's have a look at you. Arms out." She takes out her tape measure and wraps it around my various dimensions in practiced strokes. "You're thin as a whip. Do we have anything you won't drown in?"

Self-conscious, I look away. I've always been slim, and despite the culinary reputation of the city, I've shed weight since coming to Paris.

She walks toward a rail of hanging dresses and begins to flip through them. I crane my neck to see. "Why do I have to change my clothes?" I ask.

Madame Leroux stops and turns to look at me, affronted. "We can't have you representing the agency in that!" She nods to my simple navy dress and continues looking for a replacement. I squeeze the coin Durandeau gave me and let my mind wander. Working for a countess, I'm probably going to serve in a great house as a maid, or maybe as a governess. Then it strikes me that the dresses hanging on the rack don't fit this fantasy. They're not made of practical cotton or wool in hues of gray or black. Instead they're colorful and fancy, made of satin and taffeta.

"These clothes don't look like uniforms, madame," I say, curious to get a hint as to my new position.

She turns around, pink-faced and triumphant, brandishing a dark green velvet dress with puffed sleeves. "That's because they're all one of a kind, silly. There's nothing uniform about my dresses." Her response doesn't shed any light.

She ties me into a corset, which feels like a punishment.

5

Then a bustle, like a tail, is fitted around my hips. I step into the skirt and the seamstress helps me with the bodice, making quick work of the umpteen tiny buttons. She nudges me toward the mirror and my face falls when I see how the color of the dress drains my complexion. I imagine what my mother would think. She loved clothes—not that she got to wear fine things working at the village store. I remember the chenille cloak she would wear to church, and I have a recollection of a calico print at a picnic. If she were alive and here right now, I'm positive she wouldn't have picked this dress. With their exaggerated poufs, the sleeves make my shoulders look broad; my nonexistent chest is flattened to oblivion. I turn to the side and see that the bustle has added inches to my rear, making my waist look even skinnier. I feel ridiculous.

There is a shuffling of feet outside the seamstress's room and I hear women's voices floating by. "You'd better get a move on and join them in the salon," says Madame Leroux. "Just one finishing touch." She opens a jewelry box and fishes out a hideous swan brooch. It's gaudy for my tastes, but maybe I don't understand Paris fashion. She pins the brooch to my dress with a grin, eyes twinkling through her faded wisps of hair.

I look once more at my reflection and decide that she couldn't have tried harder to make me look a fright. And then a dark realization begins to creep and spread like spilled ink on white parchment. I blot it out of my head.

The chorus of women's chatter rises as I approach the salon, and nerves dance in my chest. I take a quick breath and push open the mahogany door. There must be at least twenty women and girls squeezed into the room. Every seat is taken as I step around them to find space. I feel conspicuous in the new dress. A couple of women give me sidelong glances; they can't be judging my outfit too harshly, for it looks like they've also been subjected to Madame Leroux's handiwork. I'm uncertain where I should position myself until a pudgy, red-faced woman gives me a smile. I smile back, noting that her putrid, mustard-colored dress is worse than mine. I stand beside her. Maybe by comparison I look less terrible.

A trill of laughter turns my attention to the door. Durandeau enters with two rich-looking society ladies, and a hush falls over the room. My new colleagues freeze and remain motionless, staring into the distance. I study the rich ladies, who look like dolls—painted, perfect and delicate—at home in a well-furnished room. They walk among us slowly and with a deliberate ease. One lady is wearing a striking black and white dress. Her dark hair is rolled in a tight chignon. Her expression is self-satisfied: the cat that got the cream. The other lady's gown is iridescent pink like the lining of a shell. She has an easy laugh and keeps catching her reflection in the mirror over the fireplace. Durandeau scampers between them like an excited spaniel.

"Madame Vary." Durandeau addresses the lady in pink. "I have just the thing for you this week." He draws her attention to a woman with a hook nose and pointy chin. "This one's severe profile will greatly accentuate your perfect proportions."

Madame Vary steps toward my unattractive colleague, scrutinizing her closely.

Durandeau turns to the lady in black and white. "Countess Dubern, your fine eyes would captivate next to the piggy eyes of this one."

I flinch at Durandeau's words. The countess merely flashes a smile at his suggestion. The salon women remain stoic, and I'm shocked. Why don't they react to these insults?

"Madame Vary," the countess calls to her friend. "Look at me with this one? What do you think, better than the one I rented last week?"

"They're both so hideous I can't decide," Madame Vary says. "Although maybe the piggy one shows off your figure better."

That unwelcome thought is pushing through again. Panicked, I scan the room, taking in the faces of my new colleagues, until it hits me. The women differ in age, height, shape and coloring, but they do share one common characteristic: they are all, without exception, extremely unattractive—some outright ugly. My cheeks blaze; my heart combusts with shame at the realization that *I am one of them*.

Durandeau spies me across the room and breaks into a trot.

"Now, Countess, here's what I thought for your daughter." He gestures for me to come forward. "A light ornamentation of plainness. She would complement Isabelle very nicely, I think. Nothing too flashy for her Paris debut at the Rochefort ball."

I do as he says and step forward, gripping the folds of my dress. The countess glides toward me with a languid step. She is beautiful and imposing, like an actress on stage.

Durandeau continues dissecting me. "Note her hair, the color of wet straw; the upturned nose; the tarnish of freckles on the complexion; and the unremarkable eyes—bovine in expression, dull in color. Lastly the bony angles of the figure."

My heart, recovered from its initial shame, is now pierced by the barbs of his words—this inventory, this list of human flaws, *my* flaws, so casually delivered.

Her eyes smirk as she looks me up and down. "Yes, I think she'll do. It's hard to tell until we see them side by side."

Durandeau claps his hands. "Perfect. I will arrange a meeting once we've finished with her training. It's a match, I'm sure."

"You're red as a beet, *ma pauvre*!" My mustard colleague is grinning at me. I don't respond. I can't move, much less speak. Durandeau, the countess and Madame Vary have since quit the salon, and the women around me have picked up their conversations again. No one else looks bothered by the preceding selection process.

"Countess took quite a shine to you, eh?" Mustard goes on.

I look at her, aghast. "What is this job?"

She places a hand on her ample hip. "We are repoussoirs, of course. No one told you?"

I hesitate. "Repoussoir? I don't understand." But then it dawns on me. Could the name come from the verb *repousser*? To push away, to repel or repulse. "Re-pou-ssoir," I repeat. It stings when I roll the syllables over my tongue. The notion is impossible to absorb. "We are meant to repel, to repulse?" I say, horrified.

Mustard chortles. "Just your luck, getting singled out the

9

first day." She takes my arm and guides me across the salon, following the others, who are filing out of the room. "This way, *ma grande*. The dining room's just next door. Looks like you haven't seen a hot meal in a while."

Food is the least of my considerations as I'm led along the hallway with the train of salon women and girls. The only thing I can think of is getting out of this place. I pull away from her hold on my arm. "No, no, I can't. I have to be on my way now. I just came for the interview."

I can smell lunch; a waft of meat stew makes my stomach clench and burn with emptiness. I can hear the clatter of cutlery, the clink of glasses and the scraping of chairs. Under any other circumstances, I would welcome a free meal—but not here.

"Did Laurent recruit you?" she asks. "Handsome devil, isn't he? I would have signed up for the Prussian front if he'd asked me!" She lets out a snort of laughter.

My head is spinning and I can barely concentrate on my surroundings. I wish she'd stop asking me questions. "No, I saw a notice in the paper." The announcement—my mind's racing back to the wording of it. How could I have misunderstood?

"Well, that's bold of you. I like that. Yes, you'll fit in soon enough. Not all the younger ones make it past training."

I'm appalled; I'm not like her. I'm not like any of them.

She goes on. "I can tell you're made of stronger stuff. Or you will be, once we fatten you up a bit!"

I press my hands into my stomach, trying to suppress the cavernous growling. The temptation of food threatens to overcome my sense of pride.

"I can't stay. But thank you." I take a step back from the entrance to the dining room. I'm jostled and bumped as I push against the last girls heading for their lunch. "I really have to be going."

"It's rabbit stew today. Sure we can't convince you?"

"No, thank you. I'm not hungry."

She looks at me with pity, as if she can see through me. "Well then, until next time." She smiles kindly.

I nod a goodbye and practically fly down the corridor back to the seamstress's little room. I knock on the door and poke my head in. It's empty—thankfully. Trembling with hunger and humiliation, I wrestle my way out of the dress; the buttons on the back force me into some contortionist moves. I just want this damn thing off. Nothing helps me unlace the corset any faster, but what if that awful little man charges in here demanding his five francs back? That's food for a week. I can almost taste what I'll spend the money on: crusty baguette, salty ham and tangy mustard, washed down with a bowl of thick hot chocolate so rich I have to scoop out the dregs with a spoon.

I leave the borrowed clothes in a heap on the worktable—I don't care to hang anything up. Pulling my own dress over my head, I feel safe and like myself again. I slide a hand into the pocket of my dress and feel the weight of the gold coin and wonder: if I keep the money and never come back, is it stealing?

So what if it is. I decide it's compensation for the most humiliating experience of my life. Nestled in my pocket next to the coin is the job notice. I take it out, smoothing the crumpled newspaper. Where I ripped the page, I can see that the first word has been cut off. On the edge of the tear I can make out the letters $l$ and $y$. I fill in the missing letters myself.

UGLY YOUNG WOMEN WANTED FOR UNDEMANDING WORK.
PROPRIETY GUARANTEED.
APPLY IN PERSON TO THE DURANDEAU AGENCY,
27 AVENUE DE L'OPÉRA, PARIS.

# Chapter 2

Brigitte marches up to me across the black and white tiled floor. She's brandishing a shirt I ironed, and her narrow eyes are fixed on me. I look down, anticipating her reproach.

"Is this how they do things where you're from?" I glance up to see her pinched face. "Look at this." She's shaking the shirt at me. "As creased as my gran's face. You're in Paris now, mademoiselle, and we do things properly at Bromont Laundry."

I put the pile of linen I was sorting to one side and take back the shirt without complaint. Her *grand-mère* must have the smoothest complexion in Paris. But I have learned the hard way that arguing with my new colleagues makes things more difficult. I keep my head down, work hard and say little.

Brigitte stalks back to her linen. I smooth out the offending shirt and pick up the iron, carefully pressing the garment a section at a time. My colleagues are as hard on me as the soap and hot water are on my skin. Agnès, Brigitte and Clémence remind me of the squawky hens we used to keep when I was little. They are as thick as thieves, and pecking at me has become the highlight of their day. They like to spend their time gossiping, making me bear the brunt of the work. I can hear Clémence launching into one of her stories now.

"So I saw this *beau mec* at the dance hall." All her stories begin like this. "So I says to him, I says . . ." And continue like this. I shut out their chatter, which is as rough as their chapped hands.

Hot steam rises into my face as I press the shirt. In the two weeks I've worked here I've realized that a Parisian laundry is tantamount to a torture chamber—my muscles ache and I have burns on my arm from the iron and a staved finger from the wringer handle. It's hot and stuffy, with no end to the constant cycle of wash, dry, iron and fold. The vast room is populated with piles of dirty laundry, clean white linens strung up to dry and racks of ironed sheets ready to be sorted and returned to their owners. A system of pipes runs overhead like bars of a cage; it connects the sinks to a water source. Permanent condensation fogs up the windows. Even if I could see out, there's only a view of the alley and no time to daydream.

Upholding my resolution not to return to the agency of ugly dresses and uglier people, I set about trying to find an honest job. I thought with my experience in our village store that I would easily find work in one of the thousands of Paris shops. But after being turned away from shop after shop, I realized that young girls dressed in country clothes with no letters of reference can't sell chic fashions or fancy cakes. Underneath the lack of experience, the real deficiency I felt was the shame of the Durandeau interview. The memory taunted me, weighing down my confidence. I'd rather be an invisible worker than be thought of as ugly.

I hear a chorus of cackles from across the room. The coven breaks apart and they retreat to their chores. Brigitte saunters over to me and dumps a basket of clean laundry on my ironing table. I've finished re-pressing the shirt and carefully fold it in front of her, aware of her studying me.

"Maude, take this basket of linens to Restaurant l'Académie on rue de Rennes."

Respite from the henhouse. I nod briefly, trying not to look as relieved as I feel. Picking up the basket, I move swiftly to the door. I grab my shawl from the row of hooks and throw it around my shoulders.

"And remember to take back the dirty linen while you're at it," Brigitte calls after me.

"Yes, I will," I reply, my voice betraying a quiver of enthusiasm as I grasp the door handle.

It's late afternoon, when the sun is golden and casts long lilac shadows across the neighborhood of Montparnasse. After the monotone white and gray of the laundry, the outside world is a vibrant rainbow of color and light. I ended up living in this area because it's the arrondissement surrounding the train station where I first set foot. I didn't realize it was a hub of artists and writers. That doesn't mean that it's beautiful or that inspiration hangs on every tree; it just means the rent is cheap.

My basket is full. I hoist it on my hip like a heavy child and navigate the street, which is teaming with omnibuses, carriages and pedestrians. I walk past the butcher, who's taking down a brace of pheasants, and a flash of Monsieur Thierry gives me a shudder. A florist throws a pail of dirty water in the gutter and I skip out of the way, almost taking a tumble on the slippery cobblestones. I reposition the basket—the hens would have my guts for garters if I let the clean linen fall in the grimy street.

Restaurant l'Académie is a small neighborhood bistro, which sits between a barber's and a bookshop. A group of men is crammed into the small terrace out front, smoking cigars, enjoying the mild afternoon. There is a collection of wine bottles and glasses littering the tables; they must have been there a while.

"*Excusez-moi, excusez-moi,*" I say, trying to get to the door. They are all talking at once and oblivious to my presence. I lift the basket above my head to squeeze past their chairs.

When I enter the establishment, it takes a moment for my eyes to adjust to the dark room. The walls are papered a deep red and lined with paintings and bookshelves. The restaurant is empty apart from a waiter drying glasses behind the bar, a cigarette hanging from his mouth.

I walk over with a smile. "Linen delivery." I'm glad the trip wasn't farther; my arms are starting to ache, and the basket keeps sliding down my side.

He looks up and shakes his head at me. "Service entrance!"

"Pardon me?" I ask.

"Go around back, you idiot," he says.

I can feel the flush of warmth on my face. "I didn't know, I'm sorry."

"The front door is for customers only," he snaps.

Does he have to be so rude? I hike the basket up onto my hip and retrace my steps. There aren't even any customers inside—what does it matter which entrance I use? I fling open the door roughly, feeling the sting of Parisian manners.

"*Excusez-moi*," I say again to the men sprawling across the terrace. Again I am ignored.

The gentleman nearest me rises from his chair to argue with his friend. "Nonsense, Claude. This is the reason that the Second Empire's policies haven't changed today—the poor in their place and the rich getting richer."

While he's standing, I manage to nudge his empty chair aside with my foot and slip past. But then suddenly their political argument changes into a chorus of laughter and I spin around to see that the young man who just stood is now picking himself up off the floor. I gasp, realizing that it was my fault.

"*Je suis désolée*, monsieur," I say immediately.

He gets up, dusts off his jacket, then sits down. "Take the laundress." He points at me. "Thin as a rail. Barely making subsistence wages."

"Let's buy her some supper!" says another man.

Before I know what's happening, a man with a cigar pulls me toward him and with an abrupt lurch I'm sitting on his lap, my basket dropped on the floor.

"Have a drink with us," he says, locking his arms around me. I'm utterly repulsed. He smells like fried liver and onions.

"*Laissez-moi!*" I say, tugging at his arm. "Let me go!"

"*Garçon!*" he shouts. "A brandy for the washer girl." His breath is saturated with alcohol, and the overpowering smell burns my nostrils. I pull away from his face, but his grip around my waist is strong and I can't break free.

The waiter appears on the terrace. "*S'il vous plaît, messieurs*." His arms flap around like an orchestra conductor.

"*Je suis vraiment désolé*. She should not have imposed herself on you."

His words go unheeded and I begin to feel a surge of panic. I thrash my body forward, finally wrenching myself free from the drunk man, bumping into the table and knocking a glass of red wine smack into my basket of perfectly clean starched white tablecloths. Disaster.

I pounce on the basket, frantically pulling out the linen on top, trying to prevent the wine from soaking through to the layers beneath. The spreading stain is like a seal on my fate. I will surely be sacked for this, and then what? Will I have to beg or steal to live? I look up at the cigar man who grabbed me, and he is laughing. A well of anger rises from my gut.

"Have you nothing better to do than sit about and get drunk all afternoon?" I glance at the ruined tablecloths in my arms, pristine only moments ago. "Some of us have to work for a living, as pathetic as that might sound."

"Oh, *la bretonne*," says the cigar man on hearing my accent, which is stronger when I'm riled up. "What fighting words! My esteemed friends and I are actually trying to effect some change for the proletariat such as yourself."

"Cut it out, Claude," says a voice, and the young man whose chair I kicked aside approaches. He pulls a handkerchief from his pocket and offers it to me.

"*Merci*," I say, accepting it. I can't do much for the linen, but I use it to wipe my sticky hands.

The waiter grabs the basket of laundry. "Follow me," he says gruffly through his mustache. Trembling with anger, I follow the waiter through the door meant only for customers, across the restaurant and into the back kitchen. A cook is chopping vegetables and looks me up and down. The waiter removes the few clean tablecloths from the basket, checking for wine stains, and puts them in a cupboard. He picks up a pile of dirty laundry from under the sink and chucks it in my basket; then he grabs the wine-stained bundle from under my arm and adds it to the pile.

"Needless to say, we'll need an extra delivery of clean linen." He takes the basket and shoves it into my arms.

I nod feebly. What excuse can I invent to explain this to the hens?

"Next time, go around back. You're not much to look at, but when the customers drink that much wine, they're not choosy!"

The waiter gestures to the back door. I flee with my basket and stumble into the alley. My heart is thumping and my eyes prickle with tears and the stench of rotting food. I march away from the restaurant, not sure which direction I'm heading. Those men are just like gulls on the beach squawking at each other. They bicker and posture, and meanwhile, the ocean continues its endless back-and-forth, regardless of their jabbering.

The alley leads me back to the street. It's dusk now; as I walk, streetlamps come on like little orange stars. The evening air cools my temper. I breathe deeply, drinking it in. Then I hear a voice.

"*La bretonne!* Wait." I turn around. The man whose chair I kicked aside is walking briskly toward me. I brace myself, wondering when this ordeal will end.

"Here!" To my surprise he stretches out a hand filled

with francs. "A collection from all of us. The least we can do after we badgered you back there." He smiles. "What's your name?"

My defenses are still up. "I don't need your charity," I say, hoping he can't tell that I'm close to tears. "If only you and your friends had left me alone." My voice is thin and on the verge of cracking. I turn away and keep walking along the street, but he follows beside me. I keep my eyes focused straight ahead and the basket wedged between us. He doesn't say anything, but after a few paces I hear the clink of change and see the francs sitting on top of my pile of linen. I stop walking and look at the money. If the worst happens and I'm fired today, I'll need it. Survival over pride: I scoop up the coins with my free hand and slip them into my dress pocket. "My name is Maude," I say, throwing him a glance.

"Paul Villette." He smiles again.

I'm silent as we walk side by side down the street. His kind gesture makes me feel awkward, as if I owe him something.

"I'm sorry about my friends," he says eventually.

"What are you talking about?" I say harshly. "It was you who singled me out in the first place."

"I didn't realize how much they'd been drinking. Good for you, though, standing up to Claude like that." He breaks into a laugh. "Putting the world to rights is thirsty work where he's concerned."

"The world could do without his help." I steal a look at Paul. Away from his contemporaries, he appears a lot younger. He can't be more than twenty. He has scruffy brown hair

20

escaping from under his hat and a smile that reaches his hazel eyes. His suit is ill-fitting, a bit large for his slender frame, and droopy, as if he hasn't grown into it yet. His tie is loose, as if knotting it was an afterthought on his way out the door, and there are ink stains on his hands. He looks as if he could use a handout more than me.

Paul continues, "They mean well and will feel bad when they sober up." He shakes his head. "Claude needs a telling-off every so often. When we debate politics, it starts off with a civilized lunch and ends in an argument."

I suddenly feel self-conscious walking with this stranger after he witnessed an embarrassing display of emotions from me. I want to explain to him. "I really need this job," I blurt out. "I can't afford to lose it."

"They won't fire you over a few tablecloths, surely?"

"My colleagues aren't very forgiving." I nod to the basket. "Maybe they won't notice that there's more dirty linen than usual."

Dusk has turned to twilight when we reach boulevard du Montparnasse. "I'm going this way." He nods toward rue d'Odessa. "My apologies again, to you and your linen."

He raises his hat. "Come to one of our musical evenings at Café Chez Emile." He points to a café down the street. "More enjoyable than politics!" With a short bow, he turns and walks away.

My gaze follows his figure in the fading light until I realize with a jolt how late it's getting. I turn away and scurry down boulevard du Montparnasse.

When I enter the laundry, the hens are preparing to leave.

21

"Well, it took you long enough," says Agnès. She grabs the basket of dirty linen and to my horror begins sorting it. I can't watch. I look down at the floor; the checkered tiles dance before my eyes.

"Maude, why are there so many tablecloths here?" Agnès turns to me. "Their standing order is only for twenty. What are you trying to pull?"

My heart pounds. "Nothing. I'm not trying to pull anything."

"Don't get smart, mademoiselle," she replies.

"It was an accident," I say feebly. "At the restaurant some wine got spilled on the clean linen." I wait for the inevitable. They will sack me for certain.

"Having a time of it, were you?" Brigitte chimes in, hands on her hips. "Boozing it up with the regulars while we're working our fingers to the bone."

"No, that's not true." I meet their accusing stares.

"They'll want a new delivery of clean ones, I suppose," says Agnès.

Clémence rolls her eyes with disgust. "Dock her pay," she says to the others.

"We already took off what you owe for those singed pillow-cases," says Agnès, shaking her head. "Maude, at this rate *you'll* be paying *us* every week!" They laugh at the prospect, and I'm glad for the francs in my pocket.

"Well, we'll see about the new delivery tomorrow," says Agnès in a softer tone. She pulls a brown envelope from her apron. "Here's your pay," she says, handing it to me. "We can't give you many more chances, Maude."

Momentary relief: I still have a job. But then I feel the

thinness of the envelope and my heart deflates. The hens put on their coats and bonnets and head for the door. Brigitte turns back to me. "Mind, there's still a pile of ironing to be done before you go."

My workmates clatter out the door and I return to my ironing table. I'll be here all night.

It's late and chilly by the time I'm walking back home. The familiar smells of beer, gas lamps and soot are a welcome change from laundry soap. Usually I take my time on the boulevard, looking in the windows of the bars and cafés, watching the endless party, but tonight I'm cold and exhausted. Even so, when I turn onto Odessa my pace slows as I pass Café Chez Emile. I wonder when Paul and his friends have their musical evenings. I peer in the window but don't find his face in the crowd. Instead I catch sight of the woman I have come to call "the poor soul." In her usual spot near the window, she sits alone, her fingers locked around the stem of her glass. Her bonnet is tatty, her expression empty. What were her dreams when she arrived in Paris? Was she a runaway once, like me? I shudder at the thought of ending up like her, swallowed by the city and all alone.

With a sigh I keep walking, then turn down my narrow street, rue Delambre. The main door to my building clangs shut behind me and I find myself standing in near darkness, the light shining from under the concierge's door the only illumination. Dragging myself toward the dim stairwell—my garret room is five flights up—I place my hand on the stone wall, feeling my way a step at a time. My feet are heavy and ache as though a blacksmith has nailed irons to the soles of my boots. Just then I hear a door open on the ground floor behind me and I look down to find the concierge standing silhouetted against a shard of light.

"Mademoiselle Pichon. Rent is due. Tomorrow at the latest. I won't ask again."

"Yes, of course, madame." I keep climbing the stairs, away from her threatening figure. I don't even know—do I have enough to make rent?

Once in my room I can shut the world out; no one can bother me here. I toss my hat and shawl on the bed and take a seat at the wobbly dressing table. I light a candle and open the envelope containing my pay, counting out the francs; just as its paltry weight suggested, I won't have enough for October rent. I fish the francs Paul gave me out of my dress pocket and add them to the pile. Enough for rent but not enough to eat. I've only spent a couple of weeks at the laundry, yet with each day my hands become more flayed and my arms throb worse than the day before. Faces from my past crowd around me: my father, Monsieur Thierry and the rest of the village. *She tried to rise above us*, they sneer, and shake their heads. They want to see me fail. But I won't go home, I won't. I bang my fist on the dressing table. The coins jump. I sweep my arm across the surface, scattering the money to the floor.

Drunken shouts from the street below and the faint strains of cabaret music signal that night in Montparnasse is in full swing. At home the idea of coming here was an escape from life in the village; a daydream I indulged in to while away hours at the shop. I used to imagine that living in a beautiful, cosmopolitan city would rub off on me, that just by being in Paris, I too would become beautiful and cosmopolitan. I coveted this life, dressing it up in layers of fantasy and expectation, and now look at me. What am I to do: sleep on the streets?

I study my reflection in the tarnished mirror. Candlelight flickers and distorts my features, and I wonder what Durandeau saw when he looked at me. My light brown eyes are inoffensive enough. My nose tilts upward, "optimistically," my mother used to tell me with a smile. My lips are thin, my chin juts out—"willfully," my father says. My hair is neither blond nor rich brown, but something in between. And my figure isn't womanly; I'm skinny, with bony shoulders and hips.

I destroyed Durandeau's job notice weeks ago, but the words are still branded into my memory. *Ugly young women wanted for undemanding work.* I have no choice—tomorrow I will return to avenue de l'Opéra. I will become a repoussoir.

# Chapter 3

"You've come back for the job?" Durandeau spits the accusation at me. "Is that what you said? As if you left it here by accident, like an umbrella in a café. And here you stand to claim it."

We're in the dining room of his private apartment at the front of the agency. He is wrapped in a dressing gown, picking at his breakfast. "What do you have to say?"

"No, you misunderstand, monsieur." I shake my head and look pleading. "I wasn't sure if I would be a good fit . . . for the position. At first." My excuse is weak; my voice sounds small. I never imagined I'd have to beg for the job.

"You caused me much embarrassment with the Countess Dubern, vanishing like that. I don't appreciate your ingratitude, Mademoiselle Pichon." Using tiny silver tongs, he picks up a sugar cube and drops it into his coffee.

"An unattractive woman contributes nothing to society. But with my agency she has the chance to use her cursed looks to benefit others." He stirs his coffee. His swollen fingers dwarf the dainty spoon. "I'm not sure that you are deserving of such an opportunity."

I can feel my fate swinging like a pendulum. I'm terrified he's about to say no. "Please, monsieur," I beg.

Durandeau sneers. "It's a delicate balance to be a repoussoir—at first to fit in and be considered a society lady, then to repel the gaze from yourself to your more attractive client."

I nod emphatically, trying to show him I understand perfectly—even though I don't. I have no idea how this awful job works. I just know I need it badly, desperately.

"And to be honest, as a repoussoir you're not a standout," he continues. "You're unremarkable—not the type lots of clients go for." He pauses, his hawkish face searching mine. "Alas, it's not my decision." His words catch me by surprise, and I watch as he leans back in his chair, cradling his bowl of *café au lait*. "I bow to the countess." He sighs. "She chose you for her daughter, and there is still time to train you before the Rochefort ball."

I maintain a contrite expression for his benefit, but inwardly I'm rejoicing—I can live, I can live! He slurps the coffee loudly. "You will be given a base salary during your training. If your first client—in this case the countess's daughter—is satisfied with your services, you will be instated at full pay, which is base salary plus a commission on each assignment you're hired for."

He puts the bowl of coffee on the table, hauls himself out of his chair and belches. He approaches me, tightening the belt of his dressing gown under his expansive gut. He exhales coffee breath and contempt, and I have to restrain myself from gagging. "I have my eye on you, Mademoiselle Pichon."

I force a pleasant smile, realizing the implication of his words—I cannot afford to fail with the countess's daughter. "I will do my best, Monsieur Durandeau."

"Madame Girard!" he barks to the closed door, and moments later a sinewy woman dressed in black enters the room.

"Madame Girard is in charge of training," says Durandeau, returning to his breakfast. "She will deal with you from here."

As Madame Girard approaches, I decide she could pass for a nun. Her mousy hair is scraped into a tight bun, which exaggerates her stern expression—all that's missing is her wimple. She stops in front of me, yet doesn't shake my hand or utter any greeting; she simply gives me a hard stare, then addresses Durandeau.

"I will see to it that she fits in, monsieur."

Durandeau is already consumed by his newspaper. He just snorts in reply, which Madame Girard takes as her cue to show me to the door and usher me into the hallway.

"Follow me." Her tone is curt. "I'm going to take you to the repoussoir dressing room, where you will be assigned a more experienced colleague to mentor you through the training." Her perfunctory tone suggests that she has done this introduction countless times.

She pauses in front of the wall clock, pulls out her watch and checks the time, like a matron taking a patient's pulse. I hear a giggle and look to see a couple of girls lingering in the corridor. "Hortense, Emilie!" Girard shouts. "Get changed at once. There's a client coming at ten." The girls take a quick look at me before hurrying away. Standing here with Girard, I feel like the new girl in school.

"What did Monsieur Durandeau explain to you about

the position?" Girard asks me as we continue our march down the hallway, in the same direction the girls disappeared.

I think back to the countess and her friend looking at the women in the salon like accessories to wear. "To be honest, it doesn't make sense to me," I say cautiously.

She gives a short sigh. "Just as the jeweler places a thin metal foil under a gemstone to make it shine brighter, the agency places a repoussoir next to a society jewel to make her shine."

"Oh," I manage, even though the comparison leaves me clueless. How can my face change the appearance of someone else's?

Girard continues, "You will be given instruction on manners, dining, clothing, grooming and for you in particular, accent reduction." She fastens her eyes to mine. "You need to sound as though you come from Paris, not a pigsty. Do you understand?"

"Yes, Madame Girard."

We arrive at the end of a corridor and enter a noisy room where there must be at least ten or fifteen girls, who immediately stop talking and turn to stare at me. Some are around my age, others in their twenties or thirties; they sit squeezed between dressing tables, mirrors, basins and pitchers of water. Dresses are hanging up around the room, and corsets and bustles are slung over chairs like broken birdcages.

"Marie-Josée," Girard snaps at the woman in mustard I met on the day of my interview. "We can hear your fishwife laugh from the hallway. Comport yourself in a more lady-like way at all times, not just in front of clients."

Marie-Josée smiles, as though welcoming the rebuke. "You could do with a laugh yourself, Madame Girard. Loosen all that stress and responsibility you wear on your face."

I'm impressed at how bold this Marie-Josée woman is in the face of authority. Girard arches a brow and steps toward her. "Don't test my patience."

I watch Marie-Josée's reaction. She smiles lazily, unruffled, and I sense that she has scored a point.

Girard turns to address the rest of the girls. "Ladies, this is Maude Pichon, our newest repoussoir-in-training."

I scan the faces of the occupants of the cramped dressing room and they nod a welcome, smile or say *bonjour*.

"Marie-Josée," Girard says. "As you could do with a refresher of the rules, I'll assign you to be Mademoiselle Pichon's mentor." She surveys the other girls. "There's a client at ten, and training for the new girls at eleven."

After Girard leaves it's as though the room was holding its breath: immediately a rush of air and conversation fills the space. Marie-Josée comes up to me with a broad smile. In her thirties, she's rotund—as wide as she is tall—with a ruddy face, crooked teeth and a bulbous, fleshy nose, but her eyes sparkle.

"Did the skeleton give you one of her speeches?" At my confused look, she explains, "About the job, how did she describe it? Was it the rule of comparisons, Cinderella's stepsisters or the metal foil?"

The chatter subsides. I glance at the others and realize they're watching our exchange. "She said I am like a metal foil and something to do with jewels."

Marie-Josée bursts out laughing and holds out her palm. A few of the other girls reluctantly hand her money. They were taking bets on this?

"How do you always win?" asks a blond girl with heavy jowls and small eyes set too close together.

"I have a talent for guessing Girard's idiosyncrasies." Marie-Josée belts out another laugh as full as her figure.

The piggy blond girl now approaches me. "Didn't you have your interview ages ago? Why didn't you start right away?" Her tone is aggressive, as though she wants to pick a fight.

"Yes, I—you're right," I stammer, trying to think of what to say next.

"Cécile, grab that box of pastries," says Marie-Josée, coming to my rescue. "Unless you're not hungry?"

In a few moments we are all sitting around, the girls draped over the mismatched furniture, sharing the box of pastries. I am introduced to everyone, which involves my smiling a lot and saying *bonjour*. It's awkward between bites of croissant; flakes of pastry stick to my lips and between my teeth. Other than Marie-Josée, the only names I remember are Cécile, because she was mean, and another girl called Hortense because she looks like a horse with her long face and big teeth.

Cécile rips her *pain au chocolat* apart with her fingers. "So did you try to find a better job?" She raises an eyebrow. "Hard to beat the wages here, isn't it?" She pops a strand of pastry in her mouth.

"Leave the new girl alone," says Marie-Josée. "Entertain

us with your latest crush instead. Which client has introduced you to a new dream lover?"

Everyone laughs at Cécile's expense. Marie-Josée winks at me and I smile back. It's hard to believe, but for the first time in weeks I am filled with a sense of relief.

# Chapter 4

Tugged at, buttoned up and pulled apart, I am a muddle of new clothes, uncomfortable shoes and alien manners. Almost a week has passed since my return to the agency, during which time I have learned about the dizzying number of courses at a banquet, how to enter and descend a carriage with decorum, as well as countless other rules. Madame Girard says we have to be convincingly of *their* world—just physically repellent enough to make the client shine in the reflection of our ugliness.

I have also learned how much fun Marie-Josée is. In the dressing room she entertains the girls with outrageous impressions of Girard and Durandeau, and during training she ignores the lectures, pulls out her knitting and whispers gossip about her clients.

"What's the most glamorous assignment you've been on?" I ask her. We're standing in line at the Breton crêpe stand, waiting for our lunch. The agency dining room is serving *langue de boeuf* today. If there's one thing Marie-Josée detests it's beef tongue.

"My favorite assignment? That's easy—Maxim's. I ate a mountain of oysters, followed by the fattest lobster tails swimming in butter."

"Sounds delicious. Makes me hungry to think of it." I watch as the crêpe vendor flips the wafer-thin pancake on the hot-plate, then adds the ham and cheese. "What was the client like?" I ask, then immediately I wish I hadn't. A flash of the countess looking me up and down makes my appetite vanish for a moment.

"High-class. Everything was the best of the best. Including me." She laughs at her own joke. "Not like last night. Usually at les Ambassadeurs, I dance and drink champagne at a table up front. But no, this client had me stuck in the back corner drinking a *tisane*." She shakes her head. "Not a foot set on the dance floor, herbal tea, and my talents wasted."

It amuses me how Marie-Josée feels as though the social whirl involved in being a repoussoir is all for her benefit. She loves to dance and mingle with people.

The vendor folds our crêpes in half, then into quarters, and wraps them in paper. Marie-Josée hands him some coins and continues her pronouncements on agency clients. "Nouveau riche. That's the problem. They have the money but no class—all the trappings of high society but can't quite pull it off."

There are a few wooden benches nearby, and we take a seat. Marie-Josée's corpulent figure takes up most of the bench, so I'm forced to perch on the end.

"I haven't been on a real assignment yet," I say between bites. I can't imagine it, other than with a sense of dread. "Are the rich clients nice?" I ask, curious. "How do they treat you?"

"Like a new fur coat, an accessory of luxury," she says, her mouth full of crêpe. "We're meant to be seen." A string of cheese hangs from her chin. "Not like that one yesterday—I was stuck in the corner listening to her go on about a case of gout. There is an art to wearing a repoussoir. We aren't meant to be a confidante. We're meant to ornament."

I wipe the grease from my mouth with the back of my hand. Her bravado puzzles me. Marie-Josée manages to show utter disdain for the agency and its rulers, Durandeau and Girard. Yet at the same time she maintains an ardent respect for the job and a boastfulness about her capabilities as the agency's finest. She wields this double-edged sword of pride and scorn with equal measure. When I think of what it is that she is proud of, it doesn't make sense. Has she no shame or feelings to hurt? How can she not care that people call her ugly?

She catches me scrutinizing her. "What? Out with it!" she demands.

I hesitate for a moment, choosing my words carefully. "Doesn't it bother you, what the clients think? I mean, the actual reason you're invited to dances and fancy dinners?"

"With all those francs rattling in my purse? No, it certainly does not. They can think I'm the ugliest creature in France as long as I get paid," she laughs. "Do you know how many weeks I'd have to work in a laundry or a café to make what I earn in one *evening* at this lark?"

Strutting by our feet are some pigeons hoping for crumbs. They look like a tribe of Durandeaus, with their murmuring gurgles and beady head cocks. *Perfect, just perfect.* I stamp my feet and the birds scatter. "I suppose you're right. But the repoussoir . . . ," I wonder out loud. "It still seems absurd to me. Does it really work?" Nothing I've learned so far in lessons has made me believe the concept. "Don't society ladies like to be surrounded by pretty things, friends included?"

"Paris society is teeming with attractive women," says Marie-Josée. "How do you stand out? If you're a debutante, you must secure your future husband in a short season of dances, balls and operas. So how do you pull it off?"

I shrug. I have no experience with attracting men, let alone society's finest. "Start by looking your best, I suppose."

"When you've smeared on the rouge, dusted on the powder; when the hair curls to perfection and the most expensive couturiers have dressed you—what then?" she asks.

"But you can't judge a book by its cover," I say. "There's more to someone than appearance. What about the quality of the person you are, or the art of conversation?"

She erupts in a laugh. "Don't be soft! This is Paris. To attract attention, you need an advantage. That's where we come in."

Marie-Josée swallows her last bite of crêpe and rises from the bench. The wooden slats shift underneath me as they are relieved of the heavy load. "Come on, I'll show you," she says.

I follow her through the crowds of afternoon strollers and street vendors until we arrive at a fruit market where rows of canvas-covered stalls contain every type of fruit imaginable. The smell alone makes my mouth water. Marie-Josée stops in front of one stall and points to an overflowing basket of peaches. "Pick the best peach," she says.

I hesitate. "They all look alike."

"Go on," she urges.

I shrug and choose one. "Here." I hold it up. Where is this leading?

Marie Josée is rooting around at the bottom of the basket and finally pulls out her own peach. It's wrinkled and bruised. She takes my peach in one hand and her sorry one in the other. "Which one would you pick?"

"Well, that's easy," I say. It's not even a choice. "The good one, of course."

Marie-Josée's face lights up. "Right. The *good one*. It looks better than it did before! It's gone from ordinary to *good* in a flash. Nothing changed in its appearance—just the company it was keeping."

I'm looking back and forth between the peaches and I realize she's right. She laughs and places the good peach back in the basket, and with a sly glance at the fruit seller she pockets the bruised one. "But now look at the 'good one.' Can you even tell which one it was? That 'perfect' peach blends into the crowd. It looks average again, run-of-the-mill. All those peaches are one and the same."

"Girard's rule of comparisons." Of course! It's a simple concept—people make choices by comparing things all the time. I've seen it with my own eyes; customers in the village shop did it. I never thought it could apply to people too.

The fruit vendor is suddenly looming over us, his weathered face in a scowl.

Marie-Josée acknowledges him casually. "*Une belle journée*, monsieur!" She's naturally pleasant, and I almost forget about the peach in her pocket as we move into the thick of market shoppers.

"The repoussoir is hardly a new idea," she explains. "Those fancy ladies in the old Spanish court would parade around with a monkey on their arm for the same effect. The gall of Durandeau to make a franc out of it is actually to be admired, if he weren't such a slug."

We weave past the market stalls, and Marie-Josée takes my arm as we cross the boulevard, avoiding the carriages and sidestepping some horse manure.

I understand the concept, but it still doesn't add up. "What about the countess?" I ask. "She's already married and beautiful. She doesn't need a repoussoir."

Marie-Josée shakes her head. "*Au contraire!* The countess is the perfect kind of client. Even though she's married, she still wants to be thought of as beautiful. One thing I've learned at the agency time and again is that when an attractive woman sees her beauty fading with her youth, she's going to try anything to cling to it."

The countess is the most beautiful person I've ever seen. How could she be concerned about her looks?

Marie-Josée dips her hand into her pocket and retrieves the ugly peach. She sinks her teeth into it. "Tastes all right to me," she says with a grin, peach juice rolling down her chin. "We are a couple of bruised peaches, Maude!" She laughs heartily.

I know she doesn't mean to, but it hurts when she says that. She may be a bruised peach, but I don't feel that way.

"Maybe I'm just not ripe yet," I say without thinking.

"Oh, of course, *chérie*. Be positive," she replies gamely. "A must in this job." She's smiling, but I suddenly worry

I've offended her. She has accepted what she is—an ugly woman—and I'm trying to shrug off the same label.

We head toward the agency, pushing our way up the avenue against the parade of people and vendors. Marie-Josée, ever the good tour guide, points out a nice café here and a theater with cheap matinees over there. I sense that our time for sharing confidences is over. But I'm still mulling over everything she's said. I'm not ready to be one of life's castoffs, some rich girl's social advantage. I'm worth more than that, surely.

"Enough talking, ladies," says Girard, tapping her cane on the floor to get our attention. As with every lesson, the chairs in the salon are arranged like a school room, all facing the fire-place where Madame Girard stands. "This afternoon we are going to do an exercise. I want you to pair off with your mentors and list your partner's unattractive features."

Her words feel like a punch in my gut. Did I hear her correctly? I turn to Marie-Josée who's sitting next to me, but she merely sighs as if she's been asked to do something mundane and tedious. "Not this one again," she whispers. It's the kind of reaction I'd give Papa when he made me count the inventory on the shelves. I look along the row of other girls for a glimmer of emotion. Is it just me who has a thin skin?

"You need to get used to hearing Monsieur Durandeau draw attention to your appearance during selection," says Girard. "And you need to be prepared to hear how the public will talk about you when you enter a room with your client. Better to learn how to brace yourself now than to get upset when you're on a job."

She approaches a girl with dark hair at the end of our row. "For example, Emilie." She nudges Emilie's leg with her cane. "Well, stand up." Emilie reluctantly stands. She's a new girl, like me, and young, maybe eighteen or nineteen; she's sweet and quiet as a mouse whenever I see her in the dressing room. Girard scrutinizes her, their faces inches apart.

"I might say the following: the nose is long and pointy; the mouth curls down like a frown; a weak chin exaggerates the unfortunate nose; and of course, the moles on the face look witchy. Thank you, Emilie. You may be seated."

Emilie looks like Girard just slapped her. I bite my lip as if the stinging words were directed at me. Emilie says nothing. She simply sits down, and I have to look away, not wanting to catch her eye.

Marie-Josée mutters some choice words under her breath while Girard continues her lecture. "Remember, ladies: embrace your flaws." She waves her arm in a theatrical gesture. "They augment your client's beauty, and that's the sole purpose of an employee of the Durandeau Agency. Now pair off and start the exercise." She bats us away with her twiglike arms.

We spread out and scatter to the far corners of the salon. I realize that no one wants an audience for this exercise. As Marie-Josée and I gravitate toward the windows, my shoulders sink. How can this exercise be necessary? Hasn't every woman in the room already scrutinized her own face as the harshest of critics?

40

The truth is most of the time spent at the agency isn't awful, when I forget the reason I'm here. We're fed and clothed during work hours, it's better pay than the laundry, and of course the work isn't physically demanding. But every so often—like right now—the truth of the position strikes you like a blow. Sometimes you have to close off a part of yourself. It's at times like this I'd rather be ironing a pile of shirts.

Girard's shrill voice rings out. "Emilie! Look your partner in the eye, don't avoid the impact of her words. That won't do you any good."

With a sense of dread, I turn to face my mentor. "I suppose we should start," I say, studying the face in front of me. I can't believe I'm about to say cruel things to my new friend.

"I have my own twist on the exercise." Marie-Josée nudges me. "I will list my own good qualities and then it will be your turn; it's good for morale."

I smile, relieved. "How about we list each *other's* good qualities," I suggest. "I'm not much good at plumping up my own feathers."

"Good." She nods. "You go first, then." She mimics Girard's hand gestures. "Shower me with compliments!"

I look at her making light of our situation.

"Go on, love, you can't think of anything nice?" She flutters her lashes, playing the fool.

I reflect for another moment. I want what I say to count. "You like to protect people," I say. "You make this place bearable; you have an infectious warmth and you fight cruelty with laughter. You're like magic—"

"Oh, shush, that's enough." She cuts me off, taken aback. Her eyes fill up a little, but she blinks the emotion away. "My turn," she says. "Well, for someone so young, you have quite the resolve, coming to the big city all alone. You're plucky and bright and quite the little observer, with those sharp eyes of yours." I squirm with the compliments; my throat feels tight. These are the kind of things my mother would have said to me. I fight her memory. Marie-Josée goes on. "There's something else. You've a notion for bigger things here in Paris. I've a mind you don't even know what, but you'll have it."

"What do you mean?" I ask.

"I have a sense about you." She's looking at me intently. "Yes, you have your sights set on something, and you'll get it," she repeats.

The emotion I just felt cools at these last remarks. I doubt her words; how can I be meant for bigger things? Look where I am right now—a repoussoir-in-training.

The clock chimes and Girard starts bossing, cutting off our conversation. "Tomorrow morning we have dance practice in the dining room, followed by manners and customs. Ladies, you are dismissed."

In the evening after work I get off the omnibus a stop early and take my time strolling along the streets of my neighborhood. It's awash with activity and color in every direction, from the painted faces of the prostitutes to the street performers, market vendors and posters plastered on every free space.

I stop outside the bright windows of Café Chez Emile.

I've never ventured inside at night before—a girl alone at a bar isn't respectable—but I love watching the scene. Half of Paris seems to be crowding the bar tonight. The décor is simple, with wooden paneling matching the tables and chairs and not much on the walls. People are dancing where a couple of tables have been moved aside. Peering in the window, I'm looking for a glimpse of Paul. The zinc bar is lined thick with people. I'm studying those faces so closely I don't notice the band right away. But when the music stops and the customers turn, cheering and clapping for the musicians, I follow their gaze to the far corner. There, on a slightly raised platform, Paul sits behind the piano, laughing and saying something to his bandmates, a violinist and an accordion player. He nods to them and they strike up another tune. I watch for a few more moments, until I hear a sudden tapping and see a man pressing his face against the glass, beckoning me inside. I immediately step back and keep walking along the dark street.

# Chapter 5

The mood is wild with the repoussoirs this afternoon. Several of them are going to a charity event on the Champs-Élysées tonight, and boisterous laughter and chatter fill the dressing room. Madame Girard is assisting with some ambitious hairstyles, and Madame Leroux is wrestling with the hemming and fixing of gowns. Smells of perfume, powder and sweet tea mingle in the air.

As I brush my hair at one of the mirrors, I catch sight of Cécile in tears. She's sitting behind me and I watch in the reflection as her blond ringlets shudder, her heavy face red and swollen. It's unnerving to see her like this, and I take it as an ominous sign; it's evidence of how the job can treat even the toughest character. I turn around and watch as Marie-Josée approaches her.

"Oh, *ma puce*," Marie-Josée murmurs. "Come on, it won't be as bad tonight." Marie-Josée takes the handkerchief from her sleeve and wipes away the younger woman's tears.

Cécile sniffs loudly. "It's not fair. It's impossible to see him with her . . ." She trails off with a convulsion of sobs. I take my time braiding my hair, all the while listening in on their conversation, half guilty, half intrigued.

Marie-Josée continues with her mother hen words, comforting her. "I know it's hard, but it's your job to push him to the client. It's how it's supposed to be," she says.

Cécile shrugs off Marie-Josée's touch, tears streaming down her face. "She doesn't love him like I do."

Marie-Josée shakes her head at our inconsolable colleague, then begins to make her way over to me. I turn my attention to the ribbon at the end of my braid and fiddle with it, pretending I wasn't eavesdropping.

"It's always somebody's turn at tears with you young ones," says Marie-Josée. "Help me with my dress." She turns her back to me and I undo the hooks with difficulty; they're tight, and it takes some strength to unfasten them.

"What's wrong with Cécile?" I ask, prying open the last catch.

She slings the bodice over a chair, then steps out of the skirt of the dress. "Now undo a few laces on this corset," she tells me. "I can't breathe." I do as I'm told, and she sighs with relief when I manage to loosen it. "There's always one client who's a cruel mistress, Maude."

I think back to our earlier conversation and her "nouveau riche" client. "You mean the sort who doesn't know how to use a repoussoir?" I ask.

"No, worse than that," she says, taking a seat, and the stool creaks under her. "The kind who smiles and jokes with you in public, takes your arm, whispers confidences and exchanges coy smiles. But then she turns on you. You are a doll to be thrown across the room in a tantrum. Hearts will be broken and feelings trampled on. You have to be stronger than that." She nods toward Cécile, who is

45

still sniffling. I let myself stare at her for a moment and try to imagine what exactly happened. Getting caught up in a client's life until it gets under your skin—it's an impossible position for a repoussoir. I don't want that ever to be me.

There's a knock on the dressing room door and the girls stop talking for a moment. "Is everybody decent?" a calm male voice calls out to a rustle of skirts and muted squeals. "I have wages to distribute." The handsome man whom Durandeau consulted at my interview walks into the dressing room carrying a box of envelopes. The girls look as though they're experiencing a chain reaction of skipped heartbeats as he walks past them. Marie-Josée explained that Laurent is responsible for recruitment and accounts. She also told me that he is the reason many of the repoussoirs are here. His good looks and charm are Durandeau's secret weapon. It's a tricky task to recruit ugly women, but no girl can be mad at him for wooing her into the agency. No one can be mad at him for anything.

He calls out our names one by one, and the girls give him their best smiles when he hands over their pay—except Cécile, who has a friend collect her wages.

"Maude Pichon!"

A glimpse of him is a treat, but it's the brown envelope containing my pay that I'm most excited by—it's the only thing keeping me afloat in Paris.

When it's her turn, Marie-Josée saunters over to him wearing only her undergarments and a wicked smile, rolls of flesh nearly bursting out of her flimsy cotton chemise. I throw a hand over my mouth, shocked.

46

"You know, my client came down with whooping cough, so I'm free for you this weekend," she purrs in his ear. "There's a new show at le Chat Noir . . . How about it, handsome?"

There's nothing halfhearted about Marie-Josée! I have to hold in a laugh at her utterly brazen banter.

Laurent takes it in stride. He simply smiles and says, "I wish, *ma belle*, but I'm recruiting for the boss. Business is brisk, demand is high." He lowers his voice. "And I don't want to make the other girls jealous." He gives her a smile and even though it's not for me, my heart skips a beat too.

I watch carefully as he moves toward Cécile and strokes her damp cheek. "Oh, *pauvre petite*, I heard what happened last night. He's not worth those tears, so chin up, love." Cécile looks at him through swollen eyes. One residual sob escapes.

The sharp click of footsteps in the hall dampens the high spirits and turns everyone's attention to the door. It feels as if the temperature in the room cools when Durandeau enters.

Everyone avoids his gaze. I don't want to be noticed by him either, but I can't help stealing a look: impeccably dressed in evening tails, he purses his lips and straightens his bow tie in preparation for a speech.

"First the unpleasantries. Mademoiselle Carré." He glares at Cécile and I feel myself shrink back. "You have let down the agency with your hysterics on the job. You have one last chance to pull your professional self together or you will be relieved of your privilege of serving the agency."

Out of the corner of my eye I catch Marie-Josée pulling a face. How could she be so bold?

"Mademoiselle Pichon!" I jump at hearing my name. His beady eyes fix on me and I inwardly cower. "You are to rendezvous with Countess Dubern and her daughter at a boutique of ladies' fashions tomorrow afternoon. This will give the countess a chance to assess your suitability as a physical match for her daughter."

My heart stops racing; I'm glad I'm not in trouble. But now the job is real. Lessons with Girard have kept the dread of my first assignment at bay until now. "*Oui*, monsieur," I manage to say.

"Madame Leroux has a suitable outfit for you. Your transportation has been arranged from the agency by carriage at a quarter to three." He lifts his lapel to smell the gardenia in his buttonhole. "It is expected you will be a match. Don't disappoint." Without another word, Durandeau turns and heads for the door, with Laurent at his heels.

"Thank you, ladies," Laurent calls out, then blows us a kiss behind Durandeau's back as he closes the door.

As soon as they are gone, everyone relaxes back into their conversations, but I am silent. A knot is growing in my stomach at the thought of my first assignment. The countess is vastly more intimidating than training exercises. I pull up a chair next to Marie-Josée. She's sitting at one of the dressing tables, smearing cream over her jowly face.

"Don't fret, *ma grande*. You learned from the best." She smiles at me.

Her words aren't comforting. Anxiety twists in my stomach

as she reaches over and places a greasy hand on mine, her face serious for once. "Remember, Maude, you need to have a shell like stale baguette—hard as a rock." She squeezes my hand. "Don't let them in and you'll be fine."

I nod and force a smile. I want to believe her.

# Chapter 6

I have found that in anticipation of any dreaded event, time accelerates. My morning lessons flew by, and now I'm sitting in the agency carriage, which is charging through the streets of Paris toward my meeting with the countess and her daughter. I feel like a bugle should be proclaiming our passage or sounding the alarm. The urgency throbbing through life here is dizzying. I wonder when all of this newness and change will stop. I want that feeling of stillness that hangs in the air before a thunderstorm, when it feels as if the earth has stopped turning. If I could just catch my breath, steady my footing. But there is no respite. The city streaks by my window, the people no more than a blur.

All too soon the carriage slows and pulls to a stop on boulevard Haussman. The driver helps me down and points to the shop where my meeting is to take place. A ladies' hat boutique, it has a façade of wrought iron and a glass window with swirling gold lettering, which reads *Le Miroir des Modes*. Hats are on display in the window, perched on gilded treelike branches. The carriage pulls away and I'm left alone on the street, trying to find the courage to enter the establishment.

My chest tightens as I open the door to the sound of the jingling shop bell. There is only one customer paying an account and no sign of the countess and her daughter. I let out a breath I didn't know I was holding and relief washes over me. I must be early.

I move farther into the store, taking it all in. I've never been in such an elegant place. The ceilings are higher than one would expect from the street, and the walls are finished in dark wood and cream moldings. Suspended from the ceiling is a glittering chandelier illuminating all shapes and colors of ladies' hats. There are tall glass cabinets housing the more fragile creations, and slim wooden drawers left ajar display scarves arranged in rows.

I turn and catch a glimpse of my reflection in the wall of mirrors—it's like looking at a stranger, seeing myself in an agency outfit of brown gingham. It felt much smarter than my own clothes in the dressing room, but here in this fancy store, it's obvious how dull and plain I look: perfect for a repoussoir.

The customer leaves and the rosy shopgirl turns her attention to me. "*Bonjour*, mademoiselle. Let me know if you need assistance with sizes or styles."

How odd it is to be treated like a customer. "I'm meeting some friends," I tell her, and make my way to a chaise longue in front of the window display. I'm too intimidated to touch the fine hats, so I take a seat to wait for the clients. When I first arrived in Paris, it was my dream to work in a store like this, full of beautiful things, a far cry from the practical necessities of country life. No lugging sacks of potatoes and boxes of apples or restocking bottles of hoof oil and spools of flypaper. Most of all, no Papa breathing down my neck.

I stare at the exquisite hats; they look like exotic birds. I want to sweep my hand across their plumes and feel the soft feathers tickle my skin. I imagine choosing a different one to wear every day. For a few moments I forget the reason I'm actually here. Then a nagging thought pokes at me—a section of the repoussoir rule book comes to mind. I was given a copy of the turgid volume on the first day of training.

II. ii. *Alieni Appetens.* It is forbidden to covet a client's belongings, as this encourages unhealthy desires. Furthermore, any suspected theft of a client's property will result in dismissal and legal action.

It's as if the fashionable hats swivel away from me with disdain and the gloves laid out on the counter point accusing fingers. They know I don't deserve to wear them; they know I don't belong.

The tinkle of the shop bell turns my attention to the door. I'm surprised to see the countess's friend, Madame Vary. She wears peacock feathers in her hat and prances like the bird itself. "Ah, there you are, Maude," she says when she sees me.

I get up and we shake gloved hands.

"*Bonjour,*" calls out the shopgirl.

Madame Vary ignores her and looks me up and down. "Only for the countess would I get involved in such a thing. She is such a precious friend." Her warm words for the countess don't match her contemptuous tone of voice. She removes the peacock on her head and throws it behind me on the chaise longue.

"You are my late husband's second cousin's daughter, if anyone asks." And under her breath, "You look more like someone from *his* side of the family."

I don't know what she's referring to, but I realize her last comment is a slight. How could she resent me when I've barely spoken a word to her? I watch as she walks toward the mirrored wall and checks her appearance. She doesn't look like any widow I've ever seen—too pretty, too glamorous and too young. I don't like her.

"As you know, my name is Madame Vary but you may call me *tante* for this charade," she announces.

"I'm to pretend you are my aunt?" I ask.

Still gazing in the mirror, she says, "The countess will explain. Whatever you say to Isabelle, *don't* mention that agency." Then she wrenches herself from her reflection and walks toward the menagerie of hats on display. Her words leave me puzzled.

Before I can find out more, the shop door opens again and I turn to see the countess walk in with a girl my age. At first glance the daughter looks like a younger version of her mother, with the same rich, dark hair and pale skin, but when I study her more closely I see that her features are softer, less sculpted. She has the same dark eyes, though, the color of black cherry.

The Duberns greet Madame Vary, who introduces me as her late husband's relative.

The countess smiles, giving me the full benefit of her

handsome face. "Maude, how lovely to see you again." I'm surprised by how much friendlier she is now than she was at the agency.

Her daughter is not at all friendly, though. I offer her my hand, my smile feeling taut and unnatural. "A pleasure to meet you, Isabelle," I say. She barely articulates a *bonjour* in return. She might be prettier if she smiled.

Isabelle Dubern walks away from us and begins to wander around the store, looking at the merchandise. It makes no sense, her lack of interest in me—shouldn't she study *me* and not the hats? Her mother and Madame Vary were so particular when sizing up the agency girls.

The countess gestures for me to follow her daughter, so I make my way across the boutique, walking behind her like a puppy. She fingers the odd hat but doesn't try any on. My stomach is in knots, and I rehearse some phrases of conversation in my mind but manage to voice nothing. She appears completely indifferent to my presence.

The countess and Madame Vary boss the shopgirl around, their voices filling the store. "This hat with less detail." "More feathers." "This one in another color." "One with a veil." "Without the jewels." From where I'm standing, it appears that the countess goes for bold choices, Madame Vary the more frivolous and prettier styles. I have never seen such energetic customers of anything.

The minutes pass, and I feel as though I'm failing in this meeting. I hover near Isabelle and pick up a hat, turning it around and around. As I try to ascertain which is the front, Isabelle picks up a simple straw bonnet with a black ribbon and tries it on. In this instant I recall my training.

54

*Compliment your client on her appearance*. Finally, an avenue of conversation.

"That looks pretty," I say.

She glares at me. "I'm not looking for pretty."

The rebuff throws me. Then why do you need me? I think.

The countess sweeps in before I can respond. "Isabelle! Take off that ugly thing and try on something appropriate. Honestly, why do you enjoy acting the pauper?"

Isabelle removes the hat with a sigh and wanders to a display of over-the-top feathered hats. She picks up an ambitious creation with plumage in shades of pink and lilac. "How about this one, Mother?"

"Come, Isabelle, please. Must you go to the other extreme? You're not going to be riding a circus elephant."

I look away, not wanting to witness their private squabbles.

"How about this one for your daughter, madame?" The shopgirl intervenes with a gray ostrich-feather hat.

"That's more like it," the countess approves.

The shopgirl approaches Isabelle and fixes the hat in place.

"Now stand in front of the mirror," the countess orders. "Take a look." Isabelle does as she is told while the countess confides to her friend, "It's a relief to see her looking like a lady for once, and not a peasant or a schoolgirl."

But Isabelle maintains a steely resistance to the hat. "It doesn't suit me, Mother. The feathers would look better on the bird."

I stand a few paces behind Isabelle, studying her reflection.

She's pretty, but her beauty doesn't command attention, like her mother's does. And there's a defiance to her; something about the line of her jaw, how she holds her head up. I look at my own reflection in contrast. Does the comparison effect work? Do I really make her look prettier? How unnatural to want your own face to disappoint, to fall short, to repel the onlooker so much he latches on to your companion.

The countess addresses the salesgirl. "We'll take the ostrich feather and these." She points to the bounty that she and Madame Vary have picked out on the chaise longue. "You can start boxing everything up."

Isabelle removes the ostrich-feather hat and gives it to the shopgirl. She catches me looking at her. "Yes?" she says sourly.

I channel Girard. Quick, I think, compliments. "Oh, just . . . those gray feathers contrast nicely with your hair color," I say, smiling.

She rolls her eyes. "Are you a performing monkey—are you going to flatter me with every hat I try on?"

Why is she being so difficult? She knows this is my job; what does she expect? I look away, my face flushed with embarrassment. It's as though Isabelle is feigning ignorance of the purpose of our meeting. And then it hits me with a jolt: maybe she's not pretending. Maybe she doesn't know the reason I'm here. My heart quickens as I tally up the evidence: Madame Vary's playacting that I'm her relative, the tension between mother and daughter, and Isabelle's reluctance to look pretty or feminine. This whole charade is the work of the countess, I'm certain of it. Hiring a repoussoir for your daughter without her knowledge—if Isabelle Dubern were nicer to me, I'd feel sorry for her.

"I challenge you to find the ugliest hat in the shop." I turn to find her staring at me. "One that would make me look ridiculous."

I glance over at the countess and Madame Vary for help, but they are occupied with the salesgirl on the other side of the shop. I take a breath and walk around the merchandise, looking for a bad hat, the wrong hat, the odd one out. Isabelle follows at my heels. I see one decorated with masses of silk roses and a lacey veil. "This one." I point at it.

"Why don't you like it?" she asks.

"It has too much adornment, I suppose, to be tasteful." I hope I've made the right decision—is this some kind of test or trick?

She picks it up and examines it. The silk flowers crowd it like a great rosebush. Even the veil has small roses embroidered on it.

"Who do you think would wear a hat like this?" she asks me with a smile.

Relieved that we are actually conversing, I respond eagerly. "An actress, maybe. A vaudeville star, perhaps?"

A spark lights in her eyes. "Or a courtesan," she says playfully, trying on the hat herself. I laugh with too much enthusiasm, grateful to be sharing a joke with her.

Madame Vary approaches as Isabelle flaunts the hat.

"Did you find anything else before your mother settles the account?"

Isabelle's face falls. "I fell in love with this one, but your niece says I look like a prostitute."

I gasp, and Madame Vary colors, then shoots daggers at me. Isabelle makes a show of removing the hat as if it's tainted and puts it back on the display. What a vixen! How easily lies roll off her tongue.

I try to defend myself. "But, I—"

"Maude! Apologize at once." Madame Vary's voice is like acid. She touches Isabelle's arm and in a softer tone says, "I'm sure she didn't mean to be rude. Coming from the—uh, the convent, she's not accustomed to the latest fashions."

The countess calls, "Isabelle! Fetch the driver. Tell him we have boxes to put in the carriage."

"Yes, Mother." Isabelle smirks in my direction as she walks between me and Madame Vary. When Isabelle is safely out of earshot, Madame Vary grabs my wrist and hisses, "Where are your manners? I thought they trained you to behave like a lady. This isn't the cheap seats." She drops my arm and hurries out of the shop after Isabelle.

It's obvious to me that I'm not any kind of match for the countess's wretched daughter. It's all so absurd. This meeting is a disaster. Why didn't they prepare me properly for the farce? Regardless of whether she knows the truth of my position, Isabelle Dubern is mean and spiteful. I remember Marie-Josée's words: "There's always one client who's a cruel mistress."

"Maude!" The countess calls me over. My stomach plummets as I approach. Did she overhear the exchange with Isabelle? I dread hearing what she has to say, and I hold my breath.

"You and Isabelle are a match," she says, trying on a pair of midnight-blue gloves. "I want you for her debut at the

Rochefort ball. But before I let you loose on society, tomorrow night you will dine with us—to make sure you can handle yourself in a group of our friends."

She extends her arm to examine the glove.

"But I want to be crystal clear," she continues. Her voice is sharp and cold, like ice cracking. "This isn't like other agency jobs. Isabelle doesn't know what you are. As far as she's concerned, you are her new best friend." She meets my eye. "She is never to find out. You understand?" Her gaze is unflinching.

I nod slowly. I understand perfectly—the countess has given me an impossible assignment.

# Chapter 7

This is one of the few times I've been a customer at Café Chez Emile. On Saturday the agency doesn't open until noon. It's just past ten, and I'm sipping a bowl of hot chocolate, pretending to read the newspaper, but really I'm scanning the faces and searching for Paul's baggy suit in the crowd.

*Eiffel's Tower Soars Past Second Platform, Approaches 200m.* I skim the words of the article without taking them in. My hot chocolate is nearly gone and I'm about to give up, when, with a thrill of recognition, I see him walk through the door. He's with a couple of friends, and they take a table on the opposite wall. The waiter obviously knows them, as he produces their coffees without having to ask. Now is the right time, and I feel the surge of daring propelling me to action as I rise from my chair. But before I walk over to his table, something stops me in my tracks: Paul and his friends are suddenly distracted. My eyes follow theirs toward an attractive woman who's just walked in.

"Suzanne! Suzanne!" they call out to her. She waves and approaches their table. They are all pleased to see her—including Paul—and as I watch with dismay, each man jumps up and takes a turn to kiss her on both cheeks. She wears her wavy hair long and loose and carries a large canvas under her arm. Seeing them all together, I shrink back down into my seat and stare at the dregs of my hot chocolate. When I look up again, I see that she's sitting next to Paul and the painting is propped up on the banquette. It doesn't sit there for long. Paul picks it up and removes the cotton sheet covering it. I can't get a good look at the artwork, but much discussion occupies the table. Is she the artist? Whoever she is, she is the center of attention. The louder their chatter, the more invisible I feel. I put a coin on the table for the hot chocolate and slip out of the café unnoticed.

The omnibus is stopped on rue de Rennes, and even though I have time to kill, I run to catch it. I climb up to the open-air top deck as usual so I can see the view. My favorite part of the journey to work is when we're on the Pont Neuf over the Seine and I can see the two sides of Paris spread out on either side of the river. I live on the Left Bank, and everything to do with the agency and rich people, as far as I can tell, is on the Right Bank. But today when the omnibus reaches the Pont Neuf, instead of gazing at the view, I revisit the scene in the café. Why didn't I just say hello to him? I think, and a sigh escapes. The omnibus jolts and I glance up to look across the river. Eiffel's unfinished tower is rising in the distance. Not fitting in was never part of my dream of Paris.

I think back to the chain of events that led me to finally leave Poullan-sur-Mer. I had grown to hate the store, with all its practical items of country-life necessity. No frills or luxury. Nothing scented or pretty or delicate. It used to be fun when I was little and when my mother's touch could be felt in the inventory and the organization. After her death, Papa took me out of school. In his opinion I had learned enough arithmetic to be useful, and I was put to work managing the accounts. When my classmates were reading about Pompeii and Byzantium, I was counting bottles of liniment or hauling sacks of flour. If any of my friends came by the shop to see me, Papa would hover about sighing until they left. He said he didn't like me socializing while working. I bet the miser that he is didn't want me handing out extra butter or chocolate. Or maybe he was worried I would turn a blind eye if one of the little blighters lifted anything.

I had started talking to Papa about returning to school. The shop was running smoothly. I could still help out on weekends and afternoons. I wanted to learn—there was a whole world of knowledge I was missing out on. That was when he began promoting the idea of marrying me off. I would soon be turning sixteen, and this was his way of controlling me, of quashing my dreams.

The notion of running away surfaced gradually: a secret I had been unwilling to tell myself. The turning point came when I was in the cellar fetching apples from the dry store. Down there, you can hear the floorboards squeak and the muffled conversations from upstairs. Papa was out front loading supplies onto a farmer's cart, and the farmer's wife was gossiping to a friend, assuming they were alone in the store.

"She's only a young thing, and he works her six days a week for her keep," she said. "Young folk should have some time to live. Lord knows there's enough work to go around when she grows up."

I froze at her words, an apple in each hand. They were talking about me.

"Who's going to work for him for free when he marries her off?" asked the other woman.

I craned my neck toward the ceiling, straining to hear.

"Well, she'll be right across the street. I hear that Thierry has been dropping hints, wants a young wife to bear him some sons."

My heart battered against my chest. Monsieur Thierry, the butcher? But he was old and pock-faced and beat his dog. How could Papa possibly think . . .

"I suppose beggars can't be choosers. She doesn't have her mother's looks, that's for sure."

"Yes, she's plain as flour. Poor thing could have done with a mother's guidance at this age."

I felt the blood rushing to my head, pumping furiously. My stomach dropped to the floor and my knuckles turned white from gripping the apples so tightly.

"I expect it was a kindness on old Pichon's part. He wants her taken care of."

"Or he fancies that with Thierry as his son-in-law, he'll get a roast every night of the week! Sly old coot."

Suddenly I could see my quiet life mapped out, and it felt as though I had aged forty years. I would never visit Paris or dance with a gentleman or hear an opera. The whole village squeezed into that damp cellar, sucking out the air and crushing me. My fate had been decided; no one expected anything more of me.

I heard the squeak of the door and tinkle of the shop bell, followed by Father's voice. His banal comments about the weather and his pleasant tone with the customers reviled me. My fingernails pierced the flesh of the apples. If I wanted it, I had to seize life for myself. It was then that the explosive idea of running away to Paris flashed with the fizzing brightness of striking a match. And that flame remained hissing and sparking in my chest. It stayed bright and grew bigger and wouldn't be extinguished.

# Chapter 8

Saturday evening, and the agency is buzzing with activity in preparation for a busy night. Only new girls and mentors without plans are stuck in the salon, enduring another lesson with Girard.

I let her voice float over me as I watch the sky outside bruise from gold to purple. Night is rising in Paris, and I wear my dread of the impending evening like an unwanted hand-me-down. If only Marie-Josée were here to reassure me. We haven't crossed paths since yesterday, before my meeting with the Duberns. I'm desperate to tell her what happened with Isabelle, but this morning I was stuck in a fitting for my evening dress and this afternoon she went out on a repoussoir date, stretching it long enough to get out of training.

"October marks the start of the Paris season," lectures Girard. "All the rich Parisian families have returned from their country chateaus or foreign travel and are back on the social merry-go-round." I wish she would stop; her words only add to my anxiety.

"As employees of this agency, you will experience the best of everything—opening night at the theater, opulent banquets ānd exclusive balls. You will be driven everywhere by carriage, will wear costume jewels and fine clothes."

I hear a couple of snickers at that last comment. The girls take bets on whether our seamstress, Madame Leroux, is color-blind or has naturally abominable taste. Whatever the reason, her talent for making us look bad is legendary.

Girard drones on. "People not in the know will think you belong in these social circles. All you have to do is fit in and serve your client."

I can't sit still; I keep shifting in my seat. Everyone seems restless. A lot of us new girls have already been on solo dates, and the training is feeling redundant. It didn't help me in the one meeting I had with Isabelle Dubern.

"I want to finish today's lesson by discussing one of the subtleties of your role," Girard announces, then pauses to emphasize the importance of what she's about to say, but for me it just feels as though she's stopping time. Shouldn't we be done by now? I look at the clock: two minutes remain.

"A successful client-repoussoir relationship is based on the appearance of friendship—a close one."

This remark gets my attention. I haven't stopped thinking about the countess's words to me since she spoke them.

Girard goes on, "The comparison effect can only work if you can make yourself a mirror to your client, staying close enough to magnify her beauty. The client will play her part and be nice to you, treat you like a best friend, share secrets, and laugh with you. You must also play your part."

I want to shake my head. But what if your client is being duped by her mother? What if she doesn't know she has a part to play? If Girard were a little more approachable I might ask her advice, but Marie-Josée is the only person

I trust. I must speak to her before I leave for the Duberns'— she will know what to do.

"Remember, the closer you appear to your client, the better the result." Girard gestures dramatically, one hand on her heart, the other reaching out to some imaginary public. "Think of yourself as an actress on the stage . . ."

Before she can finish her speech the clock on the mantel piece chimes and the lesson is finally at an end.

I am the first out of the salon. Maybe Marie-Josée has returned while I was stuck in class. I run along the corridor to the dressing room, fling open the door and survey the room, looking for her familiar round figure. But as I stand there out of breath and searching, I realize instantly that she's not here. A few more girls drift into the dressing room and step around me. I can't face Isabelle Dubern and her intimidating mother without debriefing Marie-Josée on what happened in the hat shop. She's never afraid of clients. More than this, she feels like my good-luck charm at the agency—I just need to see her and then everything won't seem so bad.

"Maude." Madame Leroux sees me and beckons me over. She takes my outfit from the rack of gowns hanging up for this evening's dates. It's an old-lady dress, dark gray lace with matching gloves.

She holds it against me on the hanger. "It should fit better now that I lengthened the hem and took in the waist."

"Have you seen Marie-Josée today?" I ask as she hands me the dress.

"No, I haven't." She snaps her fingers, irritated. "Get a move on and get changed."

I slip off my agency day dress and she helps me on with the evening gown. I catch my reflection in the mirror—I look like a faded widow before I've even been married.

"Sit," she instructs, pointing to the stool opposite the mirror. She unravels my braid and bushes out my hair, then scrapes it into a pile on top of my head, fixing it with jabbing pins. I place a hand on the back of my bare neck; I'm not used to wearing my hair up like this. I feel exposed.

"You're done. Hortense, you're next," she calls out.

I leave the dressing room, and as I walk past the wall clock, I check the time. I have one hour until I have to leave. Come on, Marie-Josée, I think. Come back soon.

I sit alone in the agency dining room with a large napkin over my frock so as not to spill my dinner on it. The dining rules have been helpfully tacked on the wall in front of me.

**IV. i. All repoussoirs are required to eat in the agency dining room prior to working at an event where food is served. This is in response to certain individuals gorging themselves on the job, as well as hoarding leftovers in evening bags and coat pockets. Such behavior is strictly forbidden and will result in immediate dismissal.**

I don't have any appetite. I make patterns with my fork in the runny shepherd's pie. Maybe Isabelle will be friendlier to me this evening, or maybe she'll be worse. My stomach somersaults at the thought.

"What are you doing?" The voice startles me and I look up to meet Marie-Josée's twinkling eyes. She pushes my plate away. "Don't stuff yourself before a dinner. You won't have any room left."

Immediately I jump up and kiss her cheek. "I'm so glad you're back. You were gone all afternoon."

She laughs at the welcome and takes a seat. "Leroux told me you were off to the Duberns' tonight. Mind if I finish your plate?" she asks.

"Go ahead. But what about the rules? I should try to eat something."

"Poppycock!" Marie-Josée replies. "You have to enjoy the perks. Do you know how incredible the spread will be? You can't miss out." She whips off my napkin to prove her point and tucks it into the collar of her own dress. "Just don't let anyone see you pocket anything—and nothing too soft or it will spoil in your purse." She gives me a wink. "Leroux might not tell on you, but Girard always has a way of finding out."

A pulse of anxiety quickens through me as I imagine the dinner to come. "I doubt I'll be able to swallow a bite."

Marie-Josée shovels a forkful of shepherd's pie into her mouth. "Why so nervous? If you're on a second date already, yesterday must have gone well."

"That's why I've been desperate to speak to you. It didn't go well. The girl is a brat. And that's not the worst of it. I'm supposed to befriend her—not like a repoussoir—but as a real friend."

"What do you mean?" says Marie-Josée, her forehead scrunched up and a piece of potato hanging from the corner of her mouth.

"The countess is hiring me for the ball behind her daughter's back."

"What?" says Marie-Josée, wiping her lips with my napkin. "The daughter doesn't know you're a repoussoir?" This is the first time I've seen Marie-Josée look genuinely shocked.

I shake my head. "I have to pretend to be Madame Vary's niece or second cousin or something, and I'm supposed to make friends with Isabelle without giving the game away. I have to get through dinner tonight and the ball next Saturday."

Marie-Josée stops eating for a moment. "I've never heard of that happening before, the client being in the dark. They usually pick us out themselves."

"Exactly. It makes my job impossible, because Isabelle has made it plain she dislikes me."

Marie-Josée thinks for a moment. "How? Is she vain and stuck-up?"

"No, she's proud and standoffish."

"Don't kowtow to her; she'll be used to getting her way. Show some mettle." She nods at me. "I know you have it in you." She polishes off the last of my shepherd's pie.

"But stand up to her how?" I ask.

Marie-Josée doesn't have a chance to answer. Girard's nasal voice can be heard across the room, and we turn around to see Cécile point to our table. Girard hurries toward us with her mincing steps.

"Mademoiselle Pichon!" she calls out.

When she arrives at our table, she glances at my empty plate. "Good, you've finished your dinner. Monsieur Durandeau would like to speak to you before you leave. He's in his private rooms."

I nod and exchange a look with Marie-Josée. She pats my hand encouragingly, and I push back my chair and rise to go and face Durandeau.

I walk along the hall to his apartments, where a light shines under the door; I clench my fist and knock. A muffled grunt bids me to enter. I open the door to find Durandeau at his supper: filet mignon, not shepherd's pie. It smells unbelievably good.

"Monsieur Durandeau, you wanted to see me?" My voice has to compete with saliva-drenched chomping. His table is set as if it were in a restaurant, with white linen, silverware and a carafe of wine. There's even a candelabra on the table to add to the formal atmosphere.

"Second assignment in a week, and the ball next Saturday." He manages this utterance between mouthfuls. "The countess must like you."

I wonder if I should point out that the countess hired me tonight because she doesn't trust me and wanted to test me with a group of her friends. "What if . . ." I hesitate. "What if tonight doesn't go as planned and she decides not to hire me for the ball?"

His silverware clatters down on the plate. "Why would you say such a thing?"

I swallow hard. "I just wondered if a different client might be more appropriate for me."

"Give you another client?" he booms. "Impossible. The countess selected *you*, not some other girl."

"But, monsieur, I'm not sure this client is a good fit," I plead, desperate to make him understand. "Maybe when I have more experience . . ."

He points at me with his steak knife. "You want to get the commission without having to earn it, more like." He goes back to attacking his steak, sawing at it with vigor. "I would never contradict the Countess Dubern's wishes." He stabs a large hunk of meat and shovels it into his mouth. "She is from one of the most distinguished families in Paris. We're lucky to have her patronage."

"Yes, monsieur," I say. My posture sinks with compliance. He lectures me about the Duberns' noble ancestry, but I'm not listening. Watching him tear into his steak, an image surfaces in my imagination—the birth of the agency. Durandeau, seated by the window at his favorite restaurant, wolfs a filet mignon. Outside, two young women stroll by. From behind there isn't much to distinguish one from the other. They pause and look at the menu board outside, arm in arm, laughing at some private joke. The girl closer to him is average-looking, nothing special; the other girl, who was obscured by her friend, now steps forward, directly into Durandeau's line of vision. He gasps. "What a hideous creature!" An offensive type of ugliness reserved for a select few this world has seen fit to punish. He can't help but stare—he is hypnotized by this ugly girl.

Finally, when he can take no more, Durandeau looks to her friend for some relief from the visual assault. He is calmed by her features, which appear to soften and improve before his eyes. He thinks, *She is pretty this girl, not average at all.* Then the wheels turn. *Ah, the illusion of beauty—the rule of comparisons.* The lightning bolt strikes! He freezes midbite, wanting to hold on to this genius, delight and cunning creeping across his face. The quivering synapses fire to the next thought, his body a bystander to the loco-motive of ingenuity thundering through his brain. *Ugly women! An untapped resource until now!* A drizzle of steak blood drips from his mustache onto the white linen. The waiter disturbs his reverie. Durandeau waves him off impa-tiently, his expression ferocious. He resumes his analysis of the girls, greedily taking in the features of each. *Imagine if you could re-create this experience for other such average women. You could sell beauty!*

"Mademoiselle Pichon." Durandeau's voice makes me start, and I'm pulled from my imagination back into his apartment. "You will carry off the dinner tonight and you will attend the ball next week." He wipes his mouth with a crisp napkin. "Moreover, I want you to angle for another high-profile event with the family. There's a whole season to exploit."

I nod stiffly. The pressure to succeed with Isabelle Dubern feels like a hand clasping my throat, squeezing tighter with each task that's asked of me. I find it increasingly hard to breathe.

# Chapter 9

The horses stop in the courtyard of the Dubern home, and we step out of Madame Vary's carriage and approach the house. I can't help but look up in awe at the lights shining; I lose count from how many windows. The front door opens and it's as though the curtain is rising in the theater on opening night. I am walking toward the dazzle of the foot-lights, nearly paralyzed by stage fright. We pass through a marble vestibule into an imposing entrance hall. I have never set foot in such a grand home. One servant takes our cloaks and another leads us up the large, curved staircase. As we ascend I take in the paintings lining the wall; the oil paint reflects the chandelier lights, giving the somber family portraits a hint of life.

We continue down a carpeted hallway where Madame Vary smoothes the skirts of her dress and flashes a quick smile in a mirror—in her case, vanity is a burden that requires constant attention. One advantage of my position is that I don't need the reassurance of checking my own appearance. Instead I concentrate on the servant as he opens the double doors to the drawing room, and with my heart in my mouth I step over the threshold. My breath catches in my throat. Tapestries, paintings, velvet curtains and plush settees crowd the room. There is a roaring fire, and gilded mirrors catch the light from a myriad of lamps. This isn't the petty bourgeois furnishing of the agency: this is luxury.

A man whom I assume is the count is speaking to two older couples—a tableau of gray hair and pearls sipping cocktails. On seeing us, he immediately gets up and greets Madame Vary. I hover in her shadow as he takes her hand and kisses it in a low bow. Elegantly dressed in white tie and tails and patent leather shoes, he isn't tall, but he is full of charm and looks at least ten years older than the countess. He gives me a curt bow and immediately returns his attention to Madame Vary; he holds her gaze longer than politeness would require. Parisian manners or flirtation, I can't judge.

I'm introduced to everyone, but in my present state it's impossible for me to retain their long names or how they are connected to my hosts. I register only a kaleidoscope of pampered faces and fragments of conversations.

"Terrible business, he bankrupted that family; a good name thrown in the gutter," gossips one of the pearls-and-gray-hair set.

"Eiffel's tower is becoming a monstrosity indeed," says a man with military posture. "A blight on the skyline with each day that passes."

"It won't last: it will be torn down in a year and we'll get our Paris back," assures a woman with a shimmering sapphire at her throat.

Seated on a couch with Madame Vary, I wonder where Isabelle and the countess are: waiting to make an entrance, perhaps. I watch as more guests trickle in and the count plays host. Maybe Isabelle is being as enthusiastic about evening dresses as she was about hats. Finally, in a swish of skirts, the countess swans in with Isabelle in tow. Their arrival is the cue that my own performance is about to begin in earnest, and my head begins to swim with agency rules, Girard's training and Marie-Josée's advice. The countess greets her guests. In a stunning emerald-green gown, she wears the medal of handsomest woman in the room with ease. Isabelle looks less confident but is also beautiful in a magenta silk—she is touted like a mascot, her mother's protégée. They shine like jewels and I shrink back in my seat. The lace of my dowdy dress has started to make me itch.

The countess and Isabelle eventually make their way across the room to where Madame Vary and I are seated. When the countess reaches us, she looks at me with a glimmer in her eye. "Isabelle, keep Maude company while I steal her aunt away for a moment."

Madame Vary practically leaps off the settee, grateful for the rescue. The countess steers her friend across the room and I can hear her saying, "You must meet our good friend from England, Lord Blackwood."

As soon as her mother's back is turned, Isabelle looks me up and down and says, "Did Madame Vary condone that dress you're wearing, or are you in mourning?"

She's spiteful, and I fight to be polite. "I'm not one for fashion," I murmur.

"It's a wonder you're related, for that's all she cares about. But then again, you're not a blood relative of hers, are you?"

Could Isabelle know more than she lets on? She cuts through my veil of composure because she's right, of course, both about my dress—designed to underwhelm—and about my relationship to Madame Vary. But I can't let her bully me. I think of Marie-Josée's advice and decide to strike back. "I wouldn't want my aunt to dress me, if that's what you mean. I'm not a child."

Her head whips around; her eyes fasten on mine. I touched a nerve, I see. To emphasize my point, I let my eyes flicker over her tasteful dress. "Did your mother pick out yours? It's so pretty and feminine."

Her eyes harden; then she looks away. I wait for her to retaliate, but she only stares at the other guests, her expression sullen. Could this possibly be a truce?

Naturally I'm seated near Isabelle at dinner. The table is glittering with crystal and polished cutlery. Attending us is a battalion of servants, as many as there are guests. My first mistake is when I thank the servant who pours me a glass of wine. Several pairs of eyes note this aberration, and I remember, too late, Girard's affected voice reminding us that *one doesn't address the servants or make significant eye contact—servants are invisible.* The next faux pas comes with the soup course and my incorrect choice of cutlery. I glance at my neighbor and switch to the correct spoon, thinking no one noticed. But when I look up I realize Isabelle's eyes are fixed on me, watching my mistakes, one after the other.

As the dinner wears on, I am grateful that Isabelle and I aren't expected to engage in conversation but rather to listen to our elders. But my relative calm is broken when the middle-aged woman opposite asks, "Mademoiselle Pichon, is it your debut season also?"

I have a piece of smoked trout in my mouth. "Yes," I answer, swallowing hard. I feel the bit of fish lodge itself in my gullet, but I continue. "My aunt is giving me the benefit of a season in Paris." I say it just the way Madame Vary and I rehearsed in the carriage ride over.

"And where is your family from? *Vous avez un petit accent.*"

In one short utterance she has seen through the masking of my Breton accent. "I'm from a small village near . . ." Frantically I try to remember the town Monsieur Vary's family is from. But will she believe me? I begin to mouth "Dieppe," when Madame Vary speaks over me.

"My husband's family is from Deauville, in Normandy."

"Of course, I remember now," says the woman, and the flicker of suspicion passes as the conversation moves on to weather in the region. I should be grateful for the upper-class Parisian contempt of the provinces—to them, every country accent melds into one.

Marie-Josée was not wrong about the food. It's fit for royalty: watercress soup, foie gras, smoked trout, roast goose and then lamb cutlets with an unpronounceable sauce. The rich eat with a careless disregard. As each new course arrives and the previous one is removed, I note that mine is the only plate ever scraped clean. The others are messy with uneaten food. Even though Lord Blackwood accepted a second helping of goose, he took only one bite. His leftovers would be considered a feast back home. I look at his plump cheeks, paunchy belly and smooth, manicured hands and realize that this is a man who never goes without: the cupboard is never bare. Having more of something to him means merely asking a servant. I bite my lip as I look down at my plate and wonder: Is it bad manners to finish the food you're given? Could it be an upper-class rule of etiquette Girard omitted to teach us?

After dinner Isabelle and I are both camped out on the divan in the far corner. I am relieved to have made it through dinner and estimate we must have passed the halfway mark of the evening. The drawing room begins to fill up as more guests arrive for drinks and mingling. The countess works the room. She is a beacon of emerald light for the moths in white tie and tails. I get the impression that everyone wants to be near her and talk to her. Isabelle sighs loudly. Remembering the rules, I rally myself and venture to engage her in conversation.

"Are all these people friends of your family?"

"Friends?" She laughs. "You should know—society isn't about friendship, it's about alliances."

She makes it sound like warfare. "And the Englishman?" A natural enemy, surely.

"Lord Blackwood is a friend of the Prince of Wales—at least, that's what he claims. His proximity to royalty makes him godlike in my mother's eyes. Thankfully for me, he's already married."

I look over and see that the countess is indeed talking to Lord Blackwood. She is captivated, and the English lord leans in close to her.

Isabelle gets up. "Come on," she says, and pulls me to my feet. "The guests will keep her busy for a while, and we won't be missed." I glance back at the countess, concerned that we're being rude by leaving, but she is so deep in conversation she doesn't notice.

I follow Isabelle out of the brightly lit drawing room, and she leads me down the hall in the opposite direction from the grand staircase, then along a narrow passageway and down another set of stairs. This section at the back of the house feels more functional, for servants' use, perhaps.

"Where are we going?" I ask Isabelle. I look back, wondering if I could retrace my steps on my own. "Are you sure your mother won't mind us disappearing?"

"Don't be such a bore, Maude. Would you rather be stuck up there listening to their trivial conversations?"

"I suppose not."

We're on the ground floor of the house, and groping along a dark passageway, I follow her through a glass door and into a conservatory—home to exotic flowers and the smell of mildew. There are no lamps lit in this part of the house, but moonlight shines through the glass walls, revealing rows of plants and wrought iron furniture. I can see roses, lilies and gardenias. The sweet smell of honey and orange is overpowering, and I marvel at the blooms in the silvery light.

Now that we've made our escape, it comes as a relief to be away from the adults. Isabelle takes off her gloves and throws them on a table. "How I hate these long dinners." She's impervious to the beauty of her surroundings and slumps into a chair, crushing her dress. "And now that it's my season, there will be many more nights like this."

She looks like a wilted flower, drooping by the window. I don't understand; surely most rich girls anticipate their seasons with impatience and excitement.

I wander along the rows of flowers. "What are these

called?" I ask, looking at the Latin name on the card next to one grouping. "*Paphio . . .* something."

Isabelle gets up and crosses the conservatory toward me. She glances at the flower. "The orchid, *Paphiopedilum.*"

I touch one of the ivory petals. "It sounds like a disease," I say.

She laughs. "Father's obsessed with collecting rare specimens." But just as quickly her smile vanishes and her face hardens. "My parents treat me like one of these hothouse flowers. Cultivated to be beautiful, bred to decorate a rich man's home."

Her words take me by surprise. "Isn't that what the season is all about—finding a match?"

She looks at me with that clenched-jaw seriousness I've seen before, her eyes bright and fierce. "Not to anyone my mother picks." This time I don't take her changing mood personally. Her temper is directed at her parents and her season, not at me.

I leave the orchids and continue to explore the conservatory. I turn down a row of roses and pause to look at the colorful blooms. She remains in the orchid row, a corridor of flowers between us.

"You're not really the late Monsieur Vary's niece, are you?" Isabelle asks, looking across at me.

I freeze. My stomach drops. "Why do you say that?" Panic sets in; how could she see through me so quickly?

"You're from *her* side of the family, aren't you—the poor side."

My body relaxes, grateful for her wrong guess. But I keep strolling and play along. "Does it matter?" I ask.

"To your aunt it does." Isabelle keeps pace with me. Our footsteps making syncopated clicking sounds on the stone floor; I feel pursued.

"Mother says Madame Vary married above her class. But I suppose you knew that."

Having her believe I'm from a lowly background isn't dangerous for my cover, it's advantageous. After all, I am the poor relation in many ways.

She continues prying. "Maybe with your aunt's help you'll snatch a rich husband yourself this season."

I stop short. "Making a marriage isn't the reason I came to Paris." The words fly out of my mouth before I've had a chance to think them through.

"Why did you come, then?"

I turn and face her. "To see something of the world." I'm speaking in my own voice now. For the first time tonight I'm ignoring the endless rules of my profession, and it feels liberating. "I have always dreamed of something more than country life."

"What is it you want to experience?" she asks. Her dark eyes are shining in the moonlight.

I think back to the village women gossiping about me in Papa's shop. "More than what people expect of me."

"Mademoiselle Isabelle." We both look up to see a servant standing in the doorway. "The countess is asking that you return to the drawing room at once."

Isabelle sighs and returns to the table where she left her gloves. "Tonight is about showing me off to prospective parents-in-law, before she throws me at one of their sons."

Before we leave the conservatory Isabelle darts back to

the orchids and snaps off two heavy flowers from one of the exotic plants. She puts one in my hair and the other in hers, eyes gleaming. "Father will have a fit if he notices!"

We follow the servant up the grand staircase, not the back stair, to return to the drawing room. Isabelle is hard to read, and I can't help but wonder if giving me one of her father's prized orchids is an act of friendship or malice.

I stare at the ticking second hand of the gold clock on the mantel. It's after midnight, and Madame Vary and I are the only guests left. The count has retired, and Isabelle is in the dining room helping Madame Vary find an earring she lost somewhere between dessert and digestif. The countess and I are alone, sitting by the fire in the drawing room. The coals are dull red now and all the lamps put out but one; its flame flickers across her high cheekbones and perfect forehead.

Tiredness has smoothed out my nerves. In the warmth and stillness of the room, I reflect on my interactions with Isabelle. Maybe I shouldn't have been so honest with my opinions. Did I reveal too much of myself?

"You did well this evening," says the countess, contradicting my thoughts. "My daughter seems to be taken with you. I can see it."

I notice the quiet of the house now that everyone has gone. "*Merci*, Madame la Comtesse."

She smiles, reaching forward to touch the flower still in my hair. "It's fortunate the count only had eyes for Madame Vary this evening."

I look down at my lap, not wanting to meet her gaze.

It's a wonder she doesn't care that her husband flirts with her friend.

"What did you and Isabelle talk about in the conservatory?" she asks.

Her question is perfectly simple, making me feel my answer should be as effortless. But I worry what kind of response she is looking for.

"We talked about her season," I say quietly. My answer is ambiguous enough. I steal a look across at her. She removes the bracelet clamped to her gloved arm and places it on a side table.

"And what about her season?" She pulls at the fingers of her evening gloves and slides them off one by one.

Why should I hesitate to divulge anything Isabelle said to me? Technically the countess is my employer. I should just tell the truth. I take a breath. "Isabelle doesn't want to marry someone you choose for her," I say quickly.

"And what else?" Her voice is calm.

"She says you treat her like one of the count's orchids." A slight smile is the extent of her reaction, and I'm relieved—I thought she might be angry.

She reaches forward and takes my hand. "You have slim wrists like me," she says. Her sudden familiarity startles me.

"Try on my bracelet." She picks up the jeweled band from the table.

"Are you sure?" I ask, watching her fasten it around my wrist. The gesture feels too grand.

She laughs. "Just for a moment. Have you worn real jewels before?"

I shake my head. The bracelet is heavier than I imagined.

The emeralds evoke the depth of the ocean, and tiny diamonds line the edge of it like stars. I've never worn something so special. "It's exquisite," I say eventually. I wish it were mine.

The countess leans back in her chair and lifts a foot toward the dying fire. She seems more relaxed in my presence this time than on either of the other occasions we met. Is she beginning to like me?

"Isabelle's first ball is a defining moment," she says. "She has some important choices to make now that she has come of age. And those choices affect all of us in the family." Her voice is soft, and the word *family* sounds revered. "I can count on you, can't I?" she purrs.

"Of course," I say quietly, and look down at the bracelet. I unfasten the catch and hand it back to her, watching the jewels dance and sparkle in the firelight. I wonder if I'll ever get to wear something so precious again.

# Chapter 10

In the morning I wake up in my narrow bed with a feeling of drowsy contentment. The blankets are snug, and their warmth coaxes me back to slumber, but the clang of church bells rings out, and I become aware of the clatter of hooves, the jangle of bridles and the cries of vendors: Paris is awake. There is something I have to be happy about today, but in the fog between sleep and waking, I can't remember exactly what it is. I finally open my eyes and look at the window. The sagging curtains are parted, and I can see the sun chasing clouds from the sky until a square of light appears on the floorboards of my room. Glorious relief: that's what I feel. The Dubern dinner is over and done with and today I am free; it's my day off.

I struggle from under the tangle of blankets and pull myself out of bed. It's chilly this morning, so I light the stove, then dash back to bed until the room warms up. I look around my threadbare room—what a contrast to last night's setting. When I can bear the temperature, I get out of bed and pour water from the pitcher into the basin and with clenched teeth have a quick, cold wash and get dressed.

As I get ready, I ignore the mirror. When I became a repoussoir I obscured it with the dog-eared postcards and prints I brought from home. My position at Durandeau's has confirmed what I always feared. He has managed to solder into my mind with certainty that which my father always implied: that I wasn't good enough, I wasn't pretty enough, that I was unlovable. Like other facts so uncomfortable to face, I have decided to fold it away in a drawer in my heart, along with the death of my mother and other hurts. That drawer is locked shut.

I sit down at the dresser to braid my hair, peeking at my reflection between illustrations of Paris landmarks. Maman bought these lithographs before I was born. When Papa threw away most of her belongings after her death, I managed to rescue these pictures: Notre Dame Cathedral, the former Tuileries palace with the Louvre in the background and the view from the Arc de Triomphe. They formed the landscape of my daydreams before I came here. Maman used to say that one day she would travel to Paris to see these places with her own eyes, but she never got the chance.

I finish tying my braid and look up at the one photograph I have of her. She is in profile, a handsome woman with strong cheekbones and intelligent eyes—how I wish she would turn her head and look at me. She died of pneumonia brought on by bronchitis when I was ten. The doctor had to travel from a neighboring village; there wasn't much he could do by the time he climbed the worn stairs of our cottage. I reach up to touch the photograph; the shade of sepia lightens toward the edges, as though she's radiating some magical light from her soul. Again that rough stone of sorrow scrapes across my heart. I resist the sadness; I can't be pulled down with the weight of it today.

I pull my coat and bonnet off the hook by the door. *You can see Paris*, a small voice in my head says. *You should see all those places she wanted to.* The statement is like a dare, for now I only travel across the river to the Right Bank for work. For me it's the other side of Paris, not just in geography, but in social circles.

I head out and pull the door closed with a bang. Skipping down the stone steps of my building, I gather speed, taking them two at a time and then jumping the last few steps to the landing at each floor. I traveled all the way to Paris on my own: why shouldn't I explore? It's my day off, after all, and I've nowhere to be and no one to please but myself.

I alight from the omnibus across the river Seine, boundary between the Right and Left Banks. On the map the river looks like a ribbon of blue, thrown off by the wearer; its curving course an accident—it lies strewn across the city. In reality it's not pale blue but a murky, brackish brown, home to frequent boat traffic, traversed by numerous bridges.

Caught up in the tide of Sunday strollers, I continue along the quayside and then cross the street and pass under a set of stone arches until I find myself in the Carré du Louvre, a large courtyard in front of the museum. Laying eyes on it for the first time, I realize that the illustration on my dresser fails to capture the grandeur of the former palace.

Opulent and sprawling inside, the museum is crawling with visitors come to admire the most prestigious art collection in Europe. Its musty cathedral smells, trapped by centuries-old vaulted ceilings and gold columns, transport me back in time to an age when royalty ruled France. The child in me wants to pretend I'm a princess from years gone by—a welcome change from my present situation.

I purchase a map for a few centimes. The museum is bewildering: grand staircases, massive halls with painted ceilings and a never-ending maze of rooms, all of which are organized by era and style of art. I discover there's much more than paintings: sculptures and artifacts from Rome and Ancient Egypt, tapestries and even pottery and jewels. I wander through room after room, aimless, but pulled along with the throng of other visitors—bourgeois families, smart couples and well-dressed European tourists. I watch the tours, the groups of visitors who, like shoals of fish, gape in unison "across to your left" and then "up on your right" as their guide elaborates on the works of art.

Eventually I find myself in a quiet gallery lined with seascapes. The waves and swells of the ocean bring me back to the sea in Brittany, until a noise pulls me from the shores of home. Somebody is snoring. I turn from the wall of paintings and look around. It's only now I notice another patron on one of the wooden benches—a man, slumped over. Is he a vagrant? I hesitate to get any closer until I realize that there's something familiar about him. And then I recognize the ill-fitting suit topped with a mop of uncombed brown hair. My pulse quickens. How unlikely, yet there he is: my disheveled bohemian, Paul Villette.

# Chapter 11

"Monsieur Villette," I say as loudly as I dare. My steps echo across the parquet floor until I'm standing over him. His head is leaning against his shoulder, nodding slightly in time with his breathing, his lips parted.

"Paul?" I say. His eyes remain closed; his brow is smooth, all cares given over to sleep. I let myself study him for a moment. His messy hair looks darker in the dim light, and there are shadows under his eyes. I lean over and touch his shoulder. He doesn't stir. I fold my arms and consider what to do. His breathing continues, even and rhythmic.

I lean over again and prod him roughly.

His eyes snap open and a look of bewilderment crosses his face. I suppress a smile. It seems he's forgotten where he is, as though he was soaring with his dreams and now he must adjust to the steady ground of reality.

After blinking several times, he closes his eyes again and groans, "My head." He rubs his temples, then squints up at me with a confused expression. It's clear that he doesn't even recognize me. A lash of disappointment makes me smart. But why should that surprise me? We have only spoken once, and I was a faceless laundress, not a striking artist, like that woman, Suzanne.

He stretches and yawns. "I came to find her among the art. Instead she drugs me and flees, laughing at my expense."

"Find whom?" I ask. Is he talking about Suzanne? "You fell asleep," I say, and want to kick myself for stating the obvious.

"The muse," he says matter-of-factly. As if I should know what he means. "I'm searching for inspiration."

"Oh." I feel so uncultured.

Paul exhales deeply. He smells like Café Chez Emile when I walk past in the mornings. "I've seen every exhibition at all the bohemian galleries from Montmartre to Montparnasse," he says. "Today I thought I'd look at the old masters."

He's acting as if we were midway through a conversation, but the truth is I'm having trouble keeping up. Has he confused me with someone else?

"I don't know if you remember me. From l'Académie, a few weeks ago?" I sound prim and formal.

He gets up slowly, one hand on the bench for support. "Absinthe is the devil indeed." Eventually he manages to steady his gaze on me. His eyes are soft; the gallery feels warm suddenly.

"May I repay my debt?" I ask, pulling out my change purse and taking out some coins.

A look of recognition crosses his face. "Ah, the hard-working laundress. I remember now." He blinks heavily, as though he's having trouble focusing. "You're not supposed to return a tip."

"But I'd much rather," I say, holding out the coins to him.

He shakes his head and pushes my hand away. "Absolutely not."

"Well, thank you." I put the coins back in my purse, wondering what I can talk to him about next.

He sways a little on his feet.

"You don't look so well," I say, almost reaching out a hand to steady him.

He laughs. "I am not a true bohemian at all—I can't keep up with the rigors of the lifestyle."

"You mean you're hungover?" I wish I didn't sound like a schoolmistress. His manner is informal, and for some reason it makes me act the opposite.

"I just need to walk around and I'll feel better." He gestures to the paintings. "Do you care to look at the art together?"

"All right," I say, and fidget with my bonnet ribbons, which have come undone. When I dressed this morning it wasn't with thought of company. I have one better dress and bonnet. I wish I were wearing them today. But then, why should I care? He looks scruffier than I do.

We begin to stroll along the wall of paintings.

"Now tell me, mademoiselle—"

I interrupt him. "Maude."

"I remember your name." He throws me a smile. "Now tell me, Maude, are you still scolding innocent patrons at cafés?"

"I'm not a laundress anymore," I say, removing my bonnet, realizing too late that's not what a lady would do.

"They sacked you because of the tablecloths? Where's that fighting Breton spirit?"

"Actually, I left the laundry." My voice sounds more defiant than I meant it to.

He looks at me, surprised.

"I found a better position," I say, trying to justify it. But how on earth can I describe my job? I grope for a believable explanation. Clearly I can't admit the truth to him—it's shameful enough to admit it to myself.

"I'm a young lady's companion," I say. I bite my lip and glance at him to see if he's swallowed it. Can he tell that I'm hiding something?

"Ah, a governess."

I don't correct him. "Yes," I answer. I can feel the relief of the lie ease my expression.

"And is the little girl spoiled?"

"She is," I say truthfully. "But I think I can handle her." I'm not adept at expanding on a fib, so I ask, "Have you been to the Louvre before?"

"I used to come often, until I discovered the contemporary galleries. But it's nice to come to such a grand place to see art, don't you think?"

His relaxed manner is rubbing off on me. I want to know more about him, and feel bold enough to ask. "What did you mean before, about the muse?"

"I'm a musician, and when I'm stuck with composing I like to plunge into another art form."

I'm intrigued by this but feel unqualified to keep up my end of the conversation.

He goes on, "I thought I'd come and remind myself what the Impressionists are revolting against. Plus the benches are comfy, and it's more civilized than l'Académie," he laughs. "Everyone's not drunk by noon."

We have almost completed a tour of the room, and I

stop to look at a painting. I have no interest in it, but I'm trying to prolong our encounter. We stand side by side before a stormy seascape. The painting is a blur. I can only focus on the fact that Paul's coat sleeve is touching mine. "Why do paintings inspire you?" I ask. I'm out of my depth, but I want to understand. "Why not listen to music?"

He reflects for a moment. "I enjoy looking at paintings. It reminds me that others also toil to create."

I'm not used to being so close to a man, and I have to concentrate on appearing calm, pressing down the coil of excitement springing up inside.

He shrugs. "In a way I can appreciate it more than a symphony—I don't have to compare myself and my talents." He laughs. "Or lack thereof."

Paul seems different from other people I've met in the capital. He doesn't possess the smooth manners of the rich or the crusty suspicion I have encountered with the working classes. He has a frankness to him, an honest spontaneity that draws me in.

"So was that what I interrupted on the bench? You were soaking up inspiration." I'm teasing, and it catches me by surprise.

His eyes sparkle. "Come on. I'm wide awake, and my search for the muse continues." He takes my hand. "We are going to find a melody for my composition."

Delighted that he wants to remain in my company, I glide out of the gallery, my heart pounding from the warmth of his hand in mine.

"Portraits generally do the trick. This way." He navigates

through a small group of visitors and takes me up a flight of marble stairs to a long gallery, the ceiling of which is lined with skylights.

There are several other patrons dotted around the room, and on the far wall a woman artist has set up her easel and paints, with a cloth underneath to protect the floor.

Paul turns to me. "I can hear music in certain paintings. Women evoke melodies for me. Seascapes and rivers are the string section; in battle scenes the percussion reveals itself." After saying this he gives a half smile, maybe feeling self-conscious about sharing his theory.

"That makes sense." I nod thoughtfully, as if considering his words, but my eyes are examining his appearance. When he smiles, it sends a ripple through me like a wave. He has a small scar on his cheekbone. His hands are expressive, always in motion when he talks. They look like a sculptor's work, large and strong with slender fingers; the skin is smooth with the trace of the veins underneath.

"There's Ingres's *Bather*," says Paul, gesturing to a painting of a nude woman. She's seated with her back to the viewer, her face partially visible. "It wasn't popular when he debuted it at the Salon. But tastes change, and now people can appreciate it."

I worry for a moment about whether I should feel awkward. Is it hugely inappropriate to be looking at a picture of a naked woman with a strange man? The blush rises to my cheek, but I will it away. This is art, I decide, and find my composure. I concentrate on the painting.

"What do you think?" asks Paul. He looks at me expectantly, as if I'm going to say something most original and intelligent. Does he not realize I'm only a village girl who knows nothing about art?

I clear my mind and study the painting.

"It's curious, how the artist has taken something ordinary, a private moment, and made it so striking."

"Go on," urges Paul.

"I mean, she's exposed, the bather, yet hidden." I take a step closer to examine the canvas. "And the colors—when you look up close, they appear a bit messy, haphazard." I step back from the painting, as if I need the perspective of distance, but really, I just want to stand close to him again. "Yet when you look at the whole canvas, it all fits together."

I turn to him, surprised by my own ease and confidence in his company, trying to control the excitement beneath my chest.

"You possess it," he says.

"Possess what?" I ask, hoping what follows is a compliment.

"You have that capacity to be moved by art, to be affected by beauty."

*Beauty*. That word clangs like a saucepan lid crashing to the floor. I move on to the next portrait. Another beautiful woman. Her painted eyes stare blankly out at me, and from her rosebud lips I hear her whisper, "*Repousser: to repel, to repulse, to push away.*"

No. I can't let the agency ruin this afternoon. I shrug off my negative thoughts. I turn back to Paul. "Tell me more about your music," I say cheerfully, so as not to betray my hurt pride.

For the next while we talk about his career, from the bawdy music halls where he plays now to the sought-after place at the music academy he hopes to get accepted to. The minutes gallop by. The other patrons come and go; the artist takes down her easel and packs up her box of paints. Eventually we drift out of the gallery and down the marble stairs, through the grand rooms of the first floor and out into the Carré du Louvre. The sun is casting long shadows in the square. The October chill feels fresh after the stuffy air in the museum.

We sit on a bench with the shadow of the massive museum leaning down on us. There are fewer people in the square now that it's late in the afternoon. A far-off clock tower strikes. Then Paul sighs and says, "I have a rehearsal this evening. I should be going."

"Yes, I should go too," I say, with a fizzle of disappointment. I can see the fading light reflected in his eyes as the afternoon disappears around us.

"We're playing a concert on Saturday evening at le Chat Noir. You must come."

I break into a smile. "I'd love to," I say, and then immediately realize I can't possibly go. Isabelle Dubern's ball is next Saturday. A lead weight drags down my smile. "But unfortunately, I can't . . . I have a previous engagement." How torturous to be forced to refuse.

He smiles. "Too bad. There will be other concerts, though." He rises to leave and we shake hands. "Have a pleasant week," he says. "And don't let your charge boss you around too much."

I'd almost forgotten about that. My charge: what a

deception. "Good luck with your concert, Paul." It feels nice to say his name aloud.

"*Au revoir.*" He turns away and I watch him stride across the square and through the thinning crowds of museum-goers. The spell is broken, but the magic of our meeting lingers around me like a haze. I walk out of the square and toward the river. I lean on the stone parapet, which is warm from the sun despite the crisp air. Coppery leaves rustle by my feet; the horse chestnuts and poplars have turned as autumn has taken hold of the city. The pleasure boats continue their back and forth up and down the river. Barges unload supplies on the quay. Puffs of smoke from other boats cough into the sky and meld with the white clouds. Right Bank, Left Bank, rich or poor, I decide that the river belongs to everyone.

There are closer bridges, but I walk east toward the Pont Neuf. I prefer the view from there. Paris and its procession of life. It is at such times that the city gives me a soaring feeling and I want to hold on to the perfection of the moment. But as soon as it is labeled, it is gone. Before long, my lonely garret room will bring me back down to earth.

# Chapter 12

The kettle whistles on the stove in the repoussoir dressing room. Its piping hot squeal is shrill, but it can't compete with the excited chatter of the repoussoirs discussing their weekend assignments.

Cécile is holding court. "He's a captain in the Guard, and his dress uniform is simply dashing." She is in better spirits now that another client has unwittingly provided a new love interest. Her heavy chin shudders with excitement; her bulbous nose wrinkles up when she gives a detailed account of this captain's medals. "He's sure to be made major before long. My client says it's inevitable."

Marie-Josée shows up late and bustles past the other girls. She grins at me as she takes off her coat and bonnet. "The countess didn't gobble you up for dinner, I see." The ripples of excitement in the other girls' conversations have ebbed, and all eyes turn to me.

"The Countess Dubern?" asks Cécile. I detect a hint of hostility.

"She's hiring me for her daughter's ball," I explain. "I had a trial date with her on Saturday."

"You lucky thing," chimes in Hortense.

"Where did she take you?" Cécile asks.

Their scrutiny is making me uncomfortable. "Nowhere. I mean, I had dinner at their house." I shrug, trying to appear nonchalant.

Marie-Josée has taken custody of the kettle and is making a pot of tea. "Quiet dinner, my foot. The countess knows how to put on a show," she says, not helping my desire to stay unnoticed. She opens a box of madeleines and arranges them on a plate. "What did they serve? How many courses?"

She's putting me on the spot. I'm not used to being the center of attention, and I feel shy. "I can't remember how many."

"Details, please," Marie-Josée demands, taking a seat and placing the tea tray in front of us.

"Who was there?" asks Cécile.

"What did the countess wear?" asks Emilie, the hairs on her mole quivering with curiosity.

To my relief there's a knock on the dressing room door and Laurent interrupts the interrogation. "*Bonjour, mesdemoiselles.*"

The girls' focus shifts to his handsome face. "*Bonjour, Laurent,*" they chorus. He searches the room until he meets my gaze. "There you are, Maude. I have a message for you from Monsieur Durandeau."

I freeze at the mention of his name. The others look at me—they're glad his message isn't for them.

"He asks that you go and see Madame Leroux. She has to fit you for the Rochefort ball."

I stand up, grateful that it's only the seamstress I have to face and not Durandeau.

"A ball dress? How exciting!" Emilie chirps.

"Yes," sneers Cécile. "I'm sure Leroux has made you something special for the occasion."

I walk toward Laurent, who's holding the door open for me. "Actually, the countess has sent you a dress from her couturier," he says, smiling. There are gasps from around the room. "She had very specific instructions."

I glance back at my comrades, wondering how I should react. The other girls nudge each other and exchange looks. I suppose this must be a good thing. I look at Marie-Josée, who is nodding at me encouragingly.

"And of course"—Laurent puts his arm on my back, gently guiding me out of the dressing room—"the client is always right." Before the door is closed behind me, I can hear the other girls whispering.

Madame Leroux pins the waist of the new gown in stony silence. When I saw it on the hanger, I knew instantly that this gray satin dress was in a class of its own. I glance down at the bodice and full skirts, trying to examine the countess's choice.

"Keep still or I'll be sticking pins in you, not the dress," says Leroux.

Standing on a stool, I have not been permitted to look in the mirror, and given the seamstress's current mood, I fear I will be deprived of that privilege altogether.

There's a knock on the door and Marie-Josée enters. "Vivienne?" She calls Madame Leroux by her first name. "There's a lunch special on today at Chartier. Do you want to join us?" Marie-Josée has everyone charmed, even the scatty Madame Leroux.

"I would if I had the time." She throws her arms up and waves them toward the ever-increasing pile of dresses. Strands of frizzy hair escape from her bun with every gesture. "These constant fittings—I can't get anything else done." Her scissors hang from a ribbon around her waist and swing like a pendulum as she gets worked up.

Marie-Josée sighs in solidarity with Leroux, then turns her attention toward me. "Well, don't you look all dressed up with nowhere to go." She turns me around, examining the dress as I try to keep my balance on the stool. I'm desperate to see what the fuss is about.

Marie-Josée raises her eyebrows. "This is a first, Vivienne," she says.

"Never. I've never had a client send over a dress before," says Madame Leroux peevishly.

"That's one fussy countess," agrees Marie-Josée, teasing out the information.

"Durandeau says she wants something classic, not vulgar," says Leroux. "What an affront. As if I could make a vulgar gown. Now, where has that pincushion hidden itself?" She sifts through some fabrics on her worktable.

"I'll say." Marie-Josée flashes me a knowing look. "Who does she think she is?"

"I keep up with the fashions like any dressmaker." Madame Leroux throws a witchy hand toward the stack of outdated issues of the ladies' fashion bulletin *Le Petit Echo de la Mode.*

I take the chance while they're chatting and step off the stool to get a peek in the mirror. The bodice is a pale gray satin, and the skirt billows out like a cloud, finished in a layer of lace tulle. It's a pretty shade of gray, almost with a tinge of pink to it. No wonder Leroux is nettled—it's far superior to any dress of her creation. And what's more, I feel different wearing this new dress. A seed of hope is growing: perhaps the countess doesn't see me like the rest of the repoussoirs. Maybe she simply wants a friend for her difficult daughter. Otherwise why give a special dress to someone like me? It doesn't make sense that you'd want to dress up someone who's paid to be ugly.

Another knock sounds at the door, and before Leroux can answer, a trio of heads appear: Cécile, flanked by Emilie and Hortense.

"Oh, look at the dress," breathes Emilie. "Is that silk?"

Cécile walks up to me, eyeing my new gown intently. "There's a client coming at eleven for a selection. Laurent says we have to round everyone up."

Hortense reaches out to touch the material.

Madame Leroux is getting testy. "Why is everyone crowding in here?"

I hear Laurent's voice in the hall and he appears a moment later in the doorway.

"Emilie, Hortense, Cécile, it's almost time. What are you standing around for?" Then he looks behind the door and catches sight of Marie-Josée next to Leroux. "What's going on in here—secret workers' meeting? Durandeau will have a coronary if you decide to unionize."

"I'm just trying to get my dresses done, Monsieur Laurent," says Leroux, flustered.

"Well, everyone out, and leave Madame Leroux to her work."

My colleagues protest with a round of moans, but the crowd breaks up and they file out of the seamstress's room, dragging their heels.

"I'll be right there, Laurent. Once I change out of this dress," I say.

When I get to the salon the door is closed, which means the client has already arrived. Wearing a plain agency dress again, I open the door quietly, hoping to slip in without a fuss. My footstep on a creaky floorboard gives me away, and Durandeau's head whips around to see who's causing the disturbance.

"Excuse me, madame," Durandeau says to the client, who's strolling around the room looking at the girls. "I won't be a moment." He marches up to me, his face swollen as though his collar is throttling him. "Out! Get out," he hisses.

I'm so confused I just stand there. Shouldn't he want me to take my place with the other girls?

His eyes bulge. "You're not supposed to be in here."

Cécile, Marie-Josée and Emilie are all within earshot. Even though they remain frozen like statues, I know everyone's straining to overhear the drama.

"I know I'm late, monsieur, but—"

Durandeau cuts me off. "The countess has requested that you work exclusively for her family."

I look blankly at him, his chest puffed out, nostrils flaring, annoyed at having to explain. "She doesn't want you shown to other clients until after the ball. Now go!"

I nod feebly and make for the door, embarrassed. I can sense the other girls' eyes boring into my back.

I drift along the corridor and return to the dressing room,

where I sit alone, staring at my colleagues' belongings. We always spend the day in agency clothes, then change back into our own before we leave for the evening; until then our dresses, coats and hats are hung up. There are rows of shoes and boots, some mittens and an umbrella—all waiting for their owners to return. There is nothing to suggest from their appearance that the items belong to ugly girls—just girls, who, like me, need a job and are lucky (or unlucky enough) to fit the bill.

I think back to the day of my interview. The initial shock of contemplating a room full of unattractive women wears off eventually. Over time you get past the outer layers, the misshapen shells, and become acquainted with the soul and essence of each girl. Like any person, an ugly woman's looks are transformed by her conversation, humor, intelligence and even grace. But this all reverses during the selection process. When a client enters the salon, I've seen a girl change from her giddy, laughing self to her repoussoir guise in an instant. When she freezes like a statue, the light completely disappears from her eyes. She hides. All that's left to the outsider is that unattractive shell to judge her on. Her true self waits for the selection process to be over and her persecutors to leave the room; until that time, she is impenetrable to discovery.

No one talks about these moments, but I take note—I can feel the change happen. For it takes place in my own heart when I hear the step of a well-heeled shoe on the salon floor and Durandeau's nauseating voice.

I rinse out the teapot and tidy away the china plates. Minutes drag on. It's only now that I am separated from the rest of the girls that I can see how I've come to belong here and feel at home. Despite the unpleasantness of the job, there is comfort in the routine of the agency and the comradeship of the girls. But now I've been singled out, and I can't shake Durandeau's words. They echo in my head. *The countess chose you.*

# Chapter 13

"It is a special dance lesson today, girls," says Girard with her affected elocution. We are gathered in the dining room, the tables and chairs pushed to the sides. Each girl is partnered with another. Of course I'm paired with Marie-Josée, who actually enjoys dance practice and is surprisingly light on her feet considering her ample frame.

"Mademoiselle Pichon is to attend the official ball marking the start of the season: a first for one of our girls." Girard beams at me. I feel uncomfortable. My excitement for the new dress has been overshadowed by the pressure of such a big event.

In the village we had a dance once in the church hall. It was a chilly building not equipped for celebration or rejoicing. Still, I cradled my anticipation of the event lovingly, thinking it would be a grand affair that would change the course of sleepy rural life. Something momentous would happen that evening, I was sure. The hall was decorated with flowers, I wore my new dress—well, an old one I had made new with ribbons and lace—I drank cider and caught the eye of a boy from a neighboring village. When he led me to dance, I knew that my prophecy was becoming reality. It was only afterward he admitted it was a bet, to coax a wallflower to the floor. My hopes crushed, I spent the rest of the evening as a spectator, the promise of magic extinguished.

"Now take your partners, ladies. We shall begin with a waltz." Girard's voice squawks when she raises it. The shuffle of footsteps can be heard across the room as the girls obey orders. I turn and face Marie-Josée, putting my hand on her shoulder. She squeezes my waist, making me laugh.

"Ready, and . . . begin."

There's no music, only Girard tapping out the rhythm with her cane.

"*One*, two, three, *one*, two, three," she says breathlessly, punctuating each repetition with a thump.

As we waltz near Cécile and Hortense, I feel a sharp elbow in my back. Cécile whispers, "Watch where you're going."

Marie-Josée tuts and guides us away from them. "She's just jealous, *ma belle*," she says, twirling me around the room. "You're getting all these lovely perks and don't have to bother going to the client selections."

I feel wrongly accused. "Doesn't she understand that I don't care about those things? I'm not trying to be special or better than anyone else." I step on her toe, not paying attention to the dance. "Sorry," I say. We come to a standstill.

"Let's start over. Come on, chin up, *chérie*," says Marie-Josée. "Look at me, not your feet." She smiles at me and I feel a bit better. "Like any job in service, there are important clients and less important ones at the agency," she continues. "You are getting the high-society treatment. You're starting at the top."

"But I don't want the attention."

"It doesn't work like that. Look, not all the girls get to attend such events. Give them something, Maude."

"What do you mean?" I ask, surprised. "I'm not going to boast about the events."

"Not boast, but you have to share your experiences. If you don't, they'll think you're stuck-up. So take some notice at the ball and pay these girls some mind when they quiz you on it."

"New tempo now, girls." Girard changes the "music," but I'm distracted. I can't get the new rhythm right. Marie-Josée leads us through my missteps patiently.

"They want the details: the names of the guests, the dishes the hostess serves, a description of the clothes and jewels," she says, spinning me, her face reddening from the effort.

"Emilie, arms up, keep your frame solid!" Girard shouts.

Marie-Josée continues, "The likes of Emilie, she's only seen the inside of a café or gone for a stroll in the park—and only with lower-tier clients, at that. She hasn't been as lucky as you."

"But it's not luck," I insist. "It's a curse, such a high-profile event. It would be so much easier to walk in the park, or sit in the back of a café, out of sight."

"It's too late for that. The countess did her choosing and off to the ball you go, Cinderella."

"But I'm not Cinderella, am I? I'm supposed to be the ugly stepsister. We all are—Durandeau's *belles-soeurs*."

Girard thumps her stick out of time to get our attention. "Girls, enough talking! Concentrate on the steps. Mademoiselle

Pichon, you especially, given that you're attending a ball in a matter of days. Do you want to embarrass yourself?"

We continue dancing around the room under the scrutiny of Girard and to the unrelenting *thump, thump* of her stick.

# Chapter 14

I climb the staircase of the Dubern house behind a servant, careful not to trip on the skirts of my new dress. I had all of three seconds to look at my reflection in Leroux's workroom before being rushed out the door. Marie-Josée was out on a repoussoir date when I left the agency, so I couldn't show her the result, with the alterations complete and my hair done. Leroux wasn't interested in paying me any compliments; her lips were sewn tight after she helped me into the dress. It's absurd to admit it, but I almost felt pretty when I saw my reflection in the mirror.

I wish my mother could see me.

The gaze of Dubern relatives follows me as I advance step by step up the carpeted stair. They scrutinize me with their frozen expressions; the men are dour and the women haughty. My dress doesn't fool them. After I pass by, I imagine one portrait turning to another and asking, *Why has such an ill-bred girl been allowed to befriend our great-great-granddaughter?*

The servant leads me up another flight of stairs. I'm curious which version of Isabelle Dubern will greet me this time: the devilish cat who lashed out in the hat shop, the sullen girl who ignored me in her parents' drawing room, or that glimmer of a confidante I saw in the glass house—like one of those flowers whose petals, closed tight by day, open up to moonlight.

Walking along a hallway, I can hear raised voices.

"I will not wear it. I told you before, it's unbearable."

I recognize Isabelle's voice and I want to turn back. My question has been answered. The servant gestures toward the open door of her bedroom.

"I can't breathe." Isabelle puts her hands on her rib cage. A maid is fussing with hooks on her dress. Isabelle stamps her foot in protest, shrugging off the girl's touch. The countess is perched on the four-poster bed, watching her daughter's tantrum.

I linger in the doorway, waiting for the servant to announce me. This room isn't what I imagined for Isabelle somehow; the walls are decorated with a girlish rosebud paper; there are framed paintings of rosy children, and a collection of china dolls stare at Isabelle from a glass cabinet.

"Is that what you want? Me to faint in front of everyone?" says Isabelle.

"Enough hysterics." The countess snaps her fingers. "Cochet." She addresses the maid. "Loosen the corset a hair and see if the dress will still fit." The maid, who began to tidy up other dresses discarded on a chair, now returns to Isabelle's side. She unfastens the hooks on the bodice of the dress, then begins to loosen the corset underneath.

The countess watches closely. "You will wear the dress, Isabelle. I will have Cochet sew you into it if need be."

The room falls silent. Only the ticking of a clock on the

mantel and the sound of the maid working the corset laces can be heard.

"Madame la Comtesse," says the servant, seizing an opportunity to interrupt. "Mademoiselle Pichon has arrived."

I walk toward the countess and curtsey.

She glances at me. "*Bonsoir*, Maude. Don't you look nice," she says without feeling—not the way a compliment should be given, but as though saying something perfunctory, like "Close the door" or "Pass the butter."

"It's a shame your aunt was taken ill," she adds with a knowing look.

I didn't realize that's why I'm here alone this evening, but I play along. "Yes, she was feeling poorly." I recall the countess's remark after dinner about the count admiring the young widow. Is Madame Vary really ill or just not invited?

I look over at Isabelle. She stands silently while the maid finishes hooking up her dress. Bright white satin with chiffon folds sweeping across the low neckline and layers upon layers of skirts emphasize her neat waist. Her diamond earrings hang like giant teardrops, glittering in the lamplight. I now understand that the choice of my gray dress was expertly engineered. As beautiful as I thought it at the agency, seeing Isabelle now, I realize that I am a mere shadow—a faded bloom to her vibrant flower. The countess's grasp of the subtleties of the foil's position is far more sophisticated than the agency's.

The countess gets up from the bed and walks toward Isabelle, inspecting her daughter as a superior officer might a soldier under his command.

"Where's the necklace? Put it on," she instructs the maid.

"Mother, really, the earrings are sufficient."

"Darling," says the countess icily. "The jewels will reflect the light and brighten up your pretty face."

Isabelle scowls. Flattery doesn't soften her. She looks at me accusingly. "Maude doesn't wear carats of precious stones. Why should I?"

The countess looks at me with mock pity. "Maude suits a simpler *tenue*. I'm sure she would appreciate the chance to wear jewels if she were as lucky as you. Isn't that right, Maude?"

"I—I'm sure," I stammer, my voice croaky. "The necklace will look awfully pretty, Isabelle."

The maid takes the jewels from the box on the dressing table and places them around Isabelle's white throat—a web of rubies the color of pomegranate seeds is interlaced with shimmering diamonds.

Isabelle's jaw tightens. "I'll wear it on the condition we lend Maude something." She turns to her mother. "It's only fair."

Gripped with anxiety, I step preemptively toward the countess. "Oh, I couldn't." I shake my head emphatically.

"Come now, Isabelle. Don't be difficult," says the countess. "Cochet, fix her hair. I don't want it falling loose at the back." She's doing her best to ignore her daughter's request.

"I'm not being difficult, Mother, I'm being generous," says Isabelle. "I insist Maude be allowed to borrow something pretty. She looks positively plain."

Without knowing it, Isabelle has hit upon my intended

purpose. The countess must be silently fuming: the foil shouldn't be given jewels.

"It's not appropriate, Isabelle."

I nod. "Your mother's right. I don't need to borrow any jewels." I silently pray that Isabelle will let the matter drop.

"Mother, why not? We can easily lend her something. I have a box full of jewels."

The countess looks past her daughter and stares at her own reflection in the mirror, smoothing the neckline of her dark velvet dress.

"Very well. You may let your friend play dress-up, if that's what it takes." She shakes her head. "Everything has to be a fight with you."

Isabelle begins to rummage through the jewelry box on the dresser. "Cochet, where are Grand-Maman's pearls?" she asks. "They will go with Maude's dress."

The maid opens a drawer in the dressing table and pulls out an ivory box. Once the massive swath of pearls (five rows deep) has been secured around my undeserving neck, Isabelle spins me around to look at the result.

"Very pretty. Take a look."

The jewels feel cool and weighty against my skin. I look in the mirror on the dressing table and catch my breath: the pearls are large and dazzling and completely out of place on me. I meet the countess's gaze; her expression is one of barely masked disgust. I don't want to anger her, but how could I have refused her daughter any more than she could? To do so would have drawn attention to the insistence on my plain appearance.

"Your father will be ready to leave," says the countess.

"He's always hideously punctual, even though he hates events like these." She sweeps past me, her eyes accusing. Almost out of earshot she hisses, "Pearls before swine indeed."

The fire crackles and a loose coal falls to the hearth. Thrown by her displeasure, I walk toward the fireplace and lean down to pick up the tongs without thinking.

"Mademoiselle," says Cochet. I glance up to see her look of horror. "Geneviève will see to the fire. Don't trouble yourself in your nice dress."

I put the tongs back immediately and step away from the fire, inwardly cursing myself.

"That will be all, Cochet," Isabelle says. The maid bobs a curtsey and closes the door, and we are alone.

Isabelle glares at me. "Why did you take my mother's side about the jewels? If we're going to be friends, you cannot act like her lapdog."

"She intimidates me. I'd be scared to disagree with her." I fear my honesty will be my undoing—why couldn't I have given a more polite answer?

Isabelle's face freezes in surprise and then she slides into a laugh.

Realizing my precarious position, I touch the necklace adorning my throat. "You shouldn't have insisted I wear this, Isabelle. It's too much. I barely know your family."

"What are you saying, that you're going to vanish with the necklace into the night?" She laughs at my shocked expression. "I'm joking."

With the countess gone, Isabelle is immediately happier. I wonder if her mother is a trigger for her moods.

"I'm surprised Mother doesn't mind us going to the ball together," she says.

"Why would she object?"

Isabelle fiddles with one of her earrings. "She is normally picky about the friends I make, always wanting to pair me off with some titled girl as a best friend. The longer the name, the better; everything is for appearance's sake with her."

"Oh, I see," I murmur. "Whereas I'm a nobody." I watch Isabelle carefully. Could she be testing me? Still doubting my "poor relation" connection to Madame Vary?

"You mustn't take offense. I find you more interesting than the other debutantes."

"Why?" I'm genuinely curious.

"You have an honesty that's refreshing. And you're not obsessed with the season. It's obvious you're not from this world." She shrugs. "Yet it's not like Mother to take on a cause like you."

I have to think quickly. "I suppose she's doing my aunt a favor," I say lightly.

Isabelle shakes her head. "She doesn't do anyone favors unless there's something in it for her." She picks up her fur mantle and wraps it around her shoulders. "Shall we go?" she asks.

I nod, grateful that she doesn't expect me to justify her mother's uncharacteristic charity toward me. I follow Isabelle out of the room. Despite the drama, the necklace manages to make me feel less like one of Durandeau's repoussoirs, and I can't help but leap to the next thought: what if a young man at the ball mistakes me for a real debutante? As soon as I think this, I close the lid on the notion—I don't need that kind of dangerous thought running free in my mind. It can't do me any good.

When we reach the grand staircase, I glance at the portraits again as we pass. "Are all of these people Duberns?" I whisper to Isabelle.

"Just the dead ones."

I purse my lips to fight the smile. Isabelle is no ordinary debutante either. She has a rebel in her.

A servant is waiting at the front door with my cloak in hand. I put it on and follow the Dubern family into the night.

# Chapter 15

The carriage pulls us through the illuminated boulevards of Paris. A layer of fog wraps around the low-hanging moon and gives the streetlamps an unearthly glow. I think of the pearls under my cloak and how Durandeau would never approve. No doubt I'm breaking some agency rule.

Next to me Isabelle taps her foot lightly and tugs a finger of her gloves, pulling at a thread. I can't tell whether she's the least bit nervous or excited for the ball.

"Remember to bring up hunting with the gentlemen tonight," says the countess to her husband.

"You know I hate shooting," he says, running his thumb and forefinger down the sides of his mustache.

"I don't care. We need an invitation to a shooting party this season, for your daughter's sake."

The count ignores his wife and smiles at his daughter. "*Tu es très belle, ma fille.*"

"Yes, we did quite well, considering what we had to work with," says the countess, taking credit.

"Any excuse for you to spend money," the count responds. "There aren't enough days in the year for her to wear all those dresses I'm paying for."

I bet the count doesn't know he's paying for my wardrobe as well as his daughter's.

"Isabelle gets one season to make an impression," the countess snaps. "Do you want her looking like the poor relation?"

At that remark the count's eyes dart to mine. I look out the window to deflect his gaze. No, he wouldn't want a daughter like me.

"What kind of offers would she attract then?" the countess harps on.

They talk about Isabelle as though she's an investment or a piece of property, a chess piece to be fought over—and it can't be the first of these rows. I look at Isabelle, whose disinterested expression confirms my theory.

We pass under a set of stone arches and the horses slow to a walk in front of a floodlit building that resembles a palace. There are torches blazing along the driveway, which is lined with carriages in numbers rivaling a busy Paris boulevard.

"What is this place?" I ask Isabelle. "Is it a chateau?"

"It's just a house." Isabelle sounds bored. "It belongs to the Viscount de Rochefort."

"It's too bad his elder son is in the Orient," the countess says. "The younger one, what's his name again?"

"Xavier," says the count.

"Yes, Xavier. He's more agreeable, but of course, he won't inherit the title."

Isabelle sighs in response.

Before I mistakenly reach for the door myself, a footman in livery saves me and opens it, then helps us descend from the carriage. I stare at the family home of the Rocheforts and try to quell the queasy rolling in my stomach.

"I did find out that the Duke d'Avaray will be attending tonight. Did you hear me, Isabelle?"

"Yes, Mother." Isabelle rolls her eyes.

It's hard for me to understand how Isabelle can be so relaxed while my anxiety has advanced to a stage of pure fear. I can't even get out of a carriage without showing myself up and they're talking about fortunes and titles. My mind is reeling as we walk toward the palatial house: Will I be able to navigate the dancing and manage polite conversation? Will I say the wrong thing or have my accent questioned again?

We walk up the stone steps and pass through an elaborately carved front door. The ladies' cloaks are taken in the entrance hall, along with the men's hats, canes and overcoats. I wonder how they keep track of whose is whose.

Isabelle's parents don't hesitate for a moment about what to do or where to go. We advance with other guests up a wide marble staircase and through a vast doorway into the ballroom, and I can hear my own intake of breath. If the Dubern house felt luxurious, this place is the epitome of opulence, fit for a king or an emperor. The floor is polished, shining like a new chestnut, and couples are dancing in perfect time; the dresses are like twirling butterflies of silk, each one anchored to a dark suit and white tie. Pale mint walls are crowned with ornate moldings; bronze sconces fashioned like intertwining rose branches hold pink candles. Gilt-framed mirrors as tall as the room are interspersed between vast windows, and sugar pink settees are positioned along the walls. The light is golden and fizzing. I am speechless—it feels as if I'm walking through the pages of a fairy tale.

The girls are beautiful, a chorus of rustling skirts and laughter. I thought Isabelle looked striking, but seeing her competition, I understand Marie-Josée's peach lesson. How will Isabelle stand out in this crowd?

"Do you know all these people?" I whisper to Isabelle. There must be a hundred guests in the ballroom, all of them glittering and radiant.

"I know *of* them," she says, clearly unimpressed. "And I warn you, we'll be forced to dance, for no one here can engage us in intelligent conversation."

I shake my head, flummoxed by her complacency.

"Posture." The countess runs a finger down her daughter's spine and Isabelle makes an effort to stand straighter.

"And smile," the countess says.

Isabelle obeys.

"Don't grin, dear," the countess scolds, herself the essence of poise and grace.

Isabelle's parents approach an older couple I recognize from the Dubern dinner, who appear to be formally greeting the guests. At their side is a handsome young man with a thick brow and a conceited swagger. He sports a mustache, perhaps to add gravitas to his youthful looks.

"Monsieur le Vicomte," says the count to the older man. "Fine turnout." They shake hands.

His wife, the viscountess, shakes her head at the countess. "I can't believe our Claire and your Isabelle are already debutantes." She gestures to the young man standing next to her. "You remember my younger son, Xavier."

122

"Of course," the countess purrs, offering her hand to the young man.

"Madame la Comtesse," Xavier says, taking the countess's hand. "You look stunning, as usual. Watch out, or the gentlemen will take you for a debutante yourself."

The countess laughs, swatting at his arm in mock protest. "Honestly, Xavier," she says, delighted by his attention.

The young Rochefort exudes something that could be mistaken for charm but feels more like arrogance.

More guests arrive, and the Rocheforts turn their attention to them—but Xavier remains with us. He seeks out Isabelle. "Mademoiselle Dubern, I was hoping to see you tonight."

Isabelle gives a functional smile, one that doesn't reach her eyes. "Everything looks splendid."

"I can't take credit for a thing," he says. "Mother and Claire made all the arrangements. It's a peculiarly feminine talent, don't you think, planning a party?"

If he's trying to impress her, he's doing a poor job. Isabelle ignores his observations on the gentler sex. She introduces me instead. "This is my friend Maude Pichon."

Suddenly the focus of attention, I feel like a statue, mute and heavy, as if I were cast in bronze; my breath is shallow and my mouth is frozen in a smile.

Xavier takes my hand in a tepid grip. "The Pichon family," he says, "from . . . where did you say?"

My heart leaps and then I realize that no one said where I am from. I have to remind myself that he doesn't suspect me of being the imposter I am; he's simply trying to place me in the social hierarchy. "I'm from Normandy,"

123

I answer. At least Normandy is in the right direction to the truth—it's the province next to my home in Brittany. "A small village near Deauville. You wouldn't recognize the name, I'm sure."

He raises an eyebrow. "I daresay I wouldn't." His tone is dismissive and rude, but I can only deflect his scrutiny.

"And where are you from, Monsieur de Rochefort?" I ask.

"Paris," he sneers. "Where else?" He immediately turns toward Isabelle, snubbing me completely. "Dance with me, I insist."

"Very well," she says. But I know she's not enthusiastic. As she is led away by the young Rochefort, her eye catches mine, and her expression reads *I told you so.*

I exhale a breath, glad for a reprieve from socializing. But left alone with the count and countess, I feel like an uninvited guest. The count must be thinking the same thing, as he immediately takes his wife's arm. "Come, dear, let us leave the dancing to the young people. I want to find the general."

The countess looks irked. "How can you focus on anything other than your daughter tonight?" This first dance is a highly charged moment for her. Her gaze follows Isabelle and Xavier as though she's watching a new horse run its first race.

"She's not in mortal danger," protests the count. "She's dancing."

The countess leans toward me, her perfect features tense. "Make sure you stand beside Isabelle between dances," she whispers. I can smell her perfume: sandalwood and spice. "And don't dance yourself unless she is engaged."

I nod, both relieved that I don't have to dance and put out that I'm all but forbidden to do so.

"Whatever you do, don't leave her alone."

Before she can utter more instructions, her husband cuts in. "Edwige," says the count impatiently. "Come, I see the general."

I want to laugh when I hear the countess referred to by her Christian name: it doesn't suit her. As they walk away, I can hear the count saying, "Queer-looking girl, and what a solemn face."

I let the remark bounce off me; there's no point taking offense. Embrace your flaws, I remind myself. Now that I have been abandoned by my party, I can truly watch the dancing. And it's glorious. Everyone moves like clockwork; and not just when they're dancing. I observe the groups of people, catch fragments of conversations and snatches of gestures. It's an effortless display of well-executed manners and etiquette. The men know how to approach a lady, how to engage her in conversation; the ladies know how to laugh sweetly at just the right moments and when to move on graciously without giving offense. There is no Girard prompting in the wings: they all know their cues by heart, as if they were born with the knowledge.

The night wears on, and Isabelle's first dance turns into several. I wander away from the activity and take a seat on one of the settees at the edge of the floor. I realize that this is the quintessential repoussoir moment: sitting on the fringes and watching your client soak up the attention. I should be relieved that the evening is playing out as it was meant to, but I can't help feeling disappointed; despite the beauty surrounding me, the sheen has been taken off the night. How foolish to have gotten my hopes up just because I'm wearing the Dubern gown and pearls. Between the dancing figures I catch sight of my reflection in one of the mirrors on the opposite wall. I don't think that what nature has given me in terms of my appearance can be improved beyond how I look tonight—this is the limit of my attractiveness, and still I am passed over.

"There you are," says a voice, and I look up to find Isabelle standing over me.

Next to her is the handsomest man I have ever seen.

He takes my gloved hand in his. "*Bonsoir,* mademoiselle." He kisses it. "Duke d'Avaray." My heart hiccups and my cheeks warm. I study his immaculate appearance: dark blond hair, intense blue eyes, a strong nose and fine jaw. Unlike most of the men in the room, he wears a military uniform— he stands out from the fray in his blue jacket and red epaulettes. What's most surprising is that Isabelle appears perfectly nonchalant. She doesn't betray any excitement or flutters of the heart in front of this Adonis.

Xavier then joins our party with a pretty strawberry-blond girl whose head is piled high with curls. She turns out to be his sister, Claire. She gives me a small curtsey when we are introduced, then bats her eyes at the duke.

"Let's dance again," says Claire, trying to catch his attention.

"Tricky number, five," says Xavier, letting his eyes flicker across my face. He turns his back to me, and I understand immediately that he wants to avoid having me as a partner. I try to appear oblivious, my expression the pleasant mask I've mastered for introductions. Still, it annoys me that someone of his breeding could be so rude.

The duke turns to ask Isabelle for a dance, but she preempts his question. "I'm going to sit this one out. Oh, please dance with Maude, I insist. She hasn't danced once this evening."

My stomach somersaults at the notion of disobeying the countess—not to mention the dancing itself. I can see myself treading on the duke's toes or tripping him. I turn to him, ready to make an excuse, but I'm met with a smile. He betrays no disappointment at ending up with me. Hand extended, he simply says, "Well then, shall we?" His voice sounds rich and smooth.

I hesitate, glancing across the room to see if the countess is watching. "I'm not much of a dancer," I murmur.

"Go on, Maude," says Isabelle. "You can't be a wallflower all night."

I'm about to protest again, yet the truth is, I don't want to say no. I reach for the duke's outstretched hand and a tingle shoots up my arm. I can hear Girard's stick thumping a rhythm in my head as he leads me to the center of the room—*one*, two, three, *one*, two, three.

I must look as nervous as I feel, because the duke asks, "Is this your first ball?"

"I think that's fairly obvious," I say, and blush immediately.

He grins. "Don't look down at your feet. Look at me, I've got you."

The dance begins and the duke whisks me across the floor with assurance, holding me firmly. The orchestra is loud, and I let the violin and cello chords vibrate through me. My nerves, untangled by the music, are now restrung as quivers of excitement. With his confidence on the floor, I relax into his hold on me. As I am spun around the room, I look at his impossibly handsome face, admire his poise and ease.

"There, you're doing fine," he says. He is one of those rare people who manages to extend their confidence to those around them; his every gesture is natural, his conversation fluid—awkwardness just wouldn't occur to him.

Despite my shyness I want to know more about him. I study his face. What could I possibly talk to a duke about? The gold buttons on his uniform distract me, glinting in the candlelight. "You are in the military!" I exclaim, then wish I'd kept quiet.

"My commission is almost up," he answers. "I'm going to take over the family estate."

I sense a reluctance in his voice. "It sounds as though you'd rather stay in service," I say, attempting to draw him out.

"It's that obvious?" He smiles and sighs at the same time. "My father died and I am the only son. He was the real Duke d'Avaray. I'm merely a pretender."

His modesty only makes me like him more, makes me want to reward his openness by sharing a confession of my own. "My mother died when I was ten." And as soon as I say it, I feel cheap using my mother's death as an excuse for conversation.

But the duke looks down at me with kindness. "It's a horrible feeling, losing a parent."

"Nothing prepares you for it," I murmur.

"You're right," he says, reassuring me. I catch his eye and his smile radiates warmth and lights a fire beneath my breast. In this moment, he makes me feel as though I'm shining like the jewel itself, not the lowly metal foil designed to enhance it. I don't care how I came to be here; the only thing that matters right now is that I, Maude Pichon, from Poullan-sur-Mer, am in the arms of a duke.

When the dance ends, the duke cuts in on Xavier and Claire. It doesn't matter to me—I float back to where I left Isabelle, happy for my moment. I cross the room and revel in the way every glass, curtain and candlestick appears to be standing at attention, mindful of its contribution to the occasion. And I am part of this too. The real world of Montparnasse and the agency fades from memory, as do the feelings of humiliation and loneliness. My garret room, Monsieur Durandeau and the repoussoirs seem like a fiction, and only this fairy tale is real.

Then someone grabs my arm, wrenching me from my thoughts. I turn to find the countess's face inches from mine. "Don't waste the duke's time, Maude." She smiles at another guest walking past, but her grip betrays her anger—it is firm, not friendly.

"But—" I begin to explain.

"Don't bother trying to account for your carelessness," she interrupts, then turns to lift a glass of champagne from the tray of a passing waiter. She takes a sip and seems to calm down.

"Distract that blond girl, the Rochefort sister. She has her sights set on the duke. I will not have her overshadow Isabelle."

"But how?" I ask, anxious to please her.

She thrusts the glass in my hand. "Tip a glass of champagne

down her dress, for all I care, as long as you keep her at bay for a few dances. Isabelle must be given ample time with the duke. Everyone is watching whom he pays attention to."

Her words have slapped me out of my dancing haze, and I walk with her toward Isabelle, smiling as though we have just had the most delightful conversation.

A servant is helping Isabelle to a glass of champagne.

"Enjoying yourself, *chérie*?" the countess asks her daughter.

Isabelle takes a sip. "Yes, Mother."

"Then why aren't you dancing?" she asks. "I don't want you lounging on your own. You should be in the center of the room, where everyone can see you."

Before Isabelle can answer, a portly woman distracts the countess and she's on her way back across the ballroom to another group of people.

I smile, relieved that she's gone. "Your mother is very direct," I say, taking a seat.

Isabelle lets out a small laugh. "She's exhausting. She thinks we're all on a stage, and that we must clamber over everyone else to be visible. The jewels, the too-tight corset, the marching orders for dancing."

*And the foil rented for the occasion*, I almost say out loud.

Isabelle sips her champagne and surveys the room.

"I think the duke is dancing with Mademoiselle de Rochefort, if that's who you're looking for," I say.

"Antoine d'Avaray is Mother's obsession, not mine."

His name is Antoine, I think, and repeat it silently.

Isabelle continues, "She'd love it if her daughter became a duchess."

A prickle of jealousy stings me.

"He inherited the title recently," Isabelle continues. "I swear that's why she had me come out early—I'm not eighteen until summer."

I can imagine them together, a perfectly handsome couple. It makes my dance with him seem irrelevant. "He is dashing." I look down. The envy skips across the surface of my thoughts, then sinks into shame. How pathetic—the ugly stepsister in lust.

"He's nice enough, but I'm no duchess, Maude."

Her tone is sincere and instantly makes me feel less sorry for myself. I turn to meet her pretty face, which hides that fierceness beneath. Isabelle Dubern is indeed a conundrum. "Why couldn't you be a duchess?" I ask.

She taps a finger on her champagne glass, but it doesn't make a sound under her glove. "There is a whole world beyond this ball, and a new century dawning. But for me this is all there is: a society marriage."

How can she be so reluctant to embrace her future? It's not as though she's being forced to marry an old butcher. "Is it such a terrible fate?" I ask.

"Why must I marry at all?" She looks at me intently. "Doesn't it strike you as odd that a hundred years ago the whole country got turned upside down by a revolution but nothing has really changed? I mean not for a girl like me, anyway." She drains her glass and stares into the distance.

I shake my head, bemused. "Well, I can think of worse scenarios than marrying one of the gentlemen in this room."

"It's the status that matters most to Mother, the attention surrounding a society match. It's as if my season is happening only to her and the family, without a thought for me."

"But don't you see how lucky you are?" I press.

Her head whips around. "Is that what you think? I'm the girl who has everything?" She sounds cross.

"But aren't you?"

Isabelle sighs to make it clear I don't understand. I want her to explain, but the duke and Claire join us.

"I must be getting old," says the duke, taking a seat on the other side of Isabelle. "Dancing is more exhausting than cavalry drills." Claire's face falls at this comment. As the duke and Isabelle get deeper in conversation, I stand and retreat to a chair several feet away to give them some privacy. Claire isn't so subtle. She hovers near them, waiting for a chance to interrupt.

She's not the only one watching. A bit farther away, Xavier is flirting with a buxom brunette. Despite his animated performance with her, I notice him looking over at the duke and Isabelle every now and then. Finally Claire loses patience and begins to pester the duke for another dance. I can feel the countess watching me from across the room and I know I need to act. I must distract Claire.

I take a sip of champagne. The bubbles tingle in my nose and then fizz in my head and I look down at my glass. Surely the countess didn't really mean I should douse her with it. I begin to study Claire. Observe her. What would she buy, I wonder, if she were a customer in Father's store? What would she stop to chat about? Think, Maude, think.

And it strikes me: her hair.

It is ridiculous—a mountain of corkscrew curls piled high, defying gravity. Too much time must have been spent in its architecture. It's a perfect avenue of conversation.

I get up and approach her. "Claire, I love your hair." I smile but worry—do I sound natural or tense? "It's very . . . impressive."

She perks up and takes a step toward me. "Oh, thank you." She's positively glowing as she checks that it's still in place with a dainty hand. "Mother knows the best hairdresser in Paris."

"Is that so?" I try to sound amazed.

"Yes, and he created the style just for me. You see, there are two hairpieces, at the front and on the back, to give it the volume . . ."

I nod as she drones on about how her own hair was curled and how the fake hair was attached. Behind her Isabelle and the duke rise to join the dancing and Claire is none the wiser.

"You would never know," I say with just the right amount of enthusiasm. "The hairpieces blend right in." I sip my champagne, relieved by my small victory.

I keep Claire chatting until she is asked to dance by another suitor and I'm left alone once more to watch everyone's good time. Being a spectator is my natural state.

With my second glass of champagne, the room grows warm and the candle lights soften until they blur into each other. I let the magnificence of the setting wash over me. I cannot believe where I am.

By now it's after midnight, and the banquet table is littered with picked-over food, glasses of champagne half drunk and candles shrunk to stubs. The crowd of beautiful people is thinning: the night must end. I can't think beyond this ballroom, of the world outside. To even imagine my room in the grime of Montparnasse is to be there, and I want to hold on to this beauty. I know that when I am sitting at my dressing table, brushing my hair, this night will exist only as a memory.

I walk with the Duberns down the grand staircase to the reception hall, where we are presented with our cloaks. My aunt's carriage—in other words, the agency carriage—is picking me up directly from the ball. My feet are throbbing and my neck feels bare. Per her mother's instructions, I relinquished the family jewels to Isabelle before we made our way downstairs. I suppose the countess couldn't risk leaving them in my care.

Outside, Isabelle and I walk behind her parents. The sharp air cuts through the fuzz of champagne and fatigue. I should feel glad that the hurdle of the ball is behind me, but I find there's a thread of disappointment tangled around the relief. Did I succeed for the countess tonight—enough to be hired again? I think back to Durandeau talking about "a whole season to exploit" and I find myself hoping for another experience like tonight.

"This was magical," I say.

Isabelle shrugs. "It was all right. I'm glad you enjoyed it."

I laugh. "I can't believe how indifferent you are. It was beautiful. Everything was perfect."

"Perfectly artificial. What about real life?"

I think of my garret room waiting for me. Is that how she wants to live? Does she even know what "real life" means for most people? A touch of resentment surfaces as I contemplate this. I shake my head at her. "I'd choose this over real life any day."

The Dubern carriage pulls up first and the count and countess climb in. Before we get too close to the carriage, I stop and turn to Isabelle. "What do you want, then—if dancing with good-looking men and drinking champagne bore you to tears?"

"Do you really want to know?" Her breath forms ghostly trails in the freezing air, and she pulls her mantle tight around her shoulders.

"Isabelle, get in," the countess calls from the carriage. "It's freezing!"

Isabelle studies me carefully. "Come to tea on Tuesday and I'll show you."

I watch her hurry to the carriage. In all honesty, I wouldn't mind accepting an invitation to tea, but I don't think it's the high-profile event Durandeau has in mind for my next assignment.

The door slams shut and Isabelle waves to me from the window. She doesn't know that tea will cost her mother five francs an hour.

# Chapter 16

Monday mornings are a bustling and noisy affair at the agency, and I know the dressing room will already be crammed with girls before I even open the door. I've been starved for company since the ball, and the need to share the details of my magical evening has eaten away at me ever since. I've rehearsed my descriptions of the people, the dresses and the décor. The idea is to give my colleagues a treat, a visual madeleine to brighten their day, not to gloat—or not to appear to gloat.

I hang up my coat and hat, then smile and try to make eye contact with the others. For once I welcome their gossiping. I look around for Marie-Josée, knowing she'll be the first to pounce on me for details, but she's not here yet and I sink into a chair, disappointed. Cécile is purposely ignoring me, I can tell; she keeps her back to me and talks loudly to the other girls. I get changed into an agency day dress and wait, the minutes ticking by as the girls describe their own banal assignments. It feels as though I will burst from keeping quiet. Finally I'm given an opportunity to share when sweet Emilie takes a seat at my dressing table and with wide eyes asks, "*Et alors, le bal?*"

"It was a fairy tale come to life," I tell her, unable to

keep from smiling. I can hear the excitement in my own voice, but I don't have to hide it. "Dancing, dresses and handsome men."

"And the refreshments?" asks Emilie.

"Ten different kinds of desserts and pink champagne," I say, grinning.

"*Ooh la la!* Did you try a bit of everything?" she asks. I nod, and then Hortense joins in, hungry for details.

"Who did you dance with?"

As I recount my story, the other girls gradually look up, leaving dress hooks undone and stockings unraveled to listen. Even Cécile gives up her resistance and lingers close enough to catch the details. I don't mention the moments when I was sidelined, ignored or passed over for my client. That is something they are already familiar with and no one wants reminding of.

Marie-Josée eventually arrives, out of breath. On seeing that I am the center of attention, surrounded by the others, she says, "If you're dishing about the ball, you best stop right there." She wrestles her coat off. "Not another word until I've opened this box of pastries and taken a load off. And then you'll have to start at the beginning."

Once Marie-Josée is installed with the rest of us, the pastries cut in half to share, I start over. There is a chorus of oohs and aahs from the younger girls when I describe the Duke d'Avaray; apparently he is famously handsome, and Xavier de Rochefort is known as a charmer in many Paris circles.

"His sister, Claire, is always mentioned in the society columns," Cécile adds. "She is the most sought-after debutante this year."

Marie-Josée chimes in. "Did your client behave herself? Or was she a brat to you again?"

"Isabelle was nice enough this time," I admit.

"Who did she dance with?" asks Marie-Josée.

"She had lots of partners," I say. "Xavier was very attentive. But the countess was most anxious to see her with Antoine, the Duke d'Avaray." I say his full name again, drawing it out, because talking about the duke feels as good as thinking about him.

"I bet she was," says Marie-Josée, polishing off her pastry.

"Oh, imagine if she marries the duke! What a heavenly couple," says Emilie.

The envy I felt at the ball threatens to surface. I force it down—envy is pointless in my line of work. Besides, I don't want to be like Cécile, besotted with all her clients' suitors. That would be ridiculous. "They do look good together," I agree.

"Why does the countess prefer the duke for her daughter and not Xavier de Rochefort?" asks Hortense. "He must be rich too, judging by his father's house."

It's a good point, but it never occurred to me to ask. "Isn't rich just rich?" I say. I imagine they're all equally privileged.

Cécile pulls a deck of playing cards off a shelf and fans them out. "A duke is worth more than a viscount," she says. She pulls out the king of hearts and places it face up on the dresser. "King of hearts is the duke. Someone like the Count Dubern would be the next step down," she says, putting the queen of hearts next to the king. "Now, a viscount is one rung down from that, a jack." She places the jack next to the king and queen.

"But," says Marie-Josée, pulling a ten of hearts from the deck and placing it on the dressing table. "This is Xavier de Rochefort."

"I don't understand. Why is he the ten and not the jack?" I ask.

Marie-Josée points a pudgy finger at the ten of hearts. "Xavier is the second son. His older brother becomes the viscount after their father dies. See, the brother gets the title and most of the fortune. Ten of hearts has to make do with a smaller piece of pie."

I look at the cards laid out on the dresser. "I didn't realize there were so many rules." I think back to Isabelle's words about status and what a society match means for her family.

There's a knock on the dressing room door and Laurent walks in. "Good morning, ladies. Monsieur Durandeau wants to speak with you, Maude. Urgently."

I have a bout of nerves—or could it be excitement? I'm eager for feedback from the countess. But what if she complained to Durandeau that I wore the family jewels and danced with the duke, leaving her daughter stranded?

"In his office?" I ask Laurent.

"No, he's in the salon getting fitted for a new suit."

The circle of girls surrounding me breaks apart and I follow Laurent out of the dressing room. Before I pass through the door I glance back at the others—it was nice being the center of attention for once.

As I walk beside Laurent down the corridor, doubt begins to grow, and I shorten my stride a hint. "Do you know what he wants to see me about?" I ask.

"Not a clue, *ma belle*." We arrive in front of the ominous

closed door to the salon. "But he's usually in a good mood when new clothes are concerned." Laurent winks at me, a wave of hair grazing his long lashes. He opens the door and I enter the room.

Durandeau is preening in front of the floor-length mirror, his arms outstretched, while his tailor takes his measurements. Materials like tweed and wool plaid are laid across an armchair. I look about the room, not used to seeing the space empty of girls.

"Mademoiselle Pichon. I will be with you shortly," says Durandeau. "A shooting party requires a suitable wardrobe. I may not be a good marksman, but I know how to dress the part."

I wait patiently for the tailor to finish. I should think being a decent shot is precisely the point of hunting, but what do I know about upper-class pursuits?

"The Scottish tweed is an excellent choice for the Norfolk jacket, Monsieur Durandeau," the tailor says, removing the swatches of cloth from the armchair. He gestures for me to sit down, but Durandeau, thinking the invitation is for him, takes the seat and I remain standing. The tailor exchanges a look with me before quitting the room.

"Well, you've done it, Mademoiselle Pichon!" Durandeau sinks back into the plump cushions.

My body tenses. "Done what?"

"I have just had word from the countess." He pulls a letter out of his breast pocket and waves it in front of me. "She wants you to work exclusively with her family for the whole season. What a coup!"

140

My heart leaps in a surge of excitement. "The whole season?" I ask, amazed. "How long is that?"

"From now until summer." His beady eyes are bright.

Suddenly all I can think of is the duke's handsome face and whom else I might dance with in a whole season.

"Do you know how many events you will attend?" Durandeau asks, his double chin shuddering as he speaks.

I shake my head. "I can't imagine."

"Several a week. Concerts, operas, banquets, shooting parties and even the horse races, when the weather warms up."

"Several a week until summer," I repeat. I can see Durandeau mentally tallying up how many piles of francs that will amount to. "Does this mean I'm no longer in training?" I ask, feeling bold.

"Yes, I suppose you've earned the commission. The Dubern patronage is a boon for the agency."

I'm awestruck at how quickly my life is changing. Having so many dates with Isabelle—maybe I'll be able to afford a nicer apartment and some new clothes.

"Let me read some of the countess's letter." Durandeau scans the pages. "There was a little confusion with her friend Madame Vary."

"She's supposed to be my aunt."

"The countess says she's reluctant to play along . . . They've had some falling-out."

I question how close the countess and Madame Vary really are. Did the countess just use her as a convenient way to introduce me to her circle?

Durandeau continues, "Now, this presents the problem of how you are to get access to the Dubern girl without

141

your chaperone." He leafs through the pages of neat handwriting.

"Ah. Here it is." He reads aloud.

*"I think it best if we use common sense, Monsieur Durandeau. If Madame Vary is indisposed due to poor health, let's say, we should think logically of how Mademoiselle Pichon would spend her time were she indeed her niece and not an employee of your agency. I would naturally invite Mademoiselle Pichon to spend time with Isabelle, given that the girls are the same age and both debutantes this season. Soon her appearance at social events with our family will be taken for granted and appear quite natural. In this way, she will have ample access to my daughter and the requisite events of the season, without requiring the assistance of Madame Vary's person."*

Durandeau turns the page and continues reading.

*"Furthermore, I request that Mademoiselle Pichon dress only in the clothing I provide. I shall have my personal couturier send over a suitable wardrobe for every occasion we might require her for."*

I gasp. "A special wardrobe, just for me?"

*"In response to your question, I myself will not require the services of a repoussoir for the rest of this season. As a mother, I must put my daughter's needs before my own."* Durandeau sighs at this. "More's the pity." He finishes reading. *"My distinguished sentiments, Countess Dubern."*

He smiles, taking satisfaction in reading that last sentence, despite the fact that there's not a scrap of real affection to it; it is the perfunctory way to end a letter, as we all learn in school.

Durandeau folds the sheets of notepaper back up and

looks at me. "There you have it, Mademoiselle Pichon. I didn't hold out much hope for your future at this agency, but you have exceeded expectation. You are now a permanent employee."

My heart should sink at the idea of being a permanent repoussoir, but instead I rejoice. Perhaps my approach to this job has been wrong all along—rather than dreading it, I should be open to its possibilities.

As if he can read my giddy thoughts, Durandeau hauls himself out of his chair and approaches me, his small pigeon eyes narrowing on mine. "But now that you've secured this contract, better not do anything to jeopardize it." His breath smells sour. "If I hear any complaints from the countess, the least murmur of disapproval—"

"I understand, Monsieur Durandeau."

He looks unsatisfied, not sure whether he has sufficiently intimidated me.

"The clothes will be kept in a storeroom next to Madame Leroux's workroom; she complains that she doesn't have the space required to house your new wardrobe."

I don't need to guess why she is being unaccommodating.

He waves a fat finger toward the door. "That will be all, Mademoiselle Pichon."

I curtsey and walk quickly out of the salon. I close the door behind me and lean against it, my head spinning with the thought of what's to come. My hope has turned to certainty—something marvelous is going to happen to me this season, I can feel it.

# Chapter 17

"I'm never allowed to set foot in Isabelle's schoolroom," says the countess.

She is seated at her dressing table, amid a clutter of bottles and potions, her maid assisting with the ritual of *la toilette*. I watch as her hair is unpinned and one thick lock of black silk unfurls after another.

She looks at me in the mirror. "She must hold you high in regard to let you in."

I give her a small smile. As promised, Isabelle requested that her mother invite me to tea, but before I could be shown upstairs to the schoolroom, the countess summoned me to her boudoir for a private audience.

"Cochet, you can leave us now." The maid gives me a furtive glance, puts the pile of hairpins in a jeweled box and leaves the room.

It's warm and stuffy and I still have my coat on. I shift my weight from one foot to another.

"Take a seat, Maude." The countess points to a footstool.

When I sit down, I see my own face reflected behind hers. She smiles at me. "It's time we had a little chat."

She picks up a silver hairbrush and draws it through her

mane. This is the first time I've seen her hair unpinned. It hangs in long, dark waves down her back over a loose-fitting dressing gown. She looks not quite human to me—like a statue of a Greek goddess in the Louvre.

"This season you will be privy to all sorts of information."

I nod, wondering where this is leading.

"You can help me by using your eyes and ears. There is nothing as innocuous as a plain girl. People won't even notice you are there." There's a sharp clack when she places the brush back on the vanity.

"Whom does Isabelle speak to, dance with, look at? Which gentlemen are receptive to her, who is making a play for her attention? She is silent as stone when I ask her opinion on anyone." She selects a bottle of perfume and dabs some on her neck. "You're quick. I bet you notice everything with those unremarkable eyes."

Her insult feels less cutting paired with the backhanded compliment. At least she thinks me intelligent.

She picks up another glass bottle from her collection and swivels around to hand it to me. "Here, smell this," she instructs.

I take the bottle and remove the lilac stopper, which is shaped like a flower. Somewhat hesitant, I inhale the scent. "It's pleasant," I say. "Like spring."

"I detest it. Too sweet. The count should have bought me jewels instead." She cocks her head to the side. "You can keep it, if you like."

I'm taken aback for a moment: how generous. I examine the colored glass and the flower etching on the bottle and feel a ripple of delight at how easily this luxurious token has come into my possession. "*Merci*, Madame la Comtesse," I murmur.

I look up to see her dusting a powder puff over her face, her skin becoming more like marble than human flesh. "Tell me—the ball. What did you think?" she asks.

"Oh, it was magnificent—" I begin.

She cuts me off immediately. "Yes, yes. I mean what did you think of Isabelle's suitors?"

Unsure of what she expects to hear and how honest I should be, I hesitate.

"Come on. You spent the entire evening with my daughter."

"Obviously the duke likes her," I say, watching her reaction. "And Xavier de Rochefort was keen to get her attention. But he seemed to flirt with a lot of pretty girls. I get the impression he might envy the duke."

The countess scoffs. "Well, of course. A duke is superior to the second son of a viscount. Now, what about the duke?"

"He's drawn to Isabelle, I think. They danced together often, when he wasn't dancing with Claire de Rochefort." I feel a twinge of regret; I remember all this because I was hoping he would dance with me again.

"Claire de Rochefort? Ugh! That insipid little doll." An invisible wind has blown the countess's expression to a look of disgust. "Did she make any headway with him?"

"Claire tried, but she's empty-headed," I answer, happy to support Isabelle's claim over Claire's. There is no question that Isabelle is a far superior choice. "The duke spent more time talking to Isabelle. They seemed more of a natural fit when they conversed."

146

It feels satisfying to be able to share all the things I observe, for once. The girls at the agency want only the broad brushstrokes of the players' interactions, but the countess has an eye for detail. Finally someone appreciates my habit of watching people.

The countess drums her fingernails on the dressing table. "I bet that Rochefort girl is using her brother to forward her cause. He's known the duke for years."

"Especially if Xavier wants Isabelle for himself, wouldn't he welcome his sister throwing herself at the duke?" I say.

She arches an eyebrow. "*Très bien.*" She considers me for a moment. "Very well, Maude. You can go up and see Isabelle now." The countess rings the bell for the maid; then she leans toward the mirror and pulls the skin on her face taut like a mask. "What do they say? *Old age is the revenge of the ugly ones.*"

Her remark throws me. Does she consider me a culprit, one of these *ugly ones*, cheering on the march of time against her greatest asset?

Cochet enters the room with a curtsey. "*Oui*, madame?"

"Show Maude to Isabelle's schoolroom," the countess says without looking up.

Taking my cue, I slip the perfume bottle into my coat pocket and leave the countess to her ritual.

As I follow the maid up to the top floor of the house, a whisper of doubt pesters me. I worry that when speaking with the countess, I cast Isabelle in too favorable a light with the duke. I reflect again on what passed between them at the ball and decide that every word of what I told the countess was true. I didn't lie. What gnaws at me is that I didn't tell her the whole truth—for example, that her daughter doesn't seem interested in becoming a duchess. I decide it would be daft to divulge that information. Besides, Isabelle would have to be made of stone not to eventually be won over by the duke's kind face and dashing uniform. Maybe her rebellious words are just for show.

At the top of the stairs the maid stops and points to the last door at the end of the corridor. "Mademoiselle Isabelle's schoolroom," she announces.

"*Merci*," I say, but she is already on her way down the stairs. I walk toward the schoolroom door and knock.

"Wait!" cries Isabelle's voice from inside. "Under no circumstance open the door."

I roll my eyes. She's a bit dramatic, but I do as I'm told. While I pace in the corridor I think back to our last conversation. My curiosity is piqued—what makes her different from other society girls?

Several minutes pass before the handle turns, the door opens and Isabelle is standing in the doorway of a darkened room.

"I couldn't have you open the door and let in any light," she says by way of greeting. I step into the room and find that the only illumination is a single candle, newly lit. In the gloom I can make out a large wooden workbench with all sorts of contraptions on it, and thick tapestry-like curtains are drawn across the windows. She gives no explanation for why the room is shrouded in darkness.

"Is this a witches' coven?" I ask, only partially joking. "A schoolroom for learning sorcery and spells?"

"Did the maid only walk you partway?" she asks. "The servants think this room is haunted, or that I'm possessed." Laughing, she pulls open the curtains, and a strand of hair falls loose from her braid. "I have finished with my sacrifices for today."

The windows are mucky and a shaft of sunlight makes the dust dance around us, proving the maid's aversion to the place. Now that I can see where I'm walking, I step farther into the room. Aside from the large workbench near the windows, there's a wall lined with bookshelves, and in the far corner there's a writing desk. At the opposite end of the room a couple of armchairs flank the fireplace.

I'm drawn to the bookshelves, home to objects I've never seen before: bell jars and bottles of all shapes and sizes containing various liquids; plants and drawings of botanical specimens; glass-framed butterflies and other sizeable insects. Between these curiosities are many books. I read the spines and see volumes on wide-ranging areas of study: botany, chemistry, Roman history and architecture. There is a globe at either end of the bookshelves; I reach out to spin one as I walk past.

"Sorry for the mess," says Isabelle. "I don't usually get visitors." She is shuffling papers together on the writing desk in the corner. On a shelf above the desk sits an object the size of a mantel clock, but there is neither a clock face nor hands on it. I walk toward it to get a closer look. It is made of brass, and the case open next to it is lined in forest-green velvet.

"Father's microscope," Isabelle says, seeing me staring at

149

it. "It's over a hundred years old—one of his antiques. I daresay he hasn't missed it from his study. He enjoys collecting things but has no real appreciation for their function."

"What do you use it for?" I ask, in awe.

"Studying plants."

I marvel at all her possessions. "I've never seen a schoolroom like this," I say, and as the words leave my lips I realize at once that *this* is Isabelle's room, a space furnished with her essence, stamped with her personality, just as her bedroom is a reflection of who she's *supposed* to be— feminine and sweet, her mother's invention.

I turn to the workbench dominating the room, fascinated by the odd-shaped objects littering its surface: chipped china serving dishes, iron clamps and wooden boxes with metal parts attached. Does she have a use for all these items?

"Have a seat," Isabelle says, nodding to a stool at the bench.

"What are these contraptions?" I ask, pointing to the wooden boxes.

"Cameras. Do you want to see how they work?"

"You know how to take pictures?" I ask, astonished. "Of what?"

"Anything, really. What got me interested was the chemistry behind it."

"How incredible," I say, touching the smooth surface of the wooden box in front of me.

"Shall I take your picture, would you like that?" She's up and in motion before I can reply.

"I've never had my portrait taken before." I don't feel exactly comfortable at the idea. "It seems hugely extravagant," I murmur.

"Come on, take off your coat and let me show off my 'contraptions,' as you call them."

The absurdity of my posing as her model doesn't seem to occur to her. She busies herself setting up the equipment.

I hang my coat over a stool, somewhat reluctant to make myself at home. "Your governess is ambitious with your curriculum."

"I don't have a governess anymore." Isabelle secures the wooden camera box on a stand with three legs. "Mother got rid of her once my season started; she said I wouldn't have time for schoolwork, with all the events I have to attend. But this isn't simple schoolwork, Maude." She sweeps her hair from her face. "It's my self-designed curriculum. Take the stool and sit next to the window," she says. "We need you in the light."

I obey her instructions.

Isabelle bends down behind the camera, her head obscured. "Now move the stool a few inches closer to me and a little to the right."

"How long do I have to keep still?" I ask, shifting position.

She pops her head up. "Don't worry, I won't be putting your head in a clamp. The exposure time is only a couple of seconds. Not long at all, compared to the old days."

"How do I look?" I ask her warily. "Can you see me through that thing?"

She ducks down. "I can, but you're upside down. The

151

picture will be from the top of your head, past your shoulders. A proper portrait."

I look straight at the camera, its one black eye staring back at me.

She picks up a slim wooden frame and slots it into the camera box. "Relax," says Isabelle. "Think of something pleasant and hold still."

My mind takes me back to the ball, when I reached out and took the duke's hand.

"*Un, deux, trois*," Isabelle says. Then she removes the black cap covering the lens.

I hold on to that thought. I see his smile; I feel his hand in mine.

"*C'est fini*," Isabelle announces, returning the cap to the lens.

She orders me to close the curtains and then disappears into a closet. The wooden frame, I have just learned, encases the glass plate containing the negative image of my face. The minutes tick by as I wait in complete darkness for her to develop it. The smell of chemicals seems stronger now; it burns my nose and makes my eyes water.

Does Isabelle's mother know about this? I wonder. If Marie-Josée were taking bets, I'd put my money on no.

The closet door creaks open and footsteps approach.

"Open the curtains, Maude."

I draw back the heavy drapes and the light makes me squint. I turn around to see Isabelle walking toward me, brandishing the plate. She's wearing an artist's cotton smock over her dress and a pair of India rubber gloves. Her eyes are bright, her expression eager, as she joins me by the window, holding the plate up to the light. "Have a look."

152

Despite my earlier reluctance I'm curious, and I crane my neck toward this mysterious image, a negative of myself. It's odd to think that this ghost twin I'm looking at, with white hair and face in shadow, is actually me.

"Now the exciting part—making a print," Isabelle says. "We'll need to close the curtains again and put a candle in the safe lamp—that red lantern on the bench."

"A red light?" I ask.

"The paper we print on is sensitive to daylight but not to red light."

I don't understand this, but I light the lantern and close the curtains and we are immediately bathed in a sinister, hellish glow. If I were a servant in the Dubern house, I would be suspicious of the goings-on in the schoolroom too. "You look positively ghoulish," I say. Isabelle smiles as she fiddles with a wooden frame. She places the glass negative inside, then covers it with a sheet of paper from a sealed box. Lastly, a wooden backing secures the device together. Isabelle looks at the watch pinned to her smock and opens the curtain wide. She then props up the wooden frame by the window in full sunlight.

"What's happening?" I ask, peering at the frame.

"The light develops the print. It passes through the plate, exposing the positive image onto the treated paper. It should take about ten minutes."

I shake my head, dumbfounded. "Where did you learn all this?"

"My uncle gave me his camera and some instructions." Isabelle glances at her watch. "And my governess helped me too, before Mother sent her packing. She introduced me to the world of science, ordering the books and supplies we needed—all behind Mother's back, of course."

"What did your mother think you were learning?" I ask.

"Ladylike pursuits. I would pay Geneviève the housemaid to embroider cushions and handkerchiefs and I'd take credit. Sometimes I'd bang about on the piano or practice Italian for Mother's benefit."

I shake my head. Isabelle Dubern is full of surprises—sulky rich girl, reluctant debutante and now a secret scholar. Just when I think I know who I'm dealing with, she confounds expectation.

She spends the next few minutes at the workbench pouring liquids into china trays and I am told to watch the clock. "Time's up," I say, after ten minutes has passed. Isabelle retrieves the wooden frame and peers at the progress of her contraption. I close the curtains, checking that not a chink of light remains.

We are bathed once more in the eerie red light. I watch, fascinated, as Isabelle opens the frame and glances at the paper, now darkened with an image; but before I get a good look she drops it into a tray and douses it with water. She rinses the paper, then transfers it to a tray filled with the noxious-smelling solution, agitating the liquid so that it sloshes around submerging the paper completely.

As the minutes pass I strain to see the image, but Isabelle is blocking me from getting a clear view, not to mention the red light and ripples of the liquid make it hard to see.

"We can open the curtains and blow out the safe light. The image is fixed now, so the light won't affect it."

I follow her orders while she pours water from a pitcher into another tray, drops the paper in and rinses it gently.

"Can I see it now?" I ask, dying for a look at this first and only photograph of me.

"Once it's dry," says Isabelle. "I'll order tea and we can look at my other pictures."

She lays the sopping paper on a canvas-and-wire press. "We use this drying rack," she explains. "If we simply hang it up, the paper curls as it dries."

Watching her work, I realize this is the happiest I've seen Isabelle Dubern. She moves confidently, the hint of a smile on her face. To me she looks radiant—not in the way she looked at the ball, with the poufy dress and family jewels. She's in her element.

After she rings the bell for tea, we install ourselves in the armchairs at the parlor end of the room and she fans out her portfolio of pictures on the table.

She picks up a photograph of an orchid.

"This is one of my first. I began with objects that didn't move or talk." She laughs, but I can tell she's proud of her work.

I pore over the images, coming across a portrait of a stoic-looking woman. "Who's this?"

"Madame Ferrand, our cook. She gave me all the old serving china to use for the chemicals, and she lets me steal eggs from the kitchen for my albumen."

"Her face is interesting," I say, looking at her direct gaze and the deep lines on her forehead. She is clearly no stranger to hard work; she brings to mind the villagers I know back home.

Isabelle pulls out a duplicate of the portrait. "You see how this one is faded at the edges? It's because the emulsion wasn't applied all the way to the corners. When I reprinted it, I fixed that mistake." She points at the improved print, in my hands.

"Even so, the flawed one looks beautiful," I say. It reminds me of that photograph of my mother. "The light edges give her a more radiant look, don't you think?"

She studies the two prints. "I hadn't thought of it like that." She meets my eye with a faint smile. "You have an artist's heart and not a scientist's logic."

There's a knock on the schoolroom door.

"Leave the tea outside, Geneviève," Isabelle calls impatiently.

"Mademoiselle Isabelle." It must be one of the maids, but she doesn't enter the room. "Your mother says you are to dress for visitors after your tea. They're expected in an hour."

Isabelle gets up and flings open the door, taking the tea tray from the maid.

"Countess says you are to put on the blue patterned dress. I laid it out for you." The maid peers into the room and calls to me. "Mademoiselle Maude, the countess has ordered her carriage to drop you at your aunt's."

"*Merci*," I say, my voice sounding flat. I didn't notice how quickly the afternoon was passing until now, when I don't feel in any hurry to leave.

Isabelle pushes the door closed with her foot and makes her way back to me. The cups rattle as she sets the tea tray on the table.

"I'm constantly being thwarted." She sits down with a

sigh. "Mother's always finding more events and visits to take up my time." She pours the tea. "Sugar?"

"One, please."

Isabelle stirs in the sugar and hands me the cup. We drink our tea in silence for some time. Her face is perplexed, as if she's solving a problem.

Finally she breaks the silence.

"Maude, can I ask you something?" Her eyes are fixed on her teacup and her tone is cautious.

"What is it?" I say in a half whisper.

"Before Mother got rid of her, my governess was helping me study for the *baccalauréat* exams. You need to pass to get accepted to university." She looks up and meets my gaze. "I mean to read science at the Sorbonne." Her dark eyes are wide and serious.

My eyes flit around the room: the equipment, the experiments, the self-designed curriculum—everything falls into place now. This room doesn't house the distractions of a bored debutante; there is a purpose to all of it. How bold. "A university education?" I breathe the words. It's so far from what I could ever wish for myself.

"Mother can't know," Isabelle continues. "She doesn't approve of education for girls. But you can help me study, assist with experiments and quiz me on all the facts I have to memorize." She pauses, then adds hopefully, "I thought you might like to help."

All I can think of is that the countess doesn't know. It's another secret, another layer of duplicity, and I stall for time. "With your governess gone, what does your mother think you do up here?" I ask.

"Her mind isn't curious enough to wonder." She rolls her eyes. "If I were alone in the drawing room with a gentleman for five seconds, she would demand an account. Up here"—she nods in the direction of her workbench— "there are only books and bric-a-brac. Harmless." She cracks a mischievous smile.

"But why me?" I ask her.

"You're different from other girls my age. I know I can trust you."

My heart contracts. I am a fraud. "But I don't know anything about science. In the village—I mean in the convent, we had a very simple education."

"You're curious about the world. You came to Paris to see something of it, not to get married off." She shrugs and her voice gets softer. "Maybe you're as much a misfit this season as I am."

Her words make me feel utterly treacherous. A wave of nausea washes over me and I put down my teacup.

"Will you help me, Maude?" Her dark eyes lock to mine as she waits for an answer.

A ribbon of panic swirls inside me. I try to push back thoughts of the countess—of deceiving her. She *is* my employer. But there is something about Isabelle I'm drawn to. I grip my knees, as if to hold myself together, and I force a smile. "Of course I'll help you."

Scraping together some threads of logic, I decide that helping Isabelle will solidify our friendship, which can only strengthen my role as foil. The countess couldn't disapprove of that, could she?

Isabelle looks instantly relieved. "Your portrait. It must be dry by now." She gets up, goes to the workbench and opens the canvas drying rack. She studies the photograph for a few moments, then brings it over to me. "What do you think?"

I take the fibrous paper and study the person looking back at me, the familiar, unremarkable features.

"It's odd, seeing yourself as a stranger might," I say. My eyes have a faraway look, serious and earnest. But I question the portrait. Which Maude is staring back at me: Isabelle's confidante or her repoussoir?

"I wonder if I shouldn't have exposed it a few seconds longer." Isabelle peers over my shoulder and points to one side of the photograph. "You see, some of the detail on the side of your face is missing."

"I don't think my plain face needs more detail," I say, trying to sound light. I'm cutting too close to the bone with this comment, but I can't help it.

"You're too interesting to be plain," Isabelle says with some vehemence. "Imagine if I'd taken Claire de Rochefort's portrait. Can't you just see her conceited pose, that silly hair and her dim expression?"

I can't help but laugh.

"I'll make another print for you to keep," she says, taking the photograph and placing it with the others in her portfolio. "Maude, you are officially part of my collection." She smiles broadly, and it's then that I realize the layers of Isabelle's façade have dropped away and the real girl is standing before me.

After tea, as soon as the carriage pulls away from the house and turns onto the street, I slip my hand into my coat pocket. The perfume is still there. I take out the bottle, pull out the stopper and take a sniff. It does smell sweet—heady and decadent, like luxury should. I dab a drop on my neck and one behind my ears, just like the Countess Dubern.

# Chapter 18

The Dubern carriage drops me at the agency, where I change out of my work clothes before heading home. Boulevard du Montparnasse is busy tonight. The November evening is crisp, the sky is jet-black, and twinkling lights burst out of the darkness, bringing my neighborhood to life. The activity doesn't cease when night falls in Paris. The sound of competing piano music spills out onto the sidewalk as I pass the bars and restaurants, and on every corner there are placards and posters advertising a new cabaret or music hall.

A carriage pulls up just in front of me, and I don't think anything of it until the door is flung open and a familiar voice calls out to me.

"Maude! Come with me to le Chat Noir."

It's Paul. I freeze for a moment, my heart racing. I smooth my skirt and tuck a wisp of hair behind my ear.

"Climb in!" he shouts. The horse snorts loudly and stamps a hoof, as if urging me to hurry.

I've seen posters all over my neighborhood for the famous Montmartre cabaret; it's popular with artists and is famous for its shadow-puppet plays. How I wish I could transform my outfit into something fashionable from the countess's couturier. At least I put on the perfume, I think gratefully as I climb into the carriage.

"Where were you heading?" Paul asks.

"Just home from work. I live on rue Delambre. It's not far."

"You work late, for a governess."

All I can do is smile in agreement and quickly change the subject. "How was your concert last week? I wish I could have been there."

"You enjoy music, then?"

I sigh. "I don't get to hear much in the way of concerts, really," I tell him, and look down. "I work a lot, you see."

The carriage jolts and jerks along the streets of the Left Bank, across the river and north, cutting through the Right Bank in the direction of *la butte* de Montmartre.

"A true music lover makes their own music." Paul leans in closer. "Is there a song you like to sing?"

I shake my head, laughing. "I don't sing—I'm not musical at all."

"Come on, you must know at least one song by heart." He doesn't take his eyes off me.

I think for a moment. "I know some Breton songs." I shrug, not sure whether to share. "The Breton language has music in it. To an outsider, it might sound rough and not as pretty as French, but I always think of it as more honest, somehow."

Paul leans back in the carriage with a smile on his face. "I knew it. You are *not* a governess."

My heart seizes for a moment.

"You're a poet." He grins at me.

With a secret smile I peer out the window at the winding, narrow streets and seedy venues surrounding us. Montmartre—capital of sin, vice and bohemian Paris. I feel the thrill of adventure. Finally I'll be on the inside looking out and not the other way around.

If the ball I attended with Isabelle was a display of invisible rules and perfect choreography, le Chat Noir is the complete opposite: there are no rules. Once we walk through the door, we hit a wall of smoke and noise. Out of nowhere a jolly fat man appears in front of us and booms, "Come in and sit where you please. There is no hierarchy here, except for the intellectual one." He gestures to the packed tables around us.

The place is jammed with customers; there's no room to sit. Paul takes my hand as we push through the mob of people to find somewhere to stand. I hold on tightly, feeling anchored to him against the crush of the crowd. When someone bumps me, my cheek brushes his shoulder and I wish I could freeze time.

The cabaret is decorated with a collection of oddities: coats of arms, swords, stuffed animal heads. Rows of antique tables are populated with a mix of clientele as varied as the establishment's decorations. Some look well-to-do—bourgeois, even. Others look like disheveled artistic types; their style of dress is peculiar. I even catch sight of a woman dressed in men's trousers and a collar and tie.

Out of the crowd a hand claps down on Paul's shoulder and I start. The bubble of our intimacy bursts and I recognize the man's familiar red face from l'Académie—Claude the drunkard. Paul lets go of my hand to greet his friend and I'm suddenly adrift in the sea of bohemians.

Claude ushers us to his table and introductions are made. He appears to think he's meeting me for the first time. He hails a waiter in bold military costume.

"*Et alors?*" the waiter asks, nodding in my direction.

I have no idea what is appropriate to order. Papa only drank cider at home. I glance at the other tables and see glasses of absinthe, beer and wine. "Wine," I say immediately.

"Red or white?" asks the waiter impatiently.

"Red," I blurt out. Only because that is what a woman at the next table is drinking.

"Good. A carafe of Médoc and three glasses," says Paul.

"Make that four," says a voice. We look up to see Suzanne standing at our table. "But I won't stay if you talk politics."

Paul gets up and kisses her on the cheek. My heart sinks.

Claude leans over and does the same. "Politics is my bread and butter, my dear. How else does a journalist make a living?"

Paul introduces me. It's noisy and I know Suzanne probably didn't catch my name. She gives me a droopy handshake then slides into a chair next to him. Claude lights her cigarette. Her swanlike neck cranes up as she blows smoke above our heads. She's the very definition of nonchalance.

"How was the show?" Paul asks her.

She tosses her head back. "Claude's friend from *Le Figaro* described my paintings as 'vulgar and infantile.'" A chorus of protests follows from Paul and Claude.

"To my face, he said it. *Le con!*" She inhales on her cigarette.

I'm mesmerized watching her. She breaks all the agency rules of ladylike behavior: smoking in public, cursing, the uninhibited gestures and forceful personality.

I can feel myself disappearing, drifting into the background like a younger sibling, uninvited and tagging along.

The waiter returns with a carafe of wine.

We clink our glasses together in a toast and I take a sip. It tastes sour, like vinegar but thicker, and catches in my throat. After a few more sips I decide not to let my presence be drowned by the others. "Paul, how is your composition coming along?"

I wait for him to answer. But my question hangs in the air. When he continues to sip his wine and glance around the room, I realize instantly that he hasn't heard me. It shouldn't feel like a slight, but it does.

Claude refills our glasses and then picks up the empty carafe. "*Garçon, du vin!*" he shouts, waving it in the air.

There's a stir in the bar, as the shadow play is about to start. On stage there's an elaborately framed white background, onto which characters made of black zinc cutouts are projected by colored lights. Tonight's play features a character who is supposed to resemble Sarah Bernhardt, the famous actress—the toast or scandal of Paris, depending on who is talking about her.

"You think her beautiful?" Suzanne asks the table.

"She's much too skinny," says Claude.

I feel self-conscious; I'm sure I'm even skinnier than Sarah Bernhardt.

"She's popular," offers Paul.

"Is it better to be beautiful and obscure or ugly and

popular?" asks Suzanne. She looks at me. "Maude, what do you think?"

I don't know how to respond. It feels as if she's trying to draw me out only to humiliate me. But she can't know that words like *ugly* and *beautiful* are dangerous for me; they're coated in barbs.

"Cat got your tongue?" Claude bellows.

"It depends what you consider beautiful," Paul says, coming to my rescue. "Isn't it different for everyone?"

"Maybe people are as beautiful as they need to be?" I say eventually.

Suzanne takes a sip of wine. "How very modern of you." She returns her arm to its possessive position along the back of Paul's chair.

The play begins and everyone's attention turns to the stage. I'm relieved that the conversation is over. Yet as I pretend to watch the shadow figures, all I can think about is how much more I enjoyed the carriage ride alone with Paul and that the promise of the evening eclipsed everything that followed.

# Chapter 19

"Madame Leroux!" I call out, rapping at the seamstress's door. I don't hear a response, so I look to Marie-Josée for direction.

"Just walk in." She nudges me. "Go on. I know she's in there."

I turn the handle and peek in. Marie-Josée pushes the door wide open and we find Madame Leroux unrolling a bolt of green fabric—it looks like she's drowning in the swaths enveloping her.

I walk toward her, a smile pasted on my face. "Do you have the key to the storage room?"

She looks up, irritated.

"Durandeau said my clothes from the countess are in there," I explain.

"Yes, I know where they are," says Leroux sharply. "Give me a moment."

I brought Marie-Josée with me for moral support, as well as to satisfy her curiosity. Other than the seamstress, no one at the agency has had a glimpse of my special wardrobe yet.

Leroux dumps the roll of fabric on her worktable and rummages through a drawer, pulling out odds and ends of threads, until she produces a ring of keys from the mess. She fans them out like a hand of cards.

"It's either this one"—she points to a dull-colored key—"or try this small one." She hands them over roughly.

"*Merci*, madame."

"I've got work to do. You'd best leave me to it," says Leroux, dismissing us.

"*Merci*, Vivienne." Marie-Josée tries a smile, but Leroux is unreceptive and turns her back to us, wrestling with the fabric again. It's not like her to be so indifferent to Marie-Josée.

We leave her in peace, and after the door is closed behind us, Marie-Josée exchanges a look with me. "Poor thing," she mutters. "It must be hard for her, being snubbed by Durandeau's favorite client."

I shrug; I don't much care about Madame Leroux's feelings. The storage cupboard is just next door. I find the right key and we enter the little room. In the dim light I can make out a stack of broken chairs, a lampshade and some old candlesticks. But behind the junk, looking completely out of place, is a rack of beautifully made clothes in all manner of colors and rich fabrics.

Marie-Josée lets out a shriek. *"Ooh la la!"*

I gasp. "There are so many! Will I really need them all?"

Marie-Josée shoves the broken chairs and lampshade aside and then flips through the different outfits.

"Look, there's a list with descriptions." I pull the piece of paper from its tack on the wall and read out loud.

*"Brown tweed riding jacket and skirt for*
  *country weekend.*
*"Lilac silk taffeta for opera night.*
*"Blue velvet suit for Bois du Boulogne outing."*


Then I catch sight of stacked shoe boxes and hatboxes. "My goodness!" I point. "Shoes and hats to match."

Marie-Josée dives into the stack of hatboxes and begins rifling through them. "You've hit the jackpot, my dear. Too bad the girl is unpleasant."

"Isabelle's not so bad."

Marie-Josée turns her head and gives me a knowing look. "Really?"

I distract myself with the clothes, letting my hand glide across the different fabrics hanging on the rail. "I can't believe these are all for me."

"Don't get too attached. They're yours as long as you keep the countess happy," she says, kneeling amid layers of tissue paper and box lids. "And don't let your guard down for a minute; remember, you serve at the mother's pleasure."

I sigh. "There's not much affection between mother and daughter—they aren't a thing alike," I tell her.

"Well, don't get between them if there's an ounce of bad blood. You'll be out the door and your fancy clothes stripped off quick enough to make your head spin."

"Do you ever become friendly with your clients?"

She looks up at me pointedly. "You mean beyond what's required of the job? No, I most certainly don't." She goes back to inspecting the hats. "Most of them are a right bunch of snobs, smiling at you in public and bossing you around

169

like a skivvy when no one's watching. I keep them happy, of course, but I'd never consider any of them a friend."

I could have predicted she would react like this—Marie-Josée sees everything in black-and-white: them and us. I've been hesitant to tell her that I'm actually starting to like Isabelle. She certainly wouldn't condone my helping with her secret schoolwork. But Isabelle isn't like other clients.

Marie-Josée gets up, wearing a fetching bonnet with blue velvet trim and brown feathers. It's too small, so it perches on top of her head. She sucks in her cheeks and knits her brow in her classic Girard imitation. "You women to whom nature has been so unkind." I dissolve into laughter.

The scuffle of footsteps echoes in the corridor and the door of the little storage cupboard opens wide. The other girls peer in.

I pick up the lilac taffeta dress on its hanger and hold it against me. "Isn't it the most exquisite thing you've ever seen?"

"It's beautiful," says Emilie breathlessly.

Even Cécile is impressed. "You have all the luck," she says, reaching out to stroke a fur mantle.

As we dig through the treasure trove of clothes and hats, the other girls become as giddy and excited as I am, like children on Christmas Eve.

I spin around in the tight space, still holding the lilac dress.

"It's as though you're a real lady and not a repoussoir at all," says Emilie.

Marie-Josée tuts under her breath. "Remember who you are and why you're swanning around at operas and balls in the first place. Don't get carried away, *chérie*."

170

I giggle, ignoring her, getting dizzy from spinning in circles.

"Maude, you may wear the right clothes, but you're not their equal. Mind my words."

But I'm not listening. I'm lost in folds of lavender and the dreams my new wardrobe is inspiring.

# Chapter 20

I have learned that the Parisian aristocracy has many rules, including which day of the week is preferable to attend one event over another. Tonight is the right night for opera. As the guest of the Duberns, I'm attending a performance of *Aida*—we are to watch from their private box.

The Garnier Opera House looks like the work of a baker, a white cake with swirls of pink and cream marble and rosettes of gold frosting. It is as mobbed as the train station before Christmas, but the opera crowd doesn't wear the fatigue and grime of travelers—they wear silk and lace and glimmer in the chandelier lights. Each person is a feather in this peacock's tail of Parisian society. Again Isabelle and I follow the count and countess, this time up the grand staircase. A stage in itself, this is the place to see and be seen in Paris. The vast staircase splits off in two directions and is visible from many vantage points; people looking out from balconies observe the progress of the newcomers as they ascend.

I have never been to a proper concert before, let alone an opera. Our party proceeds up another flight of stairs and along curved corridors until we finally arrive at our private box. Nothing could have prepared me for my first glimpse of the theater. The ceiling must be twice the height of our village church, and it boasts a massive chandelier dripping with golden light. I take my seat on one of the plush chairs and grip the velvet rail in front of me. Everywhere, my eye is met with red and gold.

"It's so incredible," I breathe, gazing up at the ornate ceiling.

"Garnier built it for Napoleon III, but we got rid of our emperor before he could set foot here," Isabelle says, removing her cloak. She's wearing a brilliant violet dress, which looks striking against her jet-black hair and pale skin. I am once again her insipid shadow; my lilac taffeta dress, beautiful within the agency walls, is demoted to ordinary in her presence.

"Garnier's design isn't to my taste, though." She turns to me. "Did you know he wanted to design the tower for the Exposition Universelle?"

"You mean the one Eiffel is building?"

"Yes, he was livid when Eiffel won the commission. Garnier tried to put a stop to it—formed a group called the Protestation des Artistes, who claimed that as a mere engineer, Eiffel is incapable of creating a work of beauty." Isabelle shakes her head. "He can only look to the past."

When she talks about a subject she cares for, the spark in her eye outshines any dress or piece of jewelry she wears.

Unlike Isabelle, the count and countess are not interested in the architecture of the theater. They only have eyes for the faces populating it.

"Is that the captain who invited himself to my brother's one Easter?" asks the count.

"Where?" The countess picks up her opera glasses and searches the sea of well-groomed theater patrons.

"In Montesquiou's *loge*." The count gestures toward another box like ours.

"Don't point," hisses the countess.

I look down at the stalls and the orchestra pit and watch as the musicians take their seats. Paul's face floats into my mind. I bet he would love to play here.

"Isabelle, look!" exclaims the countess, still wielding her opera glasses. "The Duke d'Avaray is sitting with the Rocheforts."

Isabelle follows her mother's gaze and so do I, my pulse quickening at the mention of the duke's name, even though I know this is Isabelle's privilege, not mine. I won't be prone to envy where the duke is concerned. I'm content to experience Isabelle's good fortune vicariously.

"We shall invite them to dine with us afterward," announces the countess. She puts her glasses on the velvet parapet and looks eagerly at her daughter. "He's been paying you some attention. We must capitalize on that."

"Must we?" Isabelle lowers her eyes and fidgets with the buttons on her gloves.

I want to pick up the opera glasses and see him for myself, but my attention is pulled to the stage. The thump of a stick signals that the performance is about to begin. I feel a quiver of anticipation as the house lights dim, and I hold my breath in the darkness. The opera is in Italian, but Isabelle explained the plot to me in the carriage ride over. A young princess is kidnapped and sold into slavery, and a military commander falls in love with her but doesn't know her true identity.

As the curtains open, the first bars of music send a shiver of goose bumps over me. Light shines on another world: another place and time in history. Logic tells me that I am looking at a stage with painted sets framed by solid marble columns in present-day France, but I feel transported back through the ages, to ancient Egypt, to hear a slave girl's story.

Music fills the theater and I am transfixed. When Aida sings, it's as though she's singing from my own heart. In the hush, in the darkness, it is as though the performance is for me alone. In my mind, the audience has vanished, and my companions in the box recede into the shadows. The language might be foreign, but I understand the story: Aida is hiding a secret in plain sight.

When the house lights brighten and the curtain closes for intermission, my gaze remains locked on the stage. I exhale a silent breath and realize that I'm gripping the arms of my seat. As the chatter rises in the box, I feel a wave of loss wash over me; the illusion is broken and I am brought back to the carpeted floor of reality—when I was soaring just moments ago. How impossible not to be affected by such music. How jarring to take on one's old form again, and continue the conversations you were engaged in before the performance started. I wish to be left alone to ruminate on this new feeling. But the magic is already fading and commonplace concerns take over.

"I can't sit through another act on an empty stomach," grumbles the count.

The countess claps her hands. "Café de la Paix for supper."

"Mother, really?" says Isabelle. "We're leaving at the intermission again?"

The countess ignores Isabelle's complaint and addresses her husband. "We'll invite the Rocheforts. Have the footman send a note to their box."

As the rest of my party rises to leave, I'm hesitant. As much as I want to set eyes on the duke again, part of me wishes I could stay and find out what happens to Aida. I finally follow the others out of the box. I drum my fingers against my skirts in memory of the music as we walk along the marble corridors.

"Will anyone else be able to enjoy our seats?" I ask Isabelle as we retrace our steps back to the foyer.

Isabelle shakes her head. "Do you know I've never seen the end of a performance?"

"But why do your parents pay for such good seats if they always leave early?"

She smiles knowingly. "It's more about who is sitting next to whom, who is wearing what and the gossip whispered in the darkness. The performance as advertised is the drama that interests them least."

"It was spectacular," I say.

She sighs. "I know. I was enjoying it too."

After we find our way back to the marbled entrance hall, the party becomes a confusion of lost members and different plans. The viscountess has a headache and wants to go home; her husband wants to stay for supper. The countess tries to encourage Claire to accompany her mother; Xavier is nowhere to be found. As Isabelle and I wait for the muddle to be sorted, my attention gravitates to the duke, my eyes following him as if he were the sole actor onstage.

He wears the same black evening dress as the other men, but his suit is crisper on his contours, the color a deeper shade of midnight. In the general milling-around I can always locate his exact movements, even in my peripheral vision. When he brushes past me, the air shifted by his presence makes the tiny hairs on my arm stand at attention, and a shiver shoots up my neck.

Eventually it is the duke who solves the riddle of Xavier de Rochefort's disappearance, guessing that he went to visit an acquaintance backstage, unaware that we would be leaving at intermission. And so before long, the party separates into those going home—the viscountess and Claire; those going immediately to Café de la Paix—the viscount, the count and the countess; and the search party for Xavier—the duke, Isabelle and me.

The duke leads the way out the main doors of the opera house and around to the side entrance. It must have rained while we were inside, as the streets are slick. Isabelle and I link arms to avoid slipping on the wet cobblestones.

The stage door is so unremarkable I would have passed it by. The duke holds it open and we step into a wall of cigarette smoke swirling around a group of orchestra players. We follow the duke through a rabbit warren of corridors full of activity: people carrying set pieces, costumes and props flit to and fro in a constant stream of bodies. The air is stuffy and smells of greasepaint, sweat and the gas from the footlights.

The duke takes us down a hallway, past some dressing rooms. There are lots of scantily clad Egyptian slave girls, and men in evening wear chatting them up like dogs outside a butcher shop. At the end of a hallway there's a staircase littered with chorus girls. One girl is sitting on the knee of a man in a black evening coat. I recognize his swagger instantly.

"Xavier!" the duke calls to his friend. "Your presence is requested at supper."

On seeing us, Xavier immediately shifts the actress off his lap. We congregate at the bottom of the stairs, looking up at her like a group of lost tourists. Her gown is flimsy and her makeup thick. Xavier greets us, flustered at having an audience for his clandestine meeting. I see a look exchange between the men: the duke's eyes are smiling as if he has just beaten Xavier in a hand of cards. He's enjoying his friend's embarrassment.

Recovering his composure, Xavier nods. "Yes, supper, I'm ravenous."

For steak or actresses? I wonder.

The girl winks a goodbye to Xavier and turns toward her friends who are decorating the other steps.

"Can we see the stage before we go?" asks Isabelle, indifferent to Xavier's less-than-proper behavior.

Delighted to be able to accommodate this request, Xavier leads the way to the wings of the stage. The curtain is closed, but there is a gap in the material through which we can peek out to the front of house, and we take turns doing so. Intermission is almost over, and I can see people taking their seats again. I gaze up at the box where we sat, thinking how curious it is to see it from down here. I was so rapt at the performance, and now I see the insides of the make-believe exposed.

"Is that how they move the set pieces?" Isabelle asks, watching a stagehand manipulate the system of ropes and pulleys. "How does it work?"

Xavier laughs. "You're not interested in the pretty dresses?"

"Not as much as you are," Isabelle retorts, sharp as a tack.

He shakes his head and smirks. "Unusual for a girl, aren't you?" He approaches the stagehand to ask him to explain the apparatus to Isabelle.

The duke and I look at painted sets from the wings until a group of chorus members flood the stage, separating us. After the people have filed past, I don't rush to rejoin the duke. I hang back and position myself so that he's standing in my line of vision. I pretend to watch the performers assemble, but in fact I'm studying the duke—the aquiline profile and strong jaw; his sweep of brow, broken up by his dark blond waves.

Suddenly Xavier is at the duke's side, and the two men immediately plunge into a heated discussion. I keep my distance in the shadows of equipment and strain to listen, catching the odd word or phrase. I assume they must be arguing about our surprising Xavier before, but what I hear doesn't add up.

"That's not the point," Xavier says. ". . . bad idea."

"Tonight . . . last chance before I leave." That's all I can make out from the duke.

Xavier shakes his head. "It's such a risk." He leaves the duke standing there and returns to find Isabelle. I look over and see that she's still occupied with the stagehand, unaware of anything else. Instinct tells me the men's discussion wasn't about her. Something else is going on, but I'm not certain what.

The duke turns around and meets my eye. He smiles, betraying no trace of his argument with Xavier. I take a few steps toward him just as I hear a shout from above and look up almost too late to see a rope being flung down from the scaffolding over our heads.

I feel a pair of hands on my shoulders pull me out of the way just in time. My heart racing, I meet the duke's face inches from mine, his hands still clutching me. I melt with the thrill of such close contact.

"Thank you," I manage to say. My heart is thumping so loudly he must be able to hear it. I'm grateful for the dim light; otherwise my emotions—lust tempered by embarrassment—would be advertised by my complexion. "Ancient Egypt." I smile, trying to cover up my inner turmoil. "It's a dangerous place."

The duke lets out a melodious laugh and I bask in the warmth of the sound. I could exist on mere scraps of attention from a man like this. I don't need to be the starring debutante. If he thinks me witty for a moment, that is enough for me.

Isabelle joins us with Xavier at her heels. "It's all so fascinating," she says, taking my arm.

"I suppose we should get to the restaurant," Xavier suggests.

The duke pulls a watch from his pocket and checks the time. "I must make my exit, stage right. I can't join the others for dinner tonight, I'm afraid. I have an early start in the morning."

"Where are you going?" I ask, hearing the disappointment in my voice.

"I sail for England tomorrow."

He kisses Isabelle on the cheek. "Would you give my apologies to your parents?"

Then he leans down to kiss me too. My face catches fire.

He raises his top hat toward his friend. "Xavier." He nods and turns to leave.

"When do you return?" Xavier calls.

"In a few weeks," the duke answers.

"Good luck!" Xavier shouts. An officious-looking man shushes him. The duke disappears into the maze of backstage passageways.

A few *weeks*. My heart deflates. Suddenly the evening has become a dreadful bore.

Café de la Paix is not anything like Café Chez Emile. It's a fancy restaurant, exuding luxury. We are shown to a semiprivate room, where we find the count, the countess and the viscount already drinking champagne, with a plate of oysters sitting between them. As I approach the table I see the countess's eyes flicker over our party, now missing one vital person.

"You've found Xavier and lost the duke." She laughs, but her eyes are burning with questions. "Maude, you sit near me," she says. But the waiter doesn't hear her and draws out a chair at the other end of the table for me.

We take our seats. I know why she's itching to talk to me, and it doesn't take her long to broach the subject. "So, where did he go?" she asks between sips of champagne.

"The duke had to leave," says Isabelle as the waiter pours her champagne.

"Well, that's obvious, dear," says the countess, trying to sound light.

I feel a surge of boldness. "He's sailing for England tomorrow." I break the news in a matter-of-fact way.

"How dreary," the countess says through tight lips. "London in November."

The first course arrives, and so begins another feast for the senses as a seemingly endless supply of dishes is produced from the kitchen: consommé aux perles, turbot de Dieppe, lobster à la Russe and rack of lamb. The wine keeps flowing. The waiters are like dancers, flitting back and forth, flashes of black and white.

The countess is irritable and impatient throughout the meal. Without the duke the glamour of our party has gone. She only has the old viscount to flirt with, not a real audience.

At one point, Isabelle catches my eye. "The *table* looks beautiful," she says.

This is my cue for our new game. Isabelle has given me a copy of something called the periodic table, a list of chemical elements and their abbreviations. I'm supposed to quiz her on them. I open my evening bag and peek at the folded paper for some letters.

"Magnificent, glittering," I reply. These words stand for the letters M and G.

"Magnesium." Isabelle whispers the correct answer, and we giggle.

The countess's head whips around. "Isabelle, what did you say, dear?"

"Mother, can I have the carriage tomorrow morning? I promised Maude I would show her some attractions. She really hasn't had much opportunity to get to know the city since she arrived."

The countess shrugs. "Why not. But stay in the carriage. I don't want you girls traipsing the streets alone."

Isabelle looks at me, her expression mischievous. "Of course, Mother."

"Where are you going to take your friend sightseeing?" Xavier asks Isabelle. He has been attentive to Isabelle throughout dinner and appears to be taking advantage of his friend's absence to make headway with her.

"The usual: Place de la Concorde, the Arc de Triomphe, Notre Dame. Or maybe the construction site of Eiffel's tower, if we have time."

"Not one of the belles of Paris," he says, and immediately glances at me. Is that a snub or a coincidence? "It looks like a factory chimney."

"I disagree completely," says Isabelle, with a helping of passion. "It's an engineering masterpiece."

Xavier shakes his head. "The tower is an embarrassment for the city."

"If Garnier had won the commission, it would be done up like a pastry, like this café or his opera house," Isabelle says.

The force of her opinions and her lack of restraint in voicing them make me smile. I glance over at the countess, who's watching the whole exchange with a look of extreme displeasure.

By the end of supper, the table looks as though a hurricane

has swept through and left the debris of a feast in its wake. The rich are careless with so many things. Outside, the opera must have just finished, as we can see crowds of well-dressed people littering the building's steps, waiting for their carriages.

"Oh, what a bother," says the countess as she's helped on with her furs. "Our driver will get caught up in the opera crowd."

The agency carriage won't be picking me up tonight. Girard decided that because I am close to the agency I should walk back. But I have to pretend for Isabelle's sake that my aunt's carriage is collecting me. Thus far Isabelle has accepted Madame Vary's missing presence from our social occasions. She hinted that her mother isn't good at keeping female friends for long—especially pretty ones.

We step into the cold night and I predict a long, drawn-out set of goodbyes. I glance at the line of carriages across the street. "I think I can see my aunt's carriage," I lie. "I should dash." I nod to my hosts and the Rocheforts. "*Bonsoir. I had a lovely evening.*"

"Come to our house at ten o'clock and we can spend the day sightseeing," Isabelle reminds me.

The adults barely register my departure.

"It will be lovely." I smile cheerily and vanish into the crowd.


It isn't until after midnight when I ring the agency bell. There is one servant on duty at night to answer the door and keep the lamps lit in the dressing room and hallways.

My footsteps echo, loud and lonely, through the building. When I get to the dressing room, there's one other girl changing. I'm relieved; I hate being the only one here at night. We're both tired, so we don't converse beyond a *"Bonsoir."* I change into my own clothes, and after the other girl leaves I pause to look at my fine dress and fur mantle, on their hanger. The humiliation I feel as a repoussoir has shifted: I used to feel it on duty, but now it is here in the dressing room, when I am stripped of my Dubern clothes and privilege, that I resent the job.

Everyone except me hangs their agency outfits outside Madame Leroux's workroom, after business hours. I carry the Dubern clothes back to my storage closet. The key sticks in the lock. I push hard and it gives. I hang the dress up but hold on to the mantle. When I stroke the plush fur I think of the duke's hands on my shoulders when we stood backstage. I slip the garment over my coat, and throwing a glance at the rail of clothes, I wonder who would miss it—I'm the only one with a key. With the mantle draped over me, I take a peek down the corridor to make sure no one is around. I lock the door of the closet, then hurry along the hallway, down the stairs and out of the agency.

# Chapter 21

It's late when I reach Montparnasse. By this time of night drunks and generally unsavory characters populate the streets, so I've taken a private cab home. It's extravagant, but since I've started working for the Duberns I've been less careful with money. I tip the driver a few centimes and he cracks the whip on his horse's rump and the carriage pulls away. I hurry to the front door of my building, but I have to climb over a vagrant taking refuge in the doorway. I can smell the liquor wafting around him and see an empty bottle of calvados at his feet.

"*Pardon*," I say as I clamber over his legs.

The man grunts, then pushes his hat back off his face. "Maude!" he shouts.

I jump back in fright.

It's Paul, completely drunk and sprawled out on the doorstep. "There you are," he says, hauling himself to a sitting position, kicking the bottle, which rolls into the gutter with a clink.

"What are you doing?" I say, relieved it's him. "How did you know where I live?"

He pulls himself to his feet unsteadily. "You said rue Delambre. I asked the concierge at each building from the corner down," he says.

I sigh. "That will make me popular with the neighbors."

"You teach your pupil awfully late. I'm a little drunk." He throws his hand against the door for balance.

"A little?" I shake my head at the state of him. "Let's get you home. Where do you live?"

He points erratically. "Edgar Quinet," he slurs. "Not far."

I sling his right arm over my shoulder and hold him at the waist with my left arm. He leans heavily on me as we weave down the street like a couple of drunken sailors.

"How did you manage to end up so drunk without Claude around?" I ask.

"You took longer than I thought, so I finished the brandy alone."

"A whole bottle? What were you toasting?"

He waves his free arm theatrically and we nearly topple over. "The end of my music career."

"Sounds a little premature, don't you think?" I'm not really taking his ramblings seriously, I'm just trying to keep us upright.

We round the corner onto boulevard Edgar Quinet. I've always wondered where he lives. Given how much time he spends at Café Chez Emile, I knew it had to be close by.

We walk with difficulty along the street until he stops abruptly in front of his building. "The keys are in here," he says, swiping at his coat, not managing to find the pocket. I fish out the keys to his apartment.

"Maude, I'm a complete failure." He sways like a poplar in the wind. "Didn't show up for my audition."

I'm fumbling with the front door, trying to prop it open

187

and keep him from falling over at the same time. "What audition's that?"

"The music academy. Why waste their time?"

"Come on." I gently pull him through the front door and we stagger toward the stairwell. "What floor are you on?"

"I'm on the third," he slurs. "They would have laughed at my composition. I know it," he adds loudly.

"Shhh," I tell him. "You don't want to wake up the concierge."

I drag him up the steps in the dim light. "Your career is just beginning. You can audition again."

"All I do is play popular music in bars. I'll never be taken seriously."

"Not with a bottle of brandy in you."

He mumbles some more but it's unintelligible. "Come on," I tell him. "We're almost there."

When we finally get to the third floor, I'm out of breath from the effort of acting as a human crutch. I try a few different keys on his chain before I find the right one and push open the door. Finally inside his apartment, Paul stumbles forward and I help him land on the settee. It's odd to suddenly be standing right in his rooms.

His head lolls back and he blinks heavily. "Sorry for the state of things."

"It's fine," I say, looking around.

The large room is a complete mess of sheet music and used glasses and dirty clothes. A piano stands near the window, dwarfing all the other furniture in the room. I rub my hands together for warmth. I light a paraffin lamp then set about cleaning the grate and building a fire while Paul dozes.

Once the temperature is more bearable, I remove my fur mantle. I pull off Paul's boots and tease his coat off his shoulders, then cover him with a blanket. His apartment has a proper kitchen area, unlike mine, but there's nothing to eat and only the dregs of alcohol to drink—save for a tin with some tea. I find the kettle, fill it with water from the pitcher and set it on the stove.

I peer over at Paul. He appears to be dozing now. While I'm waiting for the kettle to boil, I look around the room. Tacked to the walls are photographs, paintings and sketches. It's strange inspecting someone's home like this, without their knowledge; like reading their journal, or poking about in their thoughts.

Sheets of music are scattered across the floor—the labors of his compositions, covered with scribbled notations. Is this mess just a symptom of being an artist? I take a seat at the piano; an empty wine bottle sits on the keys. I put it aside and look at the piece of music open in front of me. It has a handwritten title, and I squint at the name: "*La Bretonne*." My heart quickens. But no, it can't be connected to me, can it? It must be a coincidence. As if Paul could answer my silent question, I look over at him—he's fast asleep.

I turn back to the piano and run my finger lightly across the keys without making a sound. What would it feel like to create a melody, to write a symphony—what does it take? A shiver shoots up my spine and I feel a tug in my gut, a tug of desire. I wish I could try something like this, something creative. The secret belief—the same thing Marie-Josée told me—that I was meant for bigger things, flickers across me and vanishes. Who am I fooling with these notions? I can't play a bar of music on the piano or any other instrument.

The kettle whistles and I go to the kitchen to make tea. I realize Paul isn't going to wake up anytime soon, so I pour only one cup. I sip my tea by the dull paraffin light, my fur mantle across my lap. Before I leave I write him a note and place it on top of the piano keys, where the wine bottle stood.

*Cher Paul,*

*Persist in your endeavor. If you have a talent you must use it. Continue with your compositions. They need to be written and played for others.*

I glance again at the composition called "*La Bretonne*" and struggle for some time with the signature—kind but not too forward.

*Ton amie,*
*Maude*

# Chapter 22

"Vexed. I am utterly vexed." The countess puts down her coffee cup and looks at me.

The agency carriage just dropped me at the Dubern home, and I have been escorted to the breakfast room—a bright dining room near the conservatory—to wait for Isabelle.

The countess appears to be taking the duke's trip abroad as a personal insult.

She leans back in her chair, looking sulky. "Why must he leave now, when we were making progress with his affections for Isabelle?"

"Perhaps it was urgent business that took him away from Paris. Maybe it couldn't be helped?" I shrug.

She looks up at me, still pouting. "Did he say that?"

I shake my head. "No." I lower my eyes and study her silk dressing gown. It's embroidered with gold and green birds, and the colored threads gleam in the morning light like precious stones.

The countess picks at a pastry, pulling off tiny flakes. "Didn't you witness anything of importance? Surely he would have given some hint of his affections."

She looks at me intently, desperate to hear something

positive, and I don't want to disappoint her. I search my memory, trying to come up with something, anything, for her to latch on to. "Well, there was one moment—" I stop short.

The countess drops the pastry. "Yes?"

"We were backstage looking at the sets and watching the actors take their places," I say, then bite my lip.

She leans forward in her chair. "Tell me," she says, her face looming closer to mine.

I am about to fabricate a story, but I can't help myself. "A coil of rope fell from a scaffold above Isabelle," I say. "The duke grabbed her by the shoulders and moved her to safety, clutching her firmly."

"And?" the countess demands.

I am a barefaced liar, but I continue undeterred. "There was a point when a look passed between them. I could tell it meant something." As the words leave my lips, I realize that I'm doing more than placating the countess. If I'm not the object of the duke's affection, why can't I live my fantasies through someone else, through the girl who's supposed to be the heroine of the love story?

The countess picks up her coffee cup, satisfaction spreading across her face. "That sounds promising," she says, then takes a sip. "I think we can be sure that the duke will be thinking about her while he's away. Perhaps his hasty departure was necessary to wrench himself from her quickly and not prolong the heartache of parting."

"Yes, that could be it," I say, shifting in my seat. Did I go too far?

"But the duke is not the only eligible bachelor this

season," says the countess. She taps her nail against the porcelain cup. "There are other suitors I will introduce her to over the next few weeks. The duke shouldn't become complacent about his position. Perhaps if he hears of her popularity with other contenders, it will urge him to action."

"Do you mean a proposal?" I ask, inching forward in my chair, eager for details of the love story to unfold.

The countess jumps, her attention drawn to the door. "There you are, *chérie*," she says as Isabelle walks in.

I feel sheepish when I see Isabelle in person, given what tales I've just been telling. But was any real harm done? I'm only keeping the countess happy.

"Are you ready, Maude?" Isabelle smiles at me.

"Yes," I say all too quickly, rising from my chair. "Goodbye, Madame la Comtesse."

"Goodbye, Mother," says Isabelle.

"*Amusez-vous bien*," says the countess with a limp wave.

"You can drop us at the Palais du Trocadéro," Isabelle tells the driver as we step into the carriage outside the house.

"The countess says you are not to get out and walk, mademoiselle," says the driver with a shy look, reluctant to meet Isabelle's eyes.

"Are you going to stop me?" Her tone is harsh, turning her into that girl I met in the hat shop.

The young driver flushes and closes the carriage door behind us.

It annoys me when Isabelle is sharp with the servants.

She doesn't understand that everyone is just doing what they're told to hang on to their jobs.

As we drive through the different neighborhoods, Isabelle acts as tour guide, pointing out the sights—the church of la Madeleine, the Arc de Triomphe, Place de la Concorde. It's so much more civilized than sitting wedged between ordinary folk on the omnibus. I don't have to crane my neck to catch a glimpse of the landmarks or miss out because a hefty passenger is blocking my view.

We alight from the Dubern carriage at the Palais du Trocadéro, just across the river from *le Champ-de-Mars*, the construction site of Eiffel's tower. The driver helps us unload Isabelle's photography equipment from the carriage. He gives us a solemn nod and climbs back onto the driver's seat. "I'll be right here if you ladies need anything."

Isabelle is already striding ahead with the camera case and box of plates. I turn to the driver. "Thank you. And please don't tell the countess we got out of the carriage. We won't be long."

He nods in agreement; then I chase after Isabelle, carrying the cumbersome camera stand under my arm. The sky is overcast now, and it's cold out. A brisk wind whips my skirts and bonnet ribbons.

All around this area construction for the Exposition Universelle is going on, but it is the iron structure climbing skyward, of triangular shape and lattice framework, that dominates the skyline. I catch up to Isabelle, who has now reached the bridge that leads to the site of the tower.

"This really is the best place to view it in its entirety,"

she says. "But we should cross the river and get closer. I want to see right underneath it."

I look up in wonder at the structure. "This is the first time I've seen it up close," I breathe. "It really is becoming the colossus that everyone's talking about."

Isabelle continues marching toward the tower—the equipment doesn't slow her down any—and I follow her across the bridge.

"The tower is made of iron," she explains as she walks. "Like Eiffel's new bridge constructions, because iron is flexible in strong wind." Her voice is raised against the breeze. "It's not rigid, like stone," she calls back.

"A bridge to the sky," I say, still gazing upward. "What a vision, to build that high."

"A feat of modern engineering and mathematics," she replies.

From far away, the tower always looks as though it's growing taller of its own accord, but up close I see that there must be a hundred men or more at work—some fearlessly climbing, others on scaffolding platforms and a slew on the ground. The four-legged base occupies far more space than I imagine, and the semicircles formed between the legs look like sections of a railway station facing every direction: north, south, east and west. The tower narrows as it rises, as though reaching for the clouds, its neck craning. It's a most extraordinary feeling, gazing up at this iron creature, unfinished and headless.

Below the tower is a work site with great piles of material, iron girders, wood scaffolding and even huts for the workers. Isabelle and I pause some twenty meters from the nearest foot of the structure, and Isabelle paces back and forth, looking up at the different views.

"Here." She plants her feet firmly. "We'll take the photograph right here."

I set up the tripod just as she showed me in the schoolroom; the three wooden stumps unhinge to produce three long legs on which to mount the camera. I fix them in place while she removes the camera from its protective case.

Watching Isabelle so absorbed in her equipment, it strikes me just how curious her interests really are. I reflect for a moment. "Isabelle, what drew you to science in the first place?" I ask. "It seems like another world to most people."

She stops what she's doing and looks at me, her camera in her arms. "But that's why I love it, precisely because it's all around us—it's *completely* our world." There's a brilliance in her eye and she turns to gaze up at the tower. "That wouldn't exist without mathematics and the rules of physics." She taps the wooden housing of the camera. "And we wouldn't have framed portraits of our families on the mantel if it weren't for the science of photography. I love the logic and reason, the black-and-whiteness of it all; there is no room for human moods or extremes of fancy. There's a purity to science—it's rational."

A far-off voice catches my attention and I turn to see a workman waving at us, and a couple of his friends laughing. "Eh, *les filles*, this is a work site, not a picnic lawn."

"Are you sure we should be here, Isabelle?"

"Ignore them." She is unflappable, all her attention focused on her camera.

The men shake their heads and return to their work. I look back at Isabelle. "Do you think it will be hard being one of the few women at the Sorbonne?"

"More fun than doing the season," she says, fixing the camera to the stand.

It still doesn't make sense to me, these two lives she has. "But once you're married," I press, "surely you will still have social engagements to juggle as well?"

Isabelle shakes her head. "It's hard enough to be a woman at the university, but you can't be a society wife *and* a scholar. Impossible."

A flood of disquiet swells inside me. "What do you mean?"

Isabelle looks at me as though I'm slow. "If I pass the *bac*, I won't marry," she says. She imparts this devastating piece of information as if it goes without saying, then returns to fixing the camera to its stand. I stare, mouth open and speechless.

"What?" I begin. The wind kicks up at the same moment that a surge of panic courses through me. "I didn't realize that." I can hear the concern in my own voice. It never occurred to me that Isabelle's university plans were in direct conflict with marriage; I thought it was just a secret because her mother didn't approve of higher education for women. I stand still, getting battered by the wind, suddenly realizing that by helping Isabelle, I'm actively sabotaging the countess's plans—the whole reason for my employment. The chess piece cannot play for both black and white.

"But surely you don't want to be a spinster?" It's a weak argument, but it's the first thing that comes to mind.

Isabelle merely shrugs as she removes the lens cap and wipes the glass with a cloth.

*Think—think of something,* I tell myself. "If it's freedom you want, married women enjoy more liberty than single women, don't they? You won't always need to be chaperoned, or be told you can't get out of the carriage or be alone in a drawing room with a man. Look at your mother and Madame Vary. They can come and go as they please."

Isabelle replaces the lens cap and straightens up. "As a married woman, you lose your status, your fortune—everything becomes your husband's property. Besides, look at me now." She points in the direction of the tower. "I don't have anyone's permission to be here, do I?"

She's right. I look at the iron lines soaring above me and I feel powerless both at standing next to something this vast and at perceiving my current predicament. I've given the countess the impression that the attachment between Isabelle and the duke is deepening, progressing toward a proposal, even, but Isabelle's narrative of her future couldn't be more at odds. I stare at the tower for some moments, pondering my situation. The men up top are small, like insects on a large beast, and in the distance I can see the skeletons of new constructions. Can I influence Isabelle or should I tell all to the countess? I'm sure I'll be let go if she realizes I went behind her back to help her daughter. But what will it mean for my position if Isabelle refuses a proposal of marriage—will I get sacked for that? I could just do nothing and hope that these clashing plans for

Isabelle's future don't come to a head any time soon. What a muddle.

"How long will the tower stand before they tear it down?" I say, changing the subject.

"A few years at most." She ducks down to look through the glass window at the back of the camera.

"Why do Parisians hate it so much?" I wonder aloud.

"Lots of people think it ugly and unrefined."

Those words sting. The same kind of people who hire repoussoirs by the hour, I suppose. "Perhaps something unrefined can still be beautiful," I say, more to myself than to Isabelle.

"Take a look, Maude. Tell me what you think of the framing."

I'm surprised to be asked. "Oh, I wouldn't know."

"Just look," says Isabelle, pointing to the glass.

I bend down to look at the upside-down image. I see the strong geometric patterns of the iron structure contrasting against the pale gray sky. It is an incredible feat to build it—the ambition, the imagination required.

"It looks fine," I say, straightening up. "To tear it down seems such a shame; all that Herculean effort to make something stand that tall and strong against the elements—only to raze it to the ground. It's like crushing a dream."

Isabelle selects a plate. "All the more reason to photograph it now." She pulls back the glass viewing pane so she can slot the negative housing into the back of the camera. She pulls up the wooden slide that protects the glass plate from the light. Then she points to the lens cap. "You take the picture."

I remove the black cap covering the lens, which will let light in, exposing the treated glass to the image before me. If human beings can accomplish the feat of constructing a three-hundred-meter tower, I can manage to pull off this double life for a season.

# Chapter 23

For once I am not spending an evening with Isabelle and the Duberns. The past couple of weeks I've been with them so much it's almost as though I no longer live in my grimy Montparnasse neighborhood. It's always a jolt to the eyes, seeing the squalor and run-down buildings, after the wide avenues, large houses and carriage rides of the Right Bank.

The opera evening has become a template for many nights out: the count and countess, Isabelle, a different eligible bachelor and me. We have gone to the hippodrome with a marquis, heard chamber music with an English lord and shared a carriage ride in the Bois de Boulogne with an army captain. Xavier de Rochefort has also been a frequent visitor, capitalizing on the duke's trip abroad. Isabelle looks the part, but that's about all the countess can control. Her daughter is uniformly tepid toward each gentleman, grilling them on politics and science, quizzing their general knowledge and reading habits. This frustrates the countess no end. Pressure is mounting on me to fix it.

My role in all this has been to try to please both parties, leading the life of double agent, keeping secrets from both mother and daughter. I help Isabelle with her clandestine schoolwork and humor her mother by listening to her pronouncements on Isabelle's suitors, not to mention her anticipation of the duke's return from England—the countess is getting as impatient as a pining debutante herself. It's exhausting, but I've become used to contorting myself into what people want me to be.

As for my reception in society, as soon as it's been established that I'm without fortune or connections, I'm treated with universal disinterest. Sometimes, when I feel strong, I don't mind being ignored, because it gives me the chance to observe people and guess the secrets of their characters. But other times I feel wretched. The problem with being a professional wallflower is that you have time to reflect on your own inadequacies, you're constantly reminded of your undesirable status. Just once I'd like a chance to shine.

I unlock the door to my garret room and shake off the cold, then hang up my new coat behind the door. Besides the coat I also bought a pair of fur-trimmed gloves, which match the mantle I took from the countess's wardrobe. I debated in the shop whether to splurge on the gloves or send some money home to pay back Papa—the gloves won. The mantle is draped over a chair by the dressing table. I promised myself I'd wear it just once and then return it to the agency, but I haven't been able to bring myself to part with it yet.

When Isabelle and I are not being whisked from event to event, we retreat to her schoolroom, where I've been testing her on the *baccalauréat* mock exams. In turn, she's been showing me how to use her camera and make photographic prints. To be honest, I look forward to this time in the schoolroom more than the splendid events of the Paris season. I still haven't told Marie-Josée about my non-repoussoir time with Isabelle. When I do run into my mentor in the dressing room, we gossip about agency business and the different events we've been to with clients. I disclose as little as I can about Isabelle personally. I get the feeling Marie-Josée will be disappointed if she knows I've become friends with her.

I plump down onto my bed and review today's photography lesson with Isabelle—exposure times and aperture settings. What is a photographer? Is it simply the person operating the camera, focusing the lens and mixing chemicals? Is photography merely the faithful recording of life for postcards and *cartes de visites*, or is it something more? So far I have taken one decent portrait of Isabelle and a candid picture of the scullery maids in the Dubern kitchen. I think that a good portrait reveals a suggestion of the subject's mind, and not just a representation of how they look. It's by no means easy; to snatch the right moment can feel impossible, like capturing fairies.

Perhaps I don't possess the talent of a great painter who could render life through lines of charcoal or washes of color, but I do have the gift of observation. I can see what others miss. As for skills to possess for taking pictures, this seems like the place to start. I regard the art of photography with a surging feeling that I can distill into a single word: *yes*. That first instant I saw an image I captured in the basin of chemicals, I was hooked. This discovery is pulling me forward.

Isabelle likes to focus on getting the science right. She's been experimenting with different solutions for toning the prints. But I enjoy it when the process goes awry—that feeling of wonder when a face appears on the treated paper and you don't know what to expect. I've started to question if the flaws on the finished photograph aren't an integral part of the portrait: soft focus, underexposure, poorly applied emulsion, mysterious lines and distortions . . . all of these elements can change the character of the photograph and its subject.

I feel suddenly restless, cooped up in my little room. Is this frenzy of excitement what Paul feels when he composes music? I'm eager to tell him about my new passion, but we haven't crossed paths since the night I found him drunk on my doorstep.

I get up, put on the fur mantle, grab my hat and new gloves and leave my room. Outside the temperature has dropped, and I walk quickly; the chill nips at my nose and makes my eyes water. Café Chez Emile is a likely spot to find Paul. I peer in the window and do an inventory of the faces, but he's not there. I decide to head to the neighborhood music halls on rue de la Gaîté—I know he plays at one of them on a regular basis.

I hurry along the busy street and walk into the nearest hall—le Palais. I'm shooed out almost immediately. "We don't open until six, mademoiselle!" the bartender yells at me.

There is another venue about a block down the street on the opposite side. I cross the road, darting between carriages and an omnibus. Bright lights and the smell of tobacco and wine welcome me as I walk in the door. There's a barman stocking bottles and a couple of early patrons keeping him company at the bar. I look to the raised stage where the band sits. Next to the piano, leafing through some sheet music, I see him.

"Paul!" I call out, and my stomach does a somersault when I shout his name. I walk briskly toward him.

He looks up and a smile crosses his face. "Maude! Where have you been these days?" When I reach him he kisses me on each cheek, his lips leaving an imaginary brand as my face sizzles. "I thought I saw you the other night on l'avenue de l'Opéra, getting out of a very fine-looking carriage."

I mask my surprise—he saw me in the Dubern carriage. "Oh, that sounds like the family's carriage," I say quickly. "The family I work for." It took me back to the agency one evening after the Bois de Boulogne outing because Durandeau's carriage was in use.

I fumble to change the subject of conversation. "Yes, I haven't seen you since . . ." I trail off when I realize I have to mention the night I helped him home. I don't want to say, "Since I found you on my doorstep."

"I got your note." He looks sheepish. This is the first time I've seen a crack in his confidence. I suppose he's embarrassed about being drunk, but I hope . . . Could it be something more? I think of the composition he was working on, "*La Bretonne.*" *Could* it be about me?

Recovering his composure, he says, "I made some progress on the composition. Shall I play it for you?"

Did he just read my thoughts? "Please."

He pulls a chair up for me, removes his musician's black jacket and takes his seat behind the piano. He changes the sheet music, flashes me the quickest of smiles, then focuses and begins to play.

The ripple of keys is like a stream of clear water. The melody is sweet and pure, but there is a sorrow—no, that's not the right word—a longing underneath its current. The piece pleads with my emotions, coaxing them out of their hiding place; they float to the surface. It is as though his music is coming from inside me: it isn't the acting out of a feeling, it is the feeling itself. Everything I have kept locked up—my dreams of Paris, the disappointment of my job, the fear, dread and desperation—and at the outside of it all, hope. My eyes smart; my lips quiver as the music floods over me and the longing I've always felt to make something of myself—to escape the village and find another life—pours out of me.

Paul finishes and rests his hands gently in his lap, and the room, so full of life when he played, becomes paler and smaller in the absence of the music. He looks at me. He doesn't speak, but his hazel eyes are asking what I thought.

I can barely croak a whisper. "Beautiful, Paul. It is incredibly beautiful."

"It's not finished yet. I worry that it's not the sort of thing people will like. Is it even good?"

How can he doubt himself? "You must share it, you must," I say. "It's important. What a gift, to be able to create something that can speak directly to another person without words or explanation."

"You have an artist's soul, Maude. I hope—"

"*Une bière*, Monsieur Paul?" the barman interrupts from across the room. "Maybe a drink for the young lady?"

What was he going to say? I wonder. What does he hope?

"You want something?" he asks me.

I shake my head. "No, thanks."

Paul laughs. "I shouldn't either, or it will confirm your suspicions of me as a drunken bohemian." He calls to the barman, "*Non, ça va, merci, Jules!*"

I want to share my new interest in photography with him, but I hold back. How could I ever explain that my "pupil" has taught me such a thing? Instead I ask him, "When will you play the new piece for the public?"

"I have a concert planned with some friends. We get to try out our new compositions on some rich music lovers."

"You will play wonderfully, I'm sure of it. And then one day they will play your music at the Opéra de Paris."

He leans forward and kisses my cheek. "*T'es gentille.*"

The kiss isn't like *les bises*, the greeting people give when they meet, but something more affectionate. Looking at him this close makes me want to lean forward and fall into an embrace. My gloves fall from my lap. Glad of the distraction, I bend down to pick them up and compose myself with a deep breath.

I stay for a while with Paul as the other band members appear and customers begin to trickle in. I even stay for the first dance or two. It feels easy to be in the company of Paul and his friends. There aren't the same rules of etiquette and manners as with the aristocrats. And I don't have to be on my guard all the time, figuring out what's going on beneath the smooth conversations and judging looks of the idle rich.

When I walk home afterward, I take my time. Even though it's freezing, my mantle keeps me warm. Or maybe it's the evening spent with Paul that makes me feel this way.

Later on, when I'm lying in bed, I look between the parted curtains at the night sky. Paris: what a world away from the windswept cloud of the Breton shore, where rain clouds dissolve into ocean, the horizon forever obscured—one shade of gray fading into another. There are so many ways to live here: what is my path?

# Chapter 24

Time has charged past, and it's Christmas Eve already. I am to spend the holidays with the Duberns. When a dinner guest innocently mentioned that Madame Vary had gone to the South of France to escape the cold, I had to think on my feet. I told Isabelle that my aunt's physician prescribed the trip for her health and that I didn't mind her leaving me behind. Nonetheless, Isabelle made a scene and the countess was forced to invite me to stay for the week, now that I'm supposedly alone in Paris. The countess didn't bank on having to maintain the fiction of our connection.

At the agency I have packed a trunk of clothes from my special wardrobe that I'll need for the week. It's crammed full, and I struggle with it as I make my way along the hall.

"Maude!" Laurent comes to my aid. "I'll take that downstairs for you."

"*Merci*, Laurent."

I stretch my back for a moment as he hauls the trunk along the wooden floor toward the staircase. "What have you got in here?" he calls out to me. "Are you smuggling Marie-Josée with you?"

At the mention of her name, I feel a pang of guilt. It's

been ages since we've spent time together. I've been too busy with the Duberns. Before I can wallow too much, though, I realize I've forgotten something.

"I'll be right back," I tell Laurent. I forgot the sable hat. I'm supposed to wear it tonight to Christmas Eve Mass.

I run back along the corridor toward my wardrobe.

"Maude!" I hear Marie-Josée call out behind me. She scuttles down the corridor, catching up to me outside the storage room. "You were off at quite a clip." Her face is redder than usual, and her breathing is heavy from effort.

I squeeze her arm. "I haven't seen you in forever." It is nice to see her, but I don't really have time to gossip.

I unlock the cupboard and begin rummaging through the hatboxes.

"Help me find a hat," I tell her.

"Which one?"

"Sable fur."

As we upturn boxes, Marie-Josée says, "I just wanted to make sure you're still coming over for *le Réveillon* feast tonight. My sister has been cooking up a storm all week."

She mentioned something about this a while ago, but I completely forgot until now. I stop my search for the hat for a moment and look at her. "Oh, no, I can't." I feel terrible, but what can I do? "I have to work."

"On Christmas? Surely not." She stops helping me and folds her arms. "Agency policy is we all get to leave early tonight and have the next two days off." With her ample frame squeezed into the small space, I feel a little bit cornered.

I shrug apologetically. "I would love to spend Christmas

with your family instead of working. But I have to go. Durandeau said."

And the truth is I'm quite excited about spending a week in the luxury of the Dubern home.

I continue my search for the hat, flipping open the lids of a couple more boxes, peeking beneath layers of tissue paper.

"You should speak to Durandeau about it," Marie-Josée goes on, riled up on my behalf.

"I think he's charging double for the holiday," I say. "He agreed that I'll get paid extra too." Eventually I find the hat hiding under a pile of scarves. "Here it is." It's a plush tan-colored fur with a sprig of feathers on the side—I've been hoping to wear it ever since the weather turned cold.

"I'll go with you if you want," says Marie-Josée.

"Go where?" My voice sounds sharp, though I don't mean for it to.

"To speak to Durandeau about working on Christmas."

I try to be patient. I hold the hat between us. "No, you don't have to. It would be pointless." My tone is too firm, so I temper it with a smile. "Well, I found it," I say, looking down at the hat, conveniently avoiding her eyes. I feel bad but I wish she weren't bothering me about this now. The carriage is waiting. I nod toward the door. "I suppose I should be going."

Marie-Josée takes the hint and turns to leave the box room. She hovers next to me in the hallway as I lock up. "It's a shame; we're having a roast for dinner. And the children are so looking forward to meeting you."

"That's right, you have three nieces."

She shakes her head. "Two nieces and a nephew."

I do feel guilty, even though it's not my decision. "I'm sorry. I don't have a choice, Marie-Josée." I kiss her on the cheek. "I can't say no to the Duberns."

"If you have to work, you have to work, I suppose. I just don't see a lot of you these days." Her jolly face looks hard for once. "This job has taken over your life. I just assumed Christmas would be a safe-enough bet."

The carriage is waiting for me downstairs and I feel the soft fur of the hat against the palm of my hand.

"I know, I'm sorry. Give your family my best," I say cheerily. "I'm sure you'll have a wonderful holiday."

Marie-Josée simply stands in the hallway as I turn to leave. I run to the stairs and out to the waiting carriage. I can feel her eyes on my back, watching me go.

# Chapter 25

Midnight Mass is a spectacular affair in Paris. I had no idea church could be a social scene for the aristocracy instead of the God-fearing chore I am used to. Normally I'm agitated, bottom numbed on the hard pew and counting the minutes till it's over—especially on Christmas, when there is the Réveillon feast to look forward to.

Back home I had to endure church with Papa every Sunday: as the proprietor of the general store, he liked to think of himself as one of the pillars of the community in the way a priest or a doctor is. He would insist we attend Mass together to set a good example. The lengthy sermon ate into my precious day off, but afterward I was free, and I'd spend time on the beach.

The ocean doesn't respect Sunday rules. Waves crash and pound the shore and seagulls screech into the cutting wind. It's wholly disorganized—a mess of stones, broken shells and seaweed strewn about. I would find my rock and sit by the mermaid's handprint—an indentation in the stone, shaped like a small hand—buffeted and chilled by the wind. But I didn't mind the weather. I enjoyed the drama and exhilaration of Mother Nature's Sunday sermon more than Father Leguin's.

But tonight in la Madeleine, I wonder if I'm not at the opera. There is the beauty of the building itself, the other worshippers in their furs and finery and the choir's angelic voices. The whole scene is bathed in the heavenly light from hundreds of candles. Tonight I sing with exuberance, not for Jesus's birth so much as for my own good fortune at being able to take part in the splendor.

We return home after the *Messe de minuit* to an incredible feast attended by the Duberns' extended family. There is the countess's sister—attractive, but not stunning like the countess herself—and her husband with their young boys; some other second cousins; and the count's younger brother, Isabelle's favorite uncle, who gave her the camera.

I take a sip of wine—I now know the difference between cheap wine by the carafe and a fine vintage from the count's cellar. A servant helps me to a second portion of goose, even though I know I can't finish it. The cousins make faces at each other; it's late and they are giddy with tiredness. Isabelle's uncle is seated next to me. His conversation is easy and his blue blood seems to have some bohemian spirit coursing through it. Even the countess appears softer this evening. With just the family here tonight, the atmosphere is relaxed. For once I don't have to worry about potential suitors or the countess's marriage plans for her daughter. I can just enjoy myself.

After dinner the family retires to the drawing room to exchange presents. There is a roaring fire and a Christmas tree, and a nativity scene of little painted figurines is set up on a table by the window. The room smells of spiced nuts and *vin chaud*. I don't expect to be included in the presents, but the countess beckons me over and hands me a box. On top sits a card that reads *In great appreciation of your friendship with Isabelle*. I feel the dark shadow of guilt hover overhead, because I know she's rewarding my role as a repoussoir with this token. It feels like a Christmas bonus from an employer, not a gift of true affection. When I open the box, I find, to my astonishment, a gorgeous jeweled bracelet shining against the black velvet lining of the box. It's similar to the one she let me try on a few months ago. I can't believe her generosity, and I put it on immediately.

The countess helps me with the catch. "Do you like it?" she asks, smiling.

"It's stunning. *Merci*, Madame la Comtesse." My delight at the gift blows away my guilt.

Isabelle gives me a notebook with my initials embossed in gold on the cover. "I have something else for you, but I'll give it to you later," she whispers.

"I'm so embarrassed. I didn't buy any presents," I tell her.

"You weren't supposed to," she says. "Just enjoy it."

I look around the room and then down at my new bracelet. For the first time I feel as if I really belong.

It's the wee hours of the morning by the time a maid leads me to my bedroom by lamplight. The walls are papered green with a delicate leaf print. In the center of the room is a huge dark wood four-poster bed covered with an embroidered bedspread. There is a ceramic sculpture of an Asian woman on either side of the bed on mirrored tables. Under my feet, a thick carpet of green and white flowers decorates the floor. The fire is lit, and the maid places the lamp by my bed.

"I put out some nightclothes for you, mademoiselle," the maid says. "Seems you forgot to pack any."

I realize I've never received proper nightclothes in the wardrobe from the countess—it didn't even occur to me.

"Do you need help undressing?" she asks.

She already helped me into my Christmas Eve outfit, so I'm not taken by surprise this time. "If you could undo the buttons." I turn my back to her. She has me unbuttoned and my corset untied in seconds, then helps me out of the dress and hangs it up in the closet.

"*Bonne nuit*, mademoiselle." She closes the door behind her and I am left alone for the first time in this paradise of a room, which must exceed the dimensions of my garret room twofold. It's late, but I daren't go to sleep yet. Even if I wanted to, my body is buzzing with the excitement of actually staying for a week in the Duberns' house. I wander around the room, letting my fingers glide across the furnishings, pretending I am as accustomed to them as to my own dingy dresser and chair. I take a peek behind the curtains at the night outside. It's still, unlike my neighborhood; a blanket of luxury keeps everyone snug and quiet, sleeping in their four-poster beds, under goose-down quilts.

By the window there is a walnut desk with writing paper and an inkwell. To whom would I most like to write from this vantage? I sit down, take the quill from its well, dab it on the blotting paper and put pen to paper.

*Cher Papa,*

*I want you to know I'm quite well. I am in Paris, which is everything my dreams could conjure. I have a circle of rich friends who are taking care of me.*

I begin to let my imagination run away with me.

*As a debutante I enjoy balls and banquets with a slew of prospective suitors vying for my attention. I have everything a girl could want, so you mustn't be concerned. You must accept that I don't plan to return home to Brittany. I will write again to inform you of my imminent marriage. Of course it would be out of the question to invite you to my wedding.*

> *Your daughter,*
> *Maude*

I write my address as care of the Count and Countess Dubern, to further impress. I reread my letter, crumple the paper into a ball and throw it in the fire, watching my fantasy life smolder in an instant. Even if I'd never dream of sending such a letter, it feels nice to pretend.

I get into bed underneath the quilt embroidered with flowers. I don't put out the lamp yet; I lie still, my eyes open, absorbing the riches and beauty of the room. I am an Ophelia surrounded by flowers, ready to let the old Maude die, to be reborn into a new life.

"Maude Dubern," I whisper.

Imagine if I were the count and countess's other daughter.

I pretend this is my bedroom; the dresses hanging in the wardrobe are my own. It is my highly anticipated season, and I dance with handsome suitors who appreciate my wit and intelligence. My sister, Isabelle, has beauty and charm, but even though I am the plainer, quieter sister, I can still captivate Paris society. It is in this spirit of enjoyable self-delusion that I drift off to sleep.

On Christmas morning, I'm aware of a servant in my room building a fire. I hear Geneviève enter and whisper to the other girl—a scullery maid—to be quick and leave the room before I wake. I open my eyes to Geneviève placing a breakfast tray on the bed beside me. "*Bonjour*, mademoiselle."

"What time is it, *s'il te plaît*?" I ask her using the familiar *tu*, not the formal *vous*. She's only a servant, after all.

"After ten; everyone slept late today, mademoiselle."

"Is Isabelle awake yet?"

"Yes, she's getting ready. The family gathers in the drawing room on Christmas morning. I'll be back to help you dress." She glances down at the floor next to my bed. "Seems you had a visitor during the night!"

Geneviève leaves and I pull myself out of bed. On the floor I find two gifts wrapped in silver tissue. I open them hastily, and to my amazement, I find myself holding my very own camera and a box of glass plates. *Isabelle*, I think.

# Chapter 26

"The duke has returned from London, and I have it on good authority that he will be attending this evening's concert." The countess is positively ecstatic as she relays the news to me during our stroll in the Jardin des Tuileries on Christmas afternoon.

Excitement takes hold and my heart flutters at the thought of seeing him again. Then I stop myself and examine the situation with a cool logic—the chess game of matchmaking is on again, and I'm caught in the middle.

"I hope Isabelle will find some charm to shower him with," the countess says, sighing and glancing down the path at her daughter walking with the count. Her face grows stern. "It's not attractive, such a headstrong girl. Talking about politics and science—her conversation is a douse of cold water on the flames of romance."

I follow her gaze to the figure ahead of us in the white mantle. If only the countess knew *how* headstrong her daughter is. I wonder if I could tell her about Isabelle's plans in a way that won't get me into trouble.

The countess continues, "Ideally I want an engagement announced in the spring."

I look across at her. "Spring?" I repeat. I wasn't expecting this. Spring is so soon!

"That's supposing she can hold his interest until then." She prods a gloved finger into my arm like a wand. "Your influence will be key."

Doubt is lodged in my throat. I want to speak up and temper her expectations, but what can I say? I can't *defy* her. I swallow hard. "Isabelle is an independent girl," I venture. It's as much as I can say to stand up to the countess.

"She is, but her weakness is friendship. There is already affection between them, and with your counsel to encourage her, I'm not worried."

I thought I had more time—Durandeau had mentioned the season lasting until summer, and I've been naïvely playing along, fingers crossed, hoping I can keep everyone happy. But the countess demands results. Can I encourage Isabelle to contemplate marriage as well as her studies?

"When Isabelle is engaged, your assignment will be complete. And of course, then we can arrange some kind of reward for your efforts."

"What sort of reward?" I can feel the new bracelet underneath my coat sleeve and I almost forget my predicament at the thought of receiving another token of her appreciation.

"I'll have to think about it." She pulls up the collar on her furs; the coat is trimmed with mink tails, and they sway in unison as she moves. "Of course, it depends on setting the engagement first."

\*    \*    \*

When we return from the afternoon stroll, I seek out Isabelle. I intend to test the waters for her current temperature on marriage. I've purposely avoided this topic since our day at Eiffel's tower, and she never initiates the subject of her own accord. I open the schoolroom door without knocking—the Duberns' home as familiar to me as my own now—and take a seat in one of the armchairs by the fire. Isabelle is hard at work, poring over some papers on her workbench.

"I'll be with you in a moment," she says.

"Take your time." I relax back into the armchair and gaze at the fire. What approach will be the most persuasive? I must incorporate her desire for independence and the pursuit of academics. I can't suggest she give those up.

There's a knock on the door and the butler enters, brandishing a silver tray with two glasses of steaming mulled wine.

"Something to warm you up, mesdemoiselles, after your walk." He hands me a glass and puts the other one on the table for Isabelle, then leaves the room.

I sip the fragrant hot wine; a ribbon of liquid warmth unravels down my throat and brings a glow to my cheeks. I recognize all the servants now and understand the different roles they perform. Before they were faceless and as intimidating to me as their masters; now I know different.

I take another sip of wine, spicy and sweet. The fire crackles and I lift my feet toward it and wiggle my toes inside my boots, relishing the perfection of the setting. "Pull up a chair," I call over to Isabelle.

"Sorry, I'll be right there. I'm just looking over my Latin."

I smile and shake my head. "Your capacity for understanding all those scientific terms baffles me."

"It's not terribly difficult. I just commit things to memory," she says, walking toward me and picking up her wine. She takes the armchair opposite and leans back, her face still knotted in concentration.

"After you apply to the Sorbonne, how long until you find out if you have a place?"

"By summer, I should know." She takes a sip. "I've a good mind to tell Mother right now. It would take the pressure off all her matchmaking."

I almost choke on my wine. I play out the scenario in my mind and begin to feel ill. Isabelle will tell her mother, claiming the support of her new friend Maude. I will lose my job in an instant. Propelled by fear, I think fast. "Isabelle, honestly, just wait on that," I say casually. "Wouldn't it be best to continue with your season until you absolutely have secured the place?"

She slouches back in her chair and sighs. "I suppose."

I breathe a sigh of relief.

Now that she's mentioned the obstacle of her mother, I see a way to bring up the notion of marriage in a positive light. "I was just thinking about what you said at the tower that day."

She lifts her head, curiosity piqued.

"Have you ever considered that a husband might support your studies? It would be better to be married, then, than to remain a child in your mother's house forever."

She scrutinizes me. "Whose side are you on? Have you made a pact with Mother?"

Her accuracy throws me for a moment. I shrug, trying to appear natural. "I just think you shouldn't rule it out."

She puts down her glass. "What about you? I thought you didn't come to Paris to find a husband?"

"I would marry the right person," I say sincerely. "What about the duke, for instance?" As if he just came to mind. "He's kind and appears fond of you. Now that he's back from England, imagine if he proposes—"

"I'll have to refuse him," she interrupts.

"You can't!" I say with too much feeling. It irks me that she can be utterly dismissive of such a man. "You disregard him so easily, as though you're saying no to sugar in your tea or a second helping of cake. The duke is a worthy match—good fortune and breeding."

"Maude!" She stares at me, her head cocked to the side with a puzzled expression.

My shoulders sink. Surely by insisting, I have just given myself away.

Her eyes are fixed on me like a cat's. "I declare, you like the duke." She breaks into a grin.

The color rises in my cheek and I fight to conceal my feelings. "What? No, of course not. Preposterous." But I know my words don't match my expression. It's as if she's shining a light on my hidden desires. "I mean to say, I like him for you, yes. But he's not for me."

"You do!" She laughs. "You have a secret crush. Well, he's going to be at the Christmas ball tonight. We must throw you two together." She picks up her glass and raises it in a toast. "To Maude and the duke."

What have I done? Simultaneous delight and terror strike

a chord, which clangs off-key; this is not how the countess's matchmaking is supposed to play out.

The Russian embassy is hosting a concert, followed by a Christmas ball. The music room is a dazzling space of ivory and gold. Cherubs are painted on the ceiling and carved into the moldings. The room glows with chandelier light, and rows of gilded chairs are set up to face the grand piano—a complete contrast from the music halls of Montparnasse.

Since Isabelle concocted her plan to pair me off with the duke, I have been guilty of indulging in a fantasy for the rest of the afternoon. I can't help but wonder if maybe I do belong with the aristocracy after all. Even my dress tonight—a cream chiffon silk trimmed with black lace and sequins—is the equal of Isabelle's. If the duke picked me, nothing else would matter—not the countess, the agency, my garret room or money. All my worries would evaporate into a fairy-tale life. The Duchess d'Avaray.

As the minutes tick by and the guests begin to take their seats, I worry that the duke won't show up after all. The performance is due to start any moment, and I search the well-dressed crowd for his face.

"*Mesdames et messieurs*, please take your seats," says the ambassador, and the last guests drift into the rows of chairs. Our row is composed of Isabelle's uncle, Isabelle, me and an empty seat beside me for the duke; the count, the countess and the Rocheforts are sitting in front of us. Needless to say, the seating arrangement was Isabelle's doing.

Just as I'm about to give up on him, I see a figure gliding up the aisle in my peripheral vision.

"Is this seat taken?" I turn my head to meet the radiant face of the duke himself. He kisses my cheek as he sits down next to me, and my heart can't contain itself. But when he leans across me to greet Isabelle in the same way, a voice inside me jeers, *Why you? Why would he pick Maude Pichon over a count's daughter?*

The ambassador clears his throat to get our attention.

"*Mesdames et messieurs*, at the embassy we are patrons of music, and tonight we are going to hear an original composition by a talented young musician. Please welcome Monsieur Paul Villette."

I stop breathing. I cannot believe I have just heard my friend's name spoken aloud. That name belongs in another world, another life. Surely it's a mistake. But then the musicians walk into the room to polite applause. I gasp—the piano player is indeed my Paul Villette. The floor feels as though it's rolling beneath my feet.

I shrink down as low as I can behind the mountainous hairpieces of Claire de Rochefort, immediately in front of me. In such a tiny audience it will be easy for Paul to recognize me. Or perhaps, as I'm dressed so differently, and in such an unfamiliar setting, he won't—I hope he won't.

Paul gives a short bow and takes his seat at the grand piano. Its surface shines like liquid. He glances up at the audience just as Claire de Rochefort leans in and whispers something to her mother, exposing me completely, and my eyes lock onto his. I register the slight twitch of his head, followed by a cursory glance at my neighbors in the audience. The violin and cello players take their positions and look to him for a signal to begin.

Paul fumbles on the opening bars of his piece and my heart sinks. The performance spirals downward from there and seems to last an eternity. The sweet melody he played for me at the music hall sounds cheap in this decadent setting. The audience responds negatively—there are whispers and sniggers punctuating each phrase of music, not the least of them from my friends.

"Amateurs," the duke hisses in my ear, and it cuts me to the quick. "The pianist isn't the match for that fine instrument."

As wounded as I feel for Paul, at the same time I want to distance myself from the borrowed evening jacket, messy hair and general inferiority he exudes. In truth, I feel ashamed of him. Seeing him vulnerable among these people only magnifies my own fears of not being good enough, of being discovered. I glance to my right at the duke, then to my left past Isabelle to her uncle. These men radiate confidence and grace; Paul resembles a court jester.

When the piece is finally over, all the guests leave the music room. I want to see if Paul is all right after the doomed performance, but I don't want any of the Dubern circle to know we are acquainted. I follow Isabelle and the others for a few steps toward the ballroom, but when no one is looking I steal back into the music room unnoticed.

He's standing alone, gathering his sheets of music. He looks up and I carefully make my way past the gilded chairs, unsure of what to say.

"Is everything in this city for sale?" he asks. "How many little girls are you governess to? For I only see you in the company of grown-ups." His voice is strained with emotion.

Why is he so angry with me? "Paul, I'm sorry about your performance."

"Do you think me a simpleton? God knows Paris is expensive. You wouldn't be the first to accept 'charity' of that sort. I'm surprised your patron—or is there more than one?—I'm surprised he hasn't installed you in better accommodations. Judging from his carriage, he can well afford to keep a mistress in more luxurious surroundings." He stuffs his music sheets into a leather satchel.

I gasp when it hits me what he means. "A mistress? You think . . ." Then I have to stifle a laugh. "That's ridiculous!"

"Is it so amusing? Do you have another explanation? You are certainly not a governess. Am I wrong?"

To explain . . . I realize I can't explain. I grip the back of a chair for support. "No, I am not a governess." The truth is humiliation. Worse than what he supposes. At least this way he thinks me capable of enticing a man.

"I thought you were a different sort of girl." He looks at me harshly. "You had a purity to you. I found you open and honest. But you are an actress, I take it. Are you even interested in art or music—was that an act as well?"

"Paul, stop!" I say, my voice raised. I turn back to look at the door, hoping no one has heard us. I meet his gaze again. "I was myself with you," I say in a hushed tone. "I cannot explain further. It's not what you think, but I have no other explanation to give you. It's painful to see you disappointed with me. I cannot pretend I didn't lie to you, but you mustn't accuse me of the worst."

"You must think me utterly naïve." He slams down his satchel on the piano stool. "Every woman in Paris has her talents, her skills in manipulation; every woman has her price." He closes the lid of the piano with unnecessary force and then meets my eye. "We are all prostitutes to the rich, Mademoiselle Pichon."

I feel suddenly degraded by my job all over again. Its shadow of shame has reached every corner of my life. But I'm also angry. How could he think I would stoop so low as to be a kept woman, a rich man's mistress? If that's what he truly thinks of me, then let him believe it.

I meet his glare with mine. "Yes, most desperate people would submit to something distasteful for money," I retort, my tone icy. Let him make of that what he will. "I'm sorry your music wasn't more graciously received."

I turn away and quit the room in a hurry, just as my voice falters and a sob escapes.

I fight to compose myself, then enter the ballroom. As I look for Isabelle among the guests, I notice that her parents are dancing, and I'm grateful I don't have to deal with the countess at this moment. Isabelle is with the other young people, listening to Xavier boast about some feat of horsemanship. She looks bored. Behind her I see that the duke has been commandeered by Claire. They are both in hysterics.

I join the group casually. "What's the joke?" I say, forcing a smile.

"It was the worst performance I've seen," Claire says, laughing in a high-pitched screech.

"Where on earth did the ambassador find such buffoons? Had that pianist ever touched the instrument before?" says the duke.

"It can't be easy to play in front of people." Isabelle comes to Paul's defense. "Maybe it was nerves?"

Claire rolls her eyes and bats her fan impatiently. "Nerves or not, the composition was dreadful."

"I agree with Claire—it was hideous!" I laugh out loud, throwing away any thought of Paul, his composition, what he risked to play in front of an audience—and not least the name of the piece, "*La Bretonne*."

# Chapter 27

A cold snap has Paris in its freezing grip. I follow the trickle of girls into the agency dressing room, my cheeks raw and my fingers numb. Like the others, I'm reluctant to take off my coat. One by one, we gather near the stove to thaw out. I take in the pitiful scene and compare it to the Dubern drawing room with its roaring fire and army of servants.

The glamour of the Christmas holiday is long gone. Isabelle has a cold, and we haven't been to any events for the past ten days. The fantasies I got carried away with under the Dubern roof no longer seem possible when I'm here at the agency. Or maybe they aren't possible under any circumstance. At the Christmas ball, Isabelle's matchmaking amounted to a few dances with the duke. He was charming and courteous as ever, but I could tell he preferred Isabelle's company to mine. And so despite her protest, I feigned tiredness and the Viscountess de Rochefort took me back to the Duberns' in her carriage. I didn't even mind about the failed attempt to attract the duke, for on the drive back and into the small hours of the night it was Paul's face, and not the duke's, that kept entering my thoughts.

My new camera is the one good thing that has lasted

from the Dubern Christmas into the New Year. I practiced using it in Isabelle's schoolroom, and today I brought it to work with me. I have two plates remaining and plan to use them to take pictures of the view from the dressing room.

Of course, the moment Emilie sees the camera and exclaims aloud, the girls all gather round.

"What is that, Maude?" Emilie asks, her large eyes blinking.

"A camera." I act nonchalant, but I can feel a sense of pride quicken in me.

"Do you know how it works?" says Hortense.

Cécile pushes past the others. "Where did you get it?" She reaches out to touch it.

"It's fragile," I say, pulling it from her grasp. I've anticipated this question, and I relish my answer. "It's a gift from my client."

And there: I see the shadow of envy touch their faces.

Marie-Josée joins in. "Take a picture of us," she says, nodding at me encouragingly. Immediately the girls get giddy at her suggestion and imitate poses they've seen actresses and vaudeville stars strike. I can see what she's doing: diffusing the tension, tempering the girls' jealousy by having me share the camera with them. But I'm annoyed. I don't want to waste a plate on them. I look at my friend playing the fool with the other girls. She lifts up her skirts like a cancan dancer.

"Come on, Maude." She grins at me. "Tell us what to do!"

An idea pops into my head—I could just pretend to take the picture; they don't understand the technicalities involved. I'll take the lens cap off, but if I leave the slide protecting the negative in the camera housing, the plate won't be exposed. It will seem as if I've taken their picture. They'll feel included, yet I won't have used up a plate.

"All right. Open the net curtains and let in as much light as possible," I say. They scramble to do as I ask. Meanwhile, I place the camera on a stool as a makeshift stand. "Now go to that pool of light by the window." Excited, Marie-Josée, Hortense and Cécile horse around, arguing over who should stand in the middle. Emilie hovers at the fringes of the group, smiling at their antics.

I continue going through the motions as if I were really about to take the picture. "Emilie, join the others. Go on," I say. I find the framing and set the focus; then I slide the wooden negative housing into the back of the camera. "Hold still," I tell them. I look up from the viewer and remove the lens cap. But in that moment a shaft of soft light hits their faces, giving them an ethereal glow. In that instant I suddenly recognize that the girls are unself-conscious; they are their true selves, and I want to capture the way I see them right now. Before I can stop myself, I swiftly remove the protective cover of the negative holder and the moment is recorded, almost against my will.

"Done," I say, and a sigh escapes. I replace the lens cap and feel the rush of disappointment—I only have one plate remaining.

"What is going on in here?" Durandeau is standing in the doorway of the dressing room. "Not one of you is dressed. There is a client coming in half an hour." Smiles vanish and eyes are cast down.

"What is that, Mademoiselle Pichon?"

Instinctively I pick up the camera and draw it close.

232

"A camera, Monsieur Durandeau." My voice is almost a whisper.

"Really?" He strides toward me, his chin jutting out, suspicious. "And where did you procure such an item?"

"A gift from my client, monsieur." I shrink back from his looming figure.

"Well, you can't take an agency portrait in this hovel of a room." He looks at his watch. "There's ample time. We shall all convene in the salon for a proper formal photograph."

My face flushes with indignation as I realize what he means. I don't want to waste my last plate on a picture of Durandeau. "But—"

He cuts me off immediately. "Or would you rather I confiscate the item as property of the agency?"

I shake my head, wanting to kick myself for having brought the camera here in the first place. Part of me did want to show it off to the others.

We change into our agency clothes in silence, and I realize no one wants their repoussoir portrait taken. Nevertheless, everyone gathers in the salon. The chairs are arranged in a row. Durandeau enters and takes a seat in the middle, flanked by Girard and Laurent. The remaining seats are taken by the first girls to arrive, and the rest stand behind them.

"Is this setup going to work for you, Maude?" asks Laurent.

"Let me see." I've never taken a formal group portrait before. I place the camera on a wooden plant stand as a makeshift tripod and look through the window at the upside-down image. For this many people I should really have a bigger camera with a larger plate size. "You have to bunch together to all fit in the frame," I say. The girls shuffle closer to one another while I check the focus. Then I insert the fresh plate and pull up the protective wooden slide in preparation to take the picture. I feel nervous with the whole agency looking at me expectantly.

"I'm ready," I tell Durandeau.

The image in front of me is very different from the candid smiling faces I captured minutes earlier.

"Now, ladies," says Durandeau. "Eyes forward, chins up; think of what the agency means to you." Before me, I see the faces of my colleagues harden, the shoulders sink. And shame washes over each one of them. By contrast, Durandeau's chest puffs out and his nostrils flare. He is clearly filled with his own sense of genius. Next to him, Girard looks proud; the agency is her home. On the other side of Durandeau, Laurent looks unaffected.

I see all this happen in the blink of an eye. And I feel with certainty that I am not a part of it, I am not one of them. My heart thumping, I remove the lens cover. Light floods in, and the image is captured on the glass. My last plate is gone.

After the drama of the photograph, the workday continues like any other. In the dressing room, Marie-Josée is rounding up the girls for a lunch out. I don't feel like it today. When there's a group of us we're often seated at an out-of-the-way table, ignored by the waiters until Marie-Josée gets uppity. Then we're treated rudely. Today I just want to be left alone.

I linger behind, fixing my hair as they file out of the dressing room. When the door closes behind them, I breathe a sigh of relief and drop the pins from my hand, letting them scatter on the dressing table. I look in the mirror and think of Paul. What was it that he saw in me, and why couldn't I just tell him the truth? All the layers of deception weigh me down, and when I see my own reflection, I'm not sure who I'm looking at anymore.

The dressing room door creaks open and I look up to see Marie-Josée pop her head back in.

"You not coming with us, Maude?"

Her question breaks the seal on my irritation.

"No," I snap. "I have some errands to run."

She comes over to me and puts an arm around my shoulder. I know she means to be nice, but it's all I can do not to pull away.

"It's too bad you weren't in the picture with all of us," she says.

Sensing my bad mood, she has tried to guess what might be the root of it. She couldn't be more wrong.

"I suppose someone has to be clever enough to know how to take the picture," she says kindly.

But her niceness only provokes me more. "I'm glad I wasn't in the photograph—how could anyone want this humiliation to be captured for eternity in black-and-white?" I shrug off her touch and stand up, feeling a surge of fury. "Besides, I'm not like the rest of you. The countess sees that. All she wants is a friend for her daughter, not a hideous freak of nature."

She sucks in her breath, taken aback. "Oh, be careful, Maude." She shakes her head.

I know what she thinks; I've felt it since the beginning. She resents my contract with the Duberns—why else is she always bothering me about them, cautioning me against befriending Isabelle?

"Why must I be careful, Marie-Josée?" My voice is shrill, but I can't lower it. "You're just jealous. Because the countess would never pick someone like you for her daughter."

Her eyes open wide. "Someone like me how?" She puts her hands on her hips, challenging me to utter the words. "Spit it out, girl."

"Someone as coarse as you are." It feels unnatural to lash out, but the words keep flowing from my lips, as though from someone else. "You could never belong in their world."

I'm shaking with anger and confusion. Looking at Marie-Josée's familiar face makes me realize that spewing out these caustic words isn't the release I thought it would be. But I can't unsay the words.

She grabs my arm. "Look, my girl. I'm not jealous of you. I've been in your shoes before, and it didn't end well for me. I'm trying to save you from the same disappointment."

I don't believe her. "What do you mean? You were friends with a client?"

She releases my arm and sighs heavily. "No. It was when I was in service as a lady's maid. The gentleman of the house took a shine to me. It felt good to be a favorite for once. I was young and daft. But then a kind word turned into wandering hands. And then something worse."

My mind races ahead of her, anticipating the rest of the story. "What happened?"

"I told the mistress and she fired me. No letter of reference, no savings—I was kicked to the curb."

Her eyes meet mine, her face full of emotion. I know it's cost her something to tell me this.

I look away. I feel bad for her, but at the same time I have this need to put a distance between us. So I don't soften, and I don't apologize for my outburst. If anything, she has added more fuel to my fire.

"Our situations are completely different," I tell her. My anger transforms into contempt. I meet her gaze again, my expression hard and cold.

Marie-Josée looks like a wounded animal. Realizing she hasn't won me over, she simply casts her eyes to the floor, then leaves the room.

I stand alone in the dressing room, trembling with anger. Or is it shame?

# Chapter 28

It's deep winter in the countryside outside Paris. Late January might be cold and dark, but the weather is irrelevant because I, Maude Pichon, am staying in a chateau. The Duberns, some other notables and myself have been invited to the Duke d'Avaray's country estate. The men are going to catch the last of the duck-hunting season.

The chateau is vast and elegant, a gray stone building covered with spidery vines, situated in acres of woodland and fields of grass. The formal gardens are dead and brown at this time of year, but strolling the maze of paved paths and hedgerows, I can imagine how beautiful the greenery and flowers would be in summer. For me, just to be in the countryside is a treat; I can breathe clean air and enjoy the soothing views of rolling hills, not a rooftop or chimney in sight.

Isabelle and some of the gentlemen have gone riding, but as I am a poor horsewoman, I stayed behind to enjoy the peace and quiet of the library and a roaring fire. I've never seen so many books in one place, outside of a bookshop. After my mother died, I inherited her books, mostly classics, which I reread until I knew some pages by heart, but I also found a few romance novels in her collection, which revealed something of her nature. She daydreamed beyond the confines of Poullan-sur-Mer, just as I did.

It's afternoon, when the light is fading, that the countess summons me to her bedroom and my tranquility is snatched away. For the countess there are prospective husbands to be hunted, not waterfowl. Any interaction with her lately makes me apprehensive. I've fueled her exaggerated expectations for Isabelle and the duke. He likes Isabelle, but enough to propose? I have no idea. Judging by my own foolishness with him, I know I am the last person to interpret aristocratic manners.

When I enter the countess's bedchamber she is standing in front of the armoire, arms outstretched, an evening gown in each hand.

"Come in, Maude. Take a seat. A glass of sherry, perhaps?"

She is unusually warm, which makes me cautious.

The maid hands me a glass of sherry and I take a seat on a high-backed chair. I haven't been in the countess's room at the chateau until now; naturally it's even nicer than mine, decorated with tapestries and a great oak bed with old-fashioned hangings. Entering certain rooms here is like stepping back in time, or walking through the pages of a history book.

"Which one do you prefer?" the countess asks. "Which one should I wear this evening?"

I look at the two garments, one black with a swirling pattern of gold stitching and the other a burnt-orange satin. "The orange is more original and eye-catching," I say, hoping to please.

"Yes, but tonight I want Isabelle to shine. I'll wear the

black." She hands the dresses to the maid and nods to her. "You can leave us."

After the maid has hung up the dresses and scuttled out of the room, the countess takes a seat in the armchair across from me and picks up her glass from the side table. "I have more than an inkling that Isabelle will soon receive a proposal," she says, taking a sip of sherry. "Perhaps this very week!"

She waits for me to make some positive utterance.

I hesitate for a moment. "Really? That's wonderful," I say. But it doesn't feel wonderful.

Fortunately the countess doesn't seem to notice my reticence.

"Is it the duke?" I ask, feeling a little crushed.

She looks at me as though I'm dense. "Of course it's the duke. I heard the servants gossiping about what their future mistress would be like, how she would run the house and whether she'd bring her own maid—all the usual drivel."

"How do you know it's Isabelle he means to propose to?"

The countess sets her glass down and glares at me. "Who else would it be—you?" She breaks into a laugh and covers her mouth with her hand. "I'm sorry. Forgive me." She continues laughing, tipsy on sherry. "But really, it's too amusing." She finally composes herself.

Sufficiently humiliated, I take a gulp of the putrid sherry. "What about Claire?" I say, to get back at her for hurting my feelings. "The Rocheforts are supposed to turn up this evening with the other late arrivals."

Her mouth tightens. She runs her thumb and forefinger up and down the stem of the glass, agitated. "Well, with

Claire there is the possibility of an attraction. But from what you've been telling me these past months, he appears to have little regard for her."

She cocks her head to the side, her eyes fixed on me. "Now, when the duke proposes, Isabelle will naturally seek your counsel—more than her mother's, I might add." She pauses and swirls her sherry around the glass. "I want to make sure that when that moment arises you will encourage her to give a swift and demure acceptance. As for your reward . . ." She takes a sip and continues. "The count has an aunt near Avignon who needs a companion. She's lonely in her country estate. You would be well compensated and above the rank of servant; you would be quite comfortable."

"The South of France?" I could never have imagined such a future—it's like tasting something sweet. No more Montparnasse, no more dingy garret, no more Durandeau and the repoussoirs.

But like a pinprick, the fantasy is punctured when I think of how Isabelle will react to a proposal; somehow I must prepare her mother for the worst. "What if Isabelle refuses him? I cannot *make* her say yes. She is her own person. I mean—"

A look of wrath silences me. "If he proposes, she must accept him. What other choice would she have?"

I nod in agreement and don't say another word. Clashing desires are coming to a head, instruments without a conductor playing out of time, the crescendo turning into a bad dream.

The countess rings the bell for her maid. "Now go." She waves me away. "They'll be back from their ride soon. Who knows what might have happened all this time we've been talking?"

I put my barely drunk sherry on the side table by her armchair and leave the room. When I close the door behind me, I stand for a moment in the hallway, frozen in mind and body. Is it a betrayal to encourage Isabelle to do what her mother wishes? I know how passionate she is about her studies and the future she has planned. But I must think about myself as well. I mull over the countess's words, *above the rank of servant.*

Once installed at the chateau with the count's aunt, I would be able to write my father properly. The postmistress in Poullan-sur-Mer, on reading the return address, would spread the gossip.

*Did you hear about the Pichon girl? Lives in a castle! Aristocracy—well, I never!*

I will walk the rooms of a great house steeped in the spoils of a France that no longer exists. I can almost smell the orange blossom and lavender in the formal gardens. For the first time my future would be secure.

Somehow I *have* to make sure Isabelle says yes to the duke. I continue along the corridor toward the main stairs. I must think of her as Marie-Josée would—as an assignment.

When I return to the library I find Isabelle standing on a ladder by the bookshelf, still in her riding habit.

"What are you looking for?" I ask her.

She turns her head. "There you are." She pulls a thick volume off the shelf and holds it up for me to see. "*Science in the Age of Enlightenment.*"

"Of course." I smile and sink into the vast leather couch.

Isabelle descends the ladder with the book.

"Are you wearing breeches?" I ask.

She shrugs as she walks toward me. "I hate sidesaddle. I asked the groom to lend me a pair." She collapses on the couch beside me, the book in her hands.

I shake my head at her. "And he has your fine wool riding skirt, I suppose?"

She laughs. "I plan to return them."

"Don't let your mother see you dressed so scandalously," I tease. I'm buttering her up before I broach what's really on my mind. I know I must be more forceful than last time. "Imagine, Isabelle," I venture. "If you were mistress of this house, you could wear breeches every day if you wanted."

"And get rid of all those ladies' saddles in the tack room. That would be fun."

This is my way in; I mustn't waver. "I'm serious. Don't you think you would have more freedom in every way as a duchess"—I pause—"rather than going it alone at the Sorbonne?"

She draws her brows together and shifts her position on the couch. "What are you saying? Do you not think I'll get in?" She looks dubious.

I must capitalize on her self-doubt. That's the key to breaking her resolve. "It's not that. It's just . . . it's not your world is it?" My heart races; I'm an actor, performing the role of a villain. "I mean, this is more the life you're used to," I say, gazing around the room.

Isabelle looks up from the book in her hands. "You don't think I can handle academia?"

I force a smile to my face. I must commit to these words.

"You're intelligent. It's not that I don't think you capable. It's just . . . well, the Sorbonne is a far cry from the school-room under your parents' roof, isn't it?"

She draws the book to her chest and folds her arms around it, then glares at me. "I don't like your condescending tone, and I'm confused as to your motive. Unless you think I'm not good enough for university? Are you trying to save me the embarrassment of failure?"

I sigh deeply for effect, while inside I'm beginning to feel sick. Keep going, I will myself. Push her. "I just want you to be practical. Imagine a supportive husband who encourages your private studies, who is proud of his wife, as every husband should be. And you would have the comfort and security of his protection."

"Protection? Maude, it's university, not the jungle." She pretends to laugh, but her eyes are serious. "Your choice of words . . . You don't sound like yourself."

"Isabelle," I say, forcing my tone to be warm and kind. "I'm trying to warn you, not lecture you. A proposal from the duke might happen sooner than you think." There, the element of surprise.

"I don't care." Her chin juts forward in defiance. "My answer will always be no. The sooner I can pass the entrance exams and get a place, the sooner my charade as a debutante will be over."

If only she weren't so stubborn. It's infuriating. She doesn't appreciate anything she has, the advantages she takes for granted: her appearance, her wealth and status. Why can't she see how lucky she is? It lights a fire inside me when I think of what I've had to do just to survive.

"All you've known is the gilded cage you thrash around in. How do you think you'll survive in the real world? You've never had to do anything for yourself before." Once I've started, I can't stop. It's as if I want to pick a fight now. "I think you foolish and immature to turn down a man like the duke." I realize that genuine anger is simmering inside, and I mean every word.

She stares at me, shocked and confused. Then she gets up and stomps across the room in her riding boots.

I stand up and call after. "When are you going to grow up?"

She flings the door open, but before leaving she turns to me, her expression stormy. "I thought you were my friend." Then she turns and slams the door hard.

I take a breath and let my heartbeat slow to a manageable pulse before leaving the library by another door. I *had* to do this—I tell myself. As I stride along the hallway, my pace quickens until I start to run. I hitch up my skirts and take the stairs two at a time, desperate for the solitude of my room.

An hour later the dressing bell rings and the chateau is a flurry of activity. From my window I can see that the English guests and the Rocheforts have just arrived, and now maids and valets run back and forth with valises, polished shoes, hairpins and starched collars.

I sit at the dressing table as a maid helps me get ready. My heart is leaden as she fastens the catch on my new bracelet.

"You look very nice tonight, Mademoiselle Pichon."

I see myself in the reflection, my hair pinned up in elaborate coils, my lips and cheeks stained with rouge. I am unrecognizable.

I study the girl as she tidies up the brushes and pins. Her face is honest and round with a rosy complexion, her lashes and brows fair. It's a country freshness I haven't seen in a while. Did I used to look like that?

A memory from the past floats into my consciousness. I'm standing in the cellar of Papa's shop, an apple in each hand, listening to the farmers' wives talking about me upstairs. *Thierry has been dropping hints . . . I suppose beggars can't be choosers. She doesn't have her mother's looks, that's for sure . . . Plain as flour. Poor thing.*

I am a complete hypocrite. I wouldn't listen to what people wanted for me, wouldn't fit into the box they wanted to put me in. I made my own decision to refuse a marriage prospect, defying my father and, in a way, the whole village of Poullan-sur-Mer. And now listen to the words that pour from me. I'm no better than a farmer's wife, telling Isabelle what she shouldn't set her sights on, encouraging her to do as she's told. I hold up my bracelet to the light. Tonight it feels heavier than iron.

"Do you need anything else, mademoiselle?" asks the maid.

"*Non, merci,*" I murmur.

She curtseys and leaves the room, and I struggle to make sense of everything.

What did I achieve fighting with Isabelle? Nothing more than hurting her and myself. And I did the same to Paul and Marie-Josée. My life has become so different since I started working for the Duberns.

I get up from the dressing table and move to the window, pulling back the curtain to look outside, but my own reflection is all I see in the glass. What is it that impresses me about this rich world? I think of the many things aristocrats enjoy: music, books, painting and photography. I'm drawn to them too, but not just as the furnishings of a rich person's house. Culture is the path to knowledge and the key to an examined life. At least, that's what the bohemians say.

I look beyond my reflection and out into the pitch-black of a country night. I can't get away from the questions that fill my head. Am I truly attracted to the trappings of the gilded life, or have I tricked myself? I'm in a muddle, and all I can see is what the rich possess—their winner's spoils, their aristocratic bounty. Confronted with these things, I think, That is the life I desire. But is it the box at the opera I want or the music itself?

These thoughts come from what feels like another voice inside me, one who hasn't been taken in by the glamour of the past few months, who has been paying attention to what really matters. It's not the same person who snapped at Marie-Josée and Paul. Or the same girl who made Isabelle question herself.

I think of my hosts and the guests at the chateau. Save for Isabelle, these are the sort of people who collect art but have never been really moved by it, the sort who have vast libraries of first editions the spines of which haven't been cracked. Art is a possession, a thing to be owned, and music is just a society event.

With uneasy thoughts crowding my mind, I walk downstairs to join the party in the drawing room. Isabelle pretends to be having an enjoyable conversation with Claire when I enter the room, and a stab of guilt twists in my heart. Thankfully the butler enters shortly after I do and announces that dinner is served.

As we assemble in the dining room, I am aware that for once the beauty of the setting doesn't impress me—I've had enough opulence. The duke sits at the head of the table, Countess Dubern to his right and a horsey-looking English lady to his left. Xavier is sitting next to me, the count on my other side, and Claire—not her bubbly self tonight—is sitting opposite. Isabelle is seated at the far end of the table next to the duke's cousin, the Earl of Rochester, and on her other side is Xavier's mother. It's odd that Isabelle should be seated so far from the duke, now that their engagement is imminent.

Course after course begins to come out, and I can't help thinking a simple omelet would suffice. I couldn't have imagined a few months ago that I would ever get tired of this, but I am.

The dinner conversation revolves around the idiosyncrasies of the English, and the earl is being very jovial about the teasing.

"Why is it that every Englishman likes his meat cooked to leather?" asks the count.

"I could ask why every Frenchman likes his steak still breathing," replies the earl. His cheeks are pink from alcohol, and his whiskers make him look like a walrus.

Two servants carrying silver tureens make the tour of the table. When the countess is served, I see her distorted reflection in the dish; her features melt and stretch across its contours—she is transformed into a repoussoir with a narrow forehead, bulging eyes, flaring nostrils and a rubbery mouth. How could she live, the thought strikes me, if the mirror showed her this face every morning?

In reality, the countess's features might have been cut from marble. You search for a flaw in the lines, an imperfection, a break from the symmetry—but you find none. Yet it's not the kind of beauty that hits you like a shaft of sunlight; it's not the kind of beauty that radiates and effuses something mysterious, some inner light. She has the kind of perfect beauty characterized by the deadness of stone.

"Tell us about the highlights of London," the countess demands. "If not the English cuisine, then what?" she says, draining her glass.

"Oh, a lot of catching up with old friends, some galleries." The duke pauses, appearing to compose himself. "I do have some good news to report."

My eyes dart to Isabelle. A hush falls over the table. Could he have asked her before dinner?

The countess's eyes are fixed on the duke as she hangs on his every word.

"Speak up," says Xavier.

The duke looks at the Englishwoman to his left and says, "Lady Eleanor and I are to be married."

# Chapter 29

Several things happen in unison: the walrus guffaws and thumps his fist on the table, the countess drops her knife to the floor with a clatter, champagne is produced and the unattractive soon-to-be duchess Lady Eleanor giggles. I immediately make eye contact with Isabelle, who is looking at me with a defiant smile, as if she has won a bet.

"*Félicitations*," says Isabelle's father, raising his glass in a toast. He must be oblivious to his wife's plans for their daughter, or possibly just indifferent. Xavier raises his glass with a smug expression, whereas his sister Claire looks to be fighting back tears.

I pick up my glass as well and everyone toasts the smiling couple. I take a sip of champagne and try to swallow the disappointment I feel toward the duke. It's baffling to me. How could he choose a woman like that? She would be welcome at the agency—as an employee, not a client.

For the rest of dinner, I watch the duke and his English fiancée carefully. This woman has neither beauty nor charm. She doesn't appear witty or overly intelligent. What hold does she have on the duke? Is she an ace, a trump card in the hierarchy of British nobility? Does it all just come down to status? I study his handsome face, his affable manner, and gradually it dawns on me that that's all there is. The personality I credited him with having was my own creation. In reality, there is nothing more substantial to him than confidence and an easy smile. And why shouldn't he be this way? What has he ever had to work hard at or compete for in his life? Everything has been handed to him.

We reach the cheese course and finally the end of this torturous feast is in sight. After dinner the guests glide into the drawing room and there's talk of a card game. "Antoine, how about a hand?" says Xavier. "What do they say, *Lucky in love, unlucky in cards?*"

The duke narrows his eyes at his friend. "Other way round, I think."

I take a seat far away from the others near the tall windows. It's drafty despite the huge velvet curtains. I pick up a book left on the seat, probably by Isabelle, because no one else in the house seems to read. At least with the duke's announcement, I'm relieved of my duty to convince Isabelle to accept him. Yet before long there will be another suitor the countess will want to throw her daughter at. Could I succeed in convincing her? And if so, would my reward be worth what I have to do to get it? Shame washes over me again when I think of my words to her in the library. I flick through the pages of the book she was reading. If only I hadn't fought with her this evening, we would be sitting together dissecting the duke's revelation, still friends.

"Well, you were wrong, weren't you?" I look up and see Isabelle standing over me. Her voice is prickly and I know that she hasn't let go of our fight. Still, she takes a seat beside me on the striped settee.

251

"I'm so sorry, Isabelle, about today in the library," I begin immediately.

She ignores my apology. "Turns out the duke likes his ladies as rich as Queen Victoria."

"What do you mean?" I ask. As if Isabelle or Claire aren't rich *and* beautiful.

"According to the earl, Lady Eleanor is an heiress to one of the largest fortunes in England."

"But doesn't he have enough money already?" I ask. "Unless he has some true regard for her, I mean."

"They just met. And her family owns the half of England that the Queen doesn't own." She stares at me, her expression stony. "Is that the kind of good match I should be making?"

I take a deep breath. "I didn't mean the things I said before, Isabelle. Maybe I was a bit envious of you—that's all." I look down. She doesn't respond because our conversation is interrupted.

"We shall leave this place tomorrow," the countess says as she sways over us, a glass of brandy in her hand. "I don't see any sense in our staying here another night," she slurs. Her face looks clammy; her hair is falling out of place. "Your father will inform the duke that we have to return to Paris in the morning. The gall of him, to invite us here to humiliate us." She spits the words. "It's appalling."

I've never seen her composure so broken before.

"Mother, maybe you should go to bed," Isabelle says. She gets up, pries the brandy glass from her mother's grip and puts it down. She leads her across the room to the count. An exchange takes place, and then the countess stumbles into her husband's arms and he guides her out of the drawing room.

Isabelle returns to my settee by the window, biting her lip to hide a smile. "I've never seen Mother that livid, or drunk, in public before," she whispers, becoming my confidante again.

Relief floods over me. For once the countess has helped me with her meddling. The comedy of her angry scene has lifted the tension between Isabelle and me. Grateful for the unspoken amnesty, I try to be witty. "At least she spared us tears—unlike Claire de Rochefort," I say. "No amount of perfect curls can compete with an heiress."

Isabelle laughs. "What luck. The pressure for a proposal had reached fever pitch with Mother. This just lets me off the hook until she finds someone else to latch onto." She sighs and plays with the pendant on the chain around her neck.

"Yes—it at least gives you more time." And me too, I think.

"Isabelle," calls a voice. We look over to see Xavier beckoning to Isabelle from the card table. "Join us for a hand. Take my mother's place, she's going to bed."

Acting as a good sport, Isabelle accepts the invitation, but it means Xavier ends up clinging to her for the rest of the evening, so I do my best to drift into the background. I'm dreading facing the countess's hangover—she'll surely be in a black mood tomorrow. But thankfully she can't blame me for the Lady Eleanor crisis—I hope.

Late at night, when the other guests have retired, Isabelle and I climb the grand staircase, each of us holding a lamp.

We turn down the long hallway, dark except for our lights and stop at her room.

"Well, good night, Maude." She looks down for a moment as if searching for some words to say.

"Are we really leaving tomorrow?" I ask to fill the silence.

She shakes her head. "Even if Mother remembers her threat, she's too curious about Lady Eleanor to miss anything. We can hide out in the library to escape them rehashing the gossip over and over." She gives me a small smile.

I note the "we" she used and smile back. Our friendship is a little dented but still intact. And right now, in this moment, I wish I could tell Isabelle everything and stop all the lies. But I know it's impossible—by absolving my guilty conscience, I would be risking my whole future. "Good night, then," I say, instead. And she turns to go.

My room is farther away, in the outer reaches of the north wing. I suppose guests are assigned rooms according to rank—there is no escaping the attention paid to blood and breeding. I walk quickly along the hallway and turn right, down the corridor where my room is located. I'm imagining the warmth of my bed when I hear a noise—a muffled bump and then a shuffling. I stop and the hairs on my neck stand up as I picture what could be lurking in the darkness. Cautiously I lift the lamp in front of me to see what's there and then begin walking again. I'm almost at my room. I grab the handle but pause before I enter. I think I can hear a voice coming from the far end of the passage.

Curiosity gets the better of me and I let go of the door handle and put down my lamp outside my room. Then I creep along the hallway, which leads to the servants' stair. There's the sound of rustling material and muted whispers—a man and a woman. I reach the top of the stairs in the near dark and peer over the banister to see two figures standing at the window alcove between floors. They are in a close embrace, lit by moon-light. But when I look closer I see that it's not an embrace, it's more of a struggle. The man is in an evening suit, the woman is obscured by him, but I see her housemaid's white pinafore skirts peeking out.

"*Non*, monsieur. *S'il vous plaît. Non!*" Her words send a chill down my spine.

"Stop! Leave her alone," I call out. I regret my words immediately.

The scuffling stops. The man's head whips round and he squints up at me through the darkness as the housemaid ducks out from under him. I hear her quick footsteps echo then disappear.

"Who's there?" the man says. I shrink back. He can't have seen me. I'm protected by shadows. I flee from the stairwell, along the corridor and back to the safety of my room. As soon as I'm inside I lock the door and blow out my lamp. I stand stock-still, not wanting to make a sound, my heart pounding, my throat dry. I wait for the sound of footsteps in the hall. I squeeze my eyes shut, but I can't forget the face in the moonlight staring up at me. I think back to Cécile's pack of cards explaining the aristocratic titles.

The ten of hearts. Xavier de Rochefort.

# Chapter 30

It's late morning, after breakfast, when Isabelle and I retreat to the chateau library. The men are out shooting, the ladies in some sitting room, gossiping, no doubt. This is the first chance we've had to talk since last night without the other guests around. I'm nearly bursting to tell her what I saw on the back stair. But a servant is fussing with the flue in the fireplace, and I have to wait until we're alone. I try to focus on the novel in my hand, but it's pointless—I've already read the same page four times.

Finally the servant finishes what he's doing, but just after he closes the door behind him, the countess enters the room with a flurry. "Isabelle, I have some important news to discuss with you."

Thwarted from sharing my gossip, I rise to leave so that they can be alone.

"Maude, you may stay," the countess says breathlessly.

She takes a seat in one of the large armchairs by the fire but gets up almost immediately and starts pacing in front of the hearth. I thought she would be shut up in her chamber nursing a hangover, but here she is, strutting with impatient energy. I have an uneasy feeling. Why is she acting so strangely? *Scheming* is the first word that comes to mind when I look at her—that look of restless hunger in her eye. Surely she doesn't think she can break up the duke and his English bride.

"Isabelle, dear. I have something to tell you." Her tone has changed from breathless to grave, and I swear she's enjoying the drama.

"Yes, Mother. Is Father ill? What's wrong?" asks Isabelle, putting her book aside, concern spreading across her face.

I study the countess, ready to distrust whatever she's about to say.

She stops pacing and stands still for a moment in front of the fireplace. "My dear, I have just found out a shocking piece of news."

My first thought is that she has found out about Xavier de Rochefort, and it feels like a relief to not be the only one who knows.

She goes on. "The Duke d'Avaray, our host and friend . . ." She pauses, drawing out the suspense. "He's bankrupt, ruined!" She hisses the words. "I found out from Monsieur de Rochefort after breakfast that he's been taking loans from his friends these past months."

"What?" I whisper to myself. That sounds ridiculous.

The log on the fire crackles and sparks.

"Bankrupt? That sounds like made-up gossip," Isabelle says. "What about all this?" She gestures to the chateau we are enjoying.

"The creditors are closing in, according to Xavier de Rochefort." The countess appears concerned, but I can tell that she's reveling in the details. "My girl, how lucky you are."

Isabelle looks confused. "Lucky? What do you mean?"

The countess shakes her head and sighs. "My dear child, you know nothing of the world."

She's overplaying her role a bit for my tastes.

"The whole thing is a scandal. His father left him the debts when he died, and the duke hasn't been able to get his head above water since. Not only that, he's been *gambling* what assets he could liquidate."

Could this be true? I recall the argument I overheard backstage at the theater and the comment Xavier made last night. Has he known about the duke's troubles all along?

The countess continues, "On his recent trip to London he met Lady Eleanor and became acquainted with her *vast* fortune, which is why they are now engaged. Just think—it could have been you marrying a destitute duke!"

Isabelle and I are both speechless. Gunshots ring out from the fields, breaking the silence. The shooting has begun.

"Thank goodness for Monsieur de Rochefort—what tact he displays, and what a comfort at a trying time like this!"

My stomach turns; the mention of his name brings back the vision of his face in the moonlight.

The countess sits down again and takes her daughter's hands in hers. "I do have some good news as well, though." She gives Isabelle a fake smile. "In speaking with Xavier, he revealed that due to his brother's absence in Indochina, he himself will inherit the family title. His older brother is living like a native, apparently, and refusing to return to France—he's the family black sheep, by all accounts."

Isabelle looks at her mother warily. "What do his

258

prospects mean to me?" She withdraws her hands from her mother's grasp.

The countess glances briefly at me and then looks intently at her daughter. Her voice softens. "Isabelle, Xavier de Rochefort has asked for your hand in marriage."

The rise and fall of gunshots outside tears through the silence; several solitary shots begin to increase in number, the crescendo like a smattering of applause. The world is approving of the match. I must say something. I must speak up but the words are stuck in my throat.

Isabelle has a look of shock and confusion on her face, and the revulsion I feel at the thought of their union breaks out like a cold sweat from my scalp down the back of my neck.

The countess continues, "And it couldn't come at a better time, deflecting any society gossip away from your association with the duke."

The guns keep firing.

The countess's face looks rapt with the conquest of a kill. "Your father and I are delighted."

Isabelle finds her voice. "No!" She sounds ferocious. "Mother, that's impossible. I barely like him. And why on earth did he ask you and Father before me?"

"Isabelle, calm yourself, *ma fille*. You don't have to decide this instant." The countess gives a little feminine laugh to lighten the mood. Her ploys are transparent.

She leans back in her chair. "But of course, this might be the best offer you could hope to get. Maybe the only offer." She follows this with silence, to let the meaning of her warning sink in.

I imagine the birds in the field. The guns must sound like cannon fire.

Isabelle is silent.

"I won't hear another word from you now," says the countess. She leans forward and touches her daughter's cheek tenderly. "You and Maude go for a stroll. I'm not going to interfere."

The countess rises and looks directly at me.

I want to speak up and tell them both what I saw last night, but my fear of the countess is too great. Her stare turns me to stone and I say nothing.

It's not until the door closes behind the countess that I begin to breathe again. But my mind is racing—what do I do? Isabelle gets up, returns her book to the correct place on the bookshelf and says, "Let's go for a walk. Get your mantle."

The winter light is pale and the ground is frosted over as we stroll the grounds. The shooting has died down; the party must be heading back to the chateau for lunch.

We don't speak for some time. I'm relieved because I don't have a clue what to say. On one side: my current job, my rosy future and a powerful countess. On the other: a friend and an appalling fiancé. What fate am I throwing her toward if I do the countess's bidding and nudge her to an acceptance? That's if she'd even listen to me. If she does accept, she'll be stuck in a great house with a drunken lech taking advantage of the servants. And who knows what other truths are lurking beneath his charming façade. I can't help but think of Marie-Josée's story about when she was a maid.

Isabelle is the first to break our silence. "Monsieur de Rochefort flirts with everyone. I didn't think he would be as stupid as to single me out." She shoves her hands in the pockets of her great fur coat. "Though I'm a count's daughter, so I suppose he's only being pragmatic."

At the edge of the formal gardens we continue on a woodland path. The bare trees make a lattice pattern against the sky that reminds me of Eiffel's tower.

"What kind of person do you think he is?" I ask her, but all I can think is, I am a coward. Is this as close as I'll tread to the truth?

"Pleasant enough, a little arrogant, easily bored." She kicks the hard ground. "Is that reason enough to say no?" She laughs halfheartedly.

"I thought your answer would be a definite no."

Her eyes meet mine. "Of course my answer is no." Her voice is strident. "That's what I told Mother, isn't it? It's just . . ." She stops short of finishing her thought and sighs. "I've been thinking about what you said in the library yesterday. Maybe I *am* naïve to think that if I pass an exam I can change my future."

I feel a gut punch of guilt. My treacherous words have seeped into her mind and soured her confidence.

She goes on, "And what if I don't pass? Just as you said, do I end up staying a child in my mother's house forever?"

It's as if she's a doll, placed in a box to be sold. Her decisions are being made for her; her future is in someone else's hands. I look at Isabelle and for the first time I see myself.

"You really might accept him?" I'm shocked at her broken resolve, dismayed to know I had a hand in it.

She shakes her head. "I can't believe I'm even considering it." She is beginning to sound desperate. "You probably think I should accept." She gives me a brief smile. "For someone with an artist's heart, you can be terribly practical at times."

I look down at the ground. With each step my boots break the thin layers of ice encasing dead leaves and twigs. I think about everything Isabelle has exposed me to—the techniques of photography, her knowledge of architecture, her passion and drive. My world has opened up because of her.

"I suppose it's the proper thing for a girl like me to do," she continues, resigned.

It doesn't matter the personal cost to me. If there's the least chance she might go ahead with this match, I must tell her what I know. She's my friend.

I stop walking and turn to her. "You can't marry him," I say. My voice is clear; I commit to my decision.

She looks surprised. This isn't what she was expecting.

"I found out something about Xavier de Rochefort that you must know." A crow caws at us from high up in a tree.

Isabelle's dark eyes grow large. "Tell me." She's waiting for me to speak.

"I saw him force himself on a servant."

Her face contorts in disgust. "When?"

"Last night after you went to bed. I heard a noise in the servants' stair."

Isabelle absorbs the news. "But wasn't it dark? Are you sure?"

"Absolutely. I saw his face in the moonlight, clear as day. I don't know who the housemaid was, but she got away. That time, anyway."

Our breath curls about us in the frozen air and we continue walking.

"Why didn't you tell us in the library?"

I can't meet her eyes on that question. Isabelle has brought us around to the biggest obstacle: her mother. "I didn't know how your mother would react and if I would get in trouble—why would she take my word against someone important like Xavier de Rochefort? I'm ashamed to say it, but I was worried about myself."

"Well, you've told me now, so that doesn't matter. In a way it's just what I need to go up against Mother. I'm sure when we tell her, she will break the arrangement. She will be furious, of course. Yet more plans thwarted."

Piles of dead leaves block our path and we stop.

"Until the next time," I say. "Your mother will find someone else to match you with, and then where will you be?" I can hear the hopelessness in my own voice. "This is the second botched engagement. She might get desperate, and then who knows what kind of person she'll find for candidate number three."

She shakes her head. "What do I do?"

"Tell her what you want, tell her your plans for university."

"Now?" she asks. "Before I even know if I'll get accepted?"

I nod, aware that I'm going against my best interests. I'm putting the nail in the coffin of my current position, and of course the dangled future in the South of France, but I don't have a choice. Even if our friendship began with a deception, a true friend is what Isabelle has become.

"Isabelle." I look her straight in the eye. "I believe in you and your dreams. You can study, have a career and support yourself in time. I know you can."

Isabelle nods slowly as it sinks in what she's about to do. "Face Mother and confess everything," she reflects out loud, and her eyes shine brightly. She grabs my hand. "Will you come with me?"

She doesn't know what she's asking. After this I can imagine the countess will give me my marching orders the moment we return to Paris, and the agency door will slam shut in my face once Durandeau finds out. I can see my future hanging by a thread. My resolve wavers. I squeeze her hand. "Of course I'll come with you."

She lets out a giddy shriek, then gives me a tight embrace.

Arm in arm we turn around and head back along the woodland path. Gradually, the temperature drops. The afternoon sky is anemic with the promise of snow. Against the white, the shadow of the chateau looms in the distance, and I try to control my rising panic. I cannot imagine the countess's reaction to Isabelle's decision.

# Chapter 31

We find the countess dozing in her room.

Sitting in an armchair, wrapped in a cashmere shawl, she opens her eyes, blinks for a moment, then extends her arms toward Isabelle. "Well, my darling. Did you make a decision? This is going to be an emotional day for your dear *maman.*"

We rehearsed what Isabelle would say to the countess on our way back along the garden path. Isabelle doesn't make a move toward her mother and keeps her arms locked by her sides as she recites her answer. "Mother, I absolutely refuse to marry Xavier de Rochefort. He arranged this with you like a business negotiation."

The countess's face goes blank and she drops her outstretched arms to her lap. "Really, is that so?" she says, all warmth gone from her voice. She turns to the side table and opens a silver cigarette case.

"Not only that, but Maude and I have discovered some disturbing information about Xavier," says Isabelle.

The countess lights a cigarette and blows the smoke above her head.

Now it's my turn. My hands are balled into fists so tight I can feel my nails dig into my palms. "Countess, if you let this marriage go ahead, you are throwing your daughter at the worst kind of man—someone who forces himself on a defenseless chambermaid."

"Nonsense!" She stares at me for a moment, taken aback by my treachery. "Just what are you talking about, Mademoiselle Pichon?" Her expression twists into anger, and I do my best not to shrink back.

Isabelle chimes in. "It's true, Maude saw it with her own eyes."

The countess laughs. "You're talking about the future Viscount de Rochefort." She's trying to shrug us off, but I know her feathers are more than ruffled.

She gets up and throws off her shawl, cigarette in hand. "Assuming it's even true, you take the word of a *servant* as gospel?" She shoots me a glare, and I know she means that *I* am the servant.

She takes a seat at her vanity. "Don't be naïve, Isabelle. Men are what they are. And besides, he didn't force himself on *you*—that would be unforgivable. I don't see that it matters. What's a chambermaid to us?" She takes a last puff of her cigarette and stubs it out in the ashtray.

Isabelle and I exchange a look. The countess's dismissive tone is loathsome.

She chuckles to herself. "At least we know he doesn't share the same tastes as Montesquiou—him you would catch with the valet." She pinches her cheeks to give them some color.

"The girl probably felt lucky to attract someone as important as the viscount's son. Gives her something to gossip about belowstairs."

She opens a bottle of perfume and dabs some on her

neck and behind her ears. "I mind that she wasn't discreet—at least it was only Maude who found out."

Of course, I think, because who am I? Merely a person of no consequence.

"The decision has been made, Isabelle." She turns to face us, her expression rigid. "You will marry Monsieur de Rochefort."

"I won't do it." Isabelle stands resolute. "You can't make me. I have other plans."

The countess rises and walks toward us. Isabelle has lit a fire in her eyes. "Other plans? There is one future for you and it's already mapped out."

She smells of stale tobacco laced with perfume. All I can think is *You* are the repoussoir. You repel me.

As if she can read my thoughts, she turns her attention from Isabelle to me.

"Now, Maude, since you are so helpful and full of revelations this afternoon, why don't you tell Isabelle who you really are?"

A wave of terror passes over me.

"Go on, I don't mind; you've served your purpose, what little you did." She folds her arms and watches me, enjoying how the tables have turned. "After all, the engagement is going ahead."

I open my mouth to speak but there's nothing I can say. I plead with her silently. Yes, I'm willing to sacrifice my job if it helps save Isabelle from a disastrous marriage. I expect to be ripped to shreds once the countess has an audience with me alone, but for her to tell Isabelle the truth—to reveal her own scheming—I could never have predicted her cruelty would go that far.

"Mother, what are you talking about?" Isabelle looks from her mother to me, baffled.

The countess cocks her head playfully. Her coolness terrifies me. She is so very in control that her wrath doesn't billow wildly like smoke but burns with the intensity of a white-hot poker. "Didn't you know that your little friend works for me?"

With that brief utterance my world is shattered. I want to scream. This can't be happening.

The countess addresses me. "What did you think, that you could cross me and fill my daughter's head with dangerous ideas? You were paid to do a job."

I'm light-headed; it's the same sensation as facing into a driving wind, when you feel the breath blown out of you.

Isabelle interrupts. "I don't understand. What are you talking about?" She takes a step away from me.

The countess ignores her daughter's question. "Honestly, at first I did just want a plain girl to make my daughter stand out. If you hadn't become such a confidante to her, the opportunity to become my informant wouldn't have arisen. You blazed the trail of influencing Isabelle, and took to it so naturally—you obeyed me effortlessly. This is all your own doing."

Her expression is the very same self-satisfied smirk she wore that first day of my interview in the salon.

"Would someone explain to me?" Isabelle's voice is raised.

The countess looks at her daughter. "Isabelle, dear, Maude is what's called a repoussoir—she's a foil, a plain girl hired to make you look more beautiful. I felt you needed all the help you could get this season."

268

"What?" Isabelle breathes the word, barely audible. Her face dissolves into bewilderment. None of this makes sense to her.

The countess is unmoved. "She then became my little spy. You're so secretive, and I am just a concerned mother, trying to help her daughter."

Her recklessness with Isabelle's feelings is what finally causes my anger to erupt. "Why do you pretend to care about Isabelle?" My voice is shrill and quavering. "Are you truly looking out for her future? Or is your interest in her season the chance to live it again for yourself?" I take a step toward her. My legs feel like jelly and my insides have withered, but I force myself to say what I think. "You envy your daughter. She has her youth, beauty, and her whole life to lead. You already made your choices, and you're miserable."

To reach this point of anger makes me want to cry, but I hold myself together.

The countess laughs, mocking me. "You are nothing more than filth from the streets, desperate for a morsel of what I have. You really are a repellent little creature."

Isabelle stammers, "Wh-why? Why did you do this to me?" I look back at her. She stares at her mother with horror and then looks at me, her face crumpled in an expression I've never seen before.

The countess replies calmly. "Your first season is the only one that counts. Other girls your age are positively giddy about the idea of finding a husband. I couldn't let you throw it away. Maude was to be an accessory, like Grand-Maman's jewels or a new dress. Something to make you stand out and shine like a Dubern. Then I saw how well you two got along and it seemed only sensible to keep control of you."

My heart twists in my chest at her words, as though she's managed to reach in and grab it in her talons. She claims it was my fault, and maybe it was. She found my weakness, my need for friendship and acceptance. I was her puppet. I excelled at being manipulated and in turn manipulating others.

Isabelle looks at me, her face stricken. "Maude, tell me this isn't true!"

I look her straight in the eye. The lie sits on my lips, but I can't voice it.

"It's the truth."

Shut in my room at the chateau, I look outside at the snow falling in heavy flakes, thick and lush like peony petals from the sky. It's been falling like this for hours. If I were to step into the cold night and look up, perhaps I would see a host of servants leaning out from upstairs windows scattering handfuls of petals from baskets, just for our pleasure. After everything I have seen of this gilded life, it wouldn't surprise me if the rich could summon the weather.

The maid is packing my trunk. All my clothes and jewelry, including the bracelet I was given, are to be sent to the countess's room. She lays out all the dresses on the bed and neatly folds them. It should be upsetting to see my precious wardrobe taken away, but clothes don't seem as important to me now that my future is bleaker than night.

"Do you know anything? Have they mentioned me downstairs?" I ask the maid.

She looks up sheepishly. She must have been instructed not to say anything.

"Please," I press her. "I need to know."

"Well," she sighs, smoothing out a blue velvet evening dress on the bed. "The countess said she found out you weren't Madame Vary's niece at all. The countess is saying you're a fraud—a con artist trying to swindle rich people."

"Of course," I say, sitting down on the bed next to the piles of clothes. She wants to destroy me completely.

The maid stops packing and looks at me. "The countess said she's been racked ever since she found out. Claims she didn't want to upset her daughter."

I shake my head. "What theatrics." She is taking her performance to the extreme.

The maid continues, "Said she finally had to act when she suspected you of trying to poison Mademoiselle Isabelle against her family and ruin her marriage prospects."

She lays the clothes between layers of tissue paper.

"Do you believe her?" I ask.

She chortles to herself. "Not really. She can say whatever she likes against you."

The maid is right.

"I heard her give instructions to the staff that you are to be turned out of the chateau at first light. You'll be given a servant's uniform to wear. They say you stole all these nice clothes from the people you've been conning along the way."

She closes the trunk and looks at me through pale lashes. "It's not true, is it, mademoiselle?"

271

I don't answer. I am a fraud. I did con Isabelle and try to undermine her dreams.

"What about Isabelle?" I ask. I can't imagine what she must think of me now.

"They announced her engagement to Monsieur de Rochefort tonight at dinner. At this very moment they're down there celebrating. The footman said Mademoiselle Isabelle didn't look too happy, not like a blushing bride-to-be."

I shake my head. The countess was calculating in revealing my identity. She used the shock of my betrayal to crush Isabelle's defenses. If only I could explain to Isabelle that I considered our friendship real and that in the end I was trying to protect her.

"Thank you," I say. "For sharing that with me. I know you didn't have to."

She smiles apologetically. "I'll just call for help with the trunk."

She leaves the room and moments later returns with a burly valet. I watch as they carry away my belongings. All that's left is the nightgown on my back.

A few minutes later the maid returns. "Sorry, Mademoiselle Pichon, but I've been instructed to lock you in for the night." She darts her eyes away, embarrassed to be the one relaying this. "Someone will let you out in the morning, and then you're on your own, I'm afraid."

I nod. Of course I am not to be trusted. "What's your name?" I ask her.

She looks at me, surprised to be asked. "Sophie."

"*Merci*, Sophie," I say with as much kindness as I can.

Before she closes the door, she hurries across the room and gives me a brief embrace. "*Bonne chance*, mademoiselle."

After I hear the key turn in the lock and I know I'm alone for the night, I let myself cry.

# Chapter 32

I am a dirty speck in a blanket of white.

The carriage that was supposed to drive me to the train station got stuck in the snow the moment it left the shoveled part of the driveway. The countess couldn't have planned it more perfectly if she'd tried. With the roads impassable, the driver merely shrugged; what could he do, what did he care—I was a criminal, a con artist in everyone's eyes. I'm sure he wondered why I wasn't being arrested instead of being escorted to the train station and given enough money for a fare to Paris. I was forced to get out of the carriage and walk from the chateau, the avenue of trees my only clue as to the direction of the long driveway.

I have no luggage since the countess commandeered the trunk, and Sophie was not lying about the servant's clothes. When the chambermaid opened my door in the morning she brought me a scullery maid's uniform: a thin cotton dress, wool stockings, boots too large for me and a moth-eaten wool mantle.

Marie-Josée was correct to the letter: they stripped the clothes off me and turned me out, and in a snowstorm, no less. As I trudge through the snow, it occurs to me that if the roads are blocked, the trains won't be running either.

But I press on, despite the painful bite of cold: where else have I to go?

With everything coated in white, the scratchy dark branches and faint animal tracks are the only break from the monotony. I feel as though I am walking into emptiness. I have nothing now. I have lost a true friend, Isabelle, and cut off another, Marie-Josée. And Paul—how wrongly I treated him. Why couldn't I have told him the truth?

I keep walking. My feet are turning numb; my stomach is empty. Finally I turn off the tree-lined avenue from the chateau and onto the main road to town. The snow isn't as deep here. I think of what's waiting for me in Paris. I will be fired from the agency in disgrace. I have some savings, but not much—getting used to the good life with the Duberns made me live beyond my means on my days off. I have frittered away my wages on clothes and other treats for myself. My future feels as desolate as this countryside is under snow.

The sky is lightening and the sun is trying to burn through the curtain of cloud. It makes me think of the whiteness of photography paper and the image of a face surfacing. The revelation of photography stays with me. That was real.

A twig snaps and I'm startled until I realize it's just a bird in a tree. As I walk past, it takes off. Its wing flaps sound like sheets snapping on a clothesline.

"Nothing like the feel of clean sheets, Maude Madeleine." A blustery laundry day at home, where my mother is hanging out the washing. I dispense the clothes pegs while she wrestles with the linens. Her hands are cold and red from the scrubbing. She smiles at me broadly. "Like being wrapped up in springtime." The sheets wave around her like sails, breaking up the slant of sun on her face.

Her image fades to white.

It takes me about an hour, frozen to the bone and damp through, to reach what must be the stone wall of the train station. I stop at the entrance, prying open the wrought-iron gate stuck in a drift of snow. The stationmaster's little cottage looks shut up, but a puff of smoke from the chimney tells me he's inside. I knock on the door and wait until eventually he comes out, flustered, not expecting anyone today. He sells me a ticket to Paris and lets me into the waiting room, where I am the sole passenger. It is several hours until the snow has melted off the tracks and the trains start running again. That's a long time to think over the mistakes you've made and to contemplate an uncertain future.

I arrived back in Paris late on Saturday night. One reprieve is that today is Sunday and I don't have to face Durandeau and the rest of the agency until tomorrow. I hole up in my garret room with the curtains drawn—I have no desire to venture outside. I stay in bed, not sleeping or reading but lying as still as can be, not wanting to move or feel, my insides hollowed out. I could fall in on myself. I am not sick, I am not dying, but I keep as still as I can to see what death would feel like—to disappear, to become invisible. I don't want to occupy space or a place in the world; I want to quietly vanish into my surroundings.

The rotting window frame allows a current of air to push

against the curtains, making them shiver in the breath of the draft; patterns of sunlight dance, then dissolve on the wall by my bed—a shadow play from the hand of the unseen. Could I capture that with my camera? With another wave of sadness I realize that there is no point messing about with photographs now; I'll need every franc for food and shelter, not plates and chemicals. I close my eyes to beauty and fall into an unrestful sleep.

When I wake on Monday I know I must return to the agency, even though every part of me recoils at the thought of it. My own clothes are still in the agency dressing room, not to mention my last week's pay, which is all the more vital to me now.

I pull myself together, wash, dress and brush my hair, feeling the whole time as though I'm about to attend a funeral. The route to work is familiar: the omnibus across the river, then a walk up avenue de l'Opéra. But this time it feels worse than my first day of work, worse than the first day I met Isabelle. Walking through the long hallway to the dressing room, I regret all the times I chose to keep on my Dubern outfits and swan through the agency rooms for all to see. I enjoyed feeling better than the other girls. Now I have come full circle. I want to return to being the anonymous wallflower with the muddy hem who came in for the interview so many months ago.

Everyone must have heard of my crushing defeat with the Duberns. Surely the countess will have sent word to Durandeau outlining her termination of the contract, along with her fury and her desire to have the remainder of the clothes returned. Durandeau's favorite client, his foothold in the aristocracy. These words play over and over in my mind until I finally stumble onto the question that I've been trying to avoid: how is he going to punish me?

I open the dressing room door. For a moment, when I am met with the familiar scene and the friendly faces, I feel a flood of relief, but it's short-lived. I step into the room and walk to my dressing table, and one by one the girls stop chatting and simply stare at me. That's when I know that news of my dismissal has reached everyone's ears.

And there is Cécile, standing triumphantly center stage, the rest of the repoussoir company, including Marie-Josée, present and accounted for, waiting for me to speak.

I take off my hat and sit down at my dressing table. I will save Cécile the bother of asking.

"The countess fired me," I say, looking straight ahead at my reflection in the mirror, not turning around.

"We all know that, Maude. But why?" I see Cécile in the mirror, rushing toward me, gleeful and hungry for details.

"I wouldn't do as I was told," I answer simply. "That pretty much ended my contract."

Cécile wasn't expecting such a vague answer. "That's it? But what did you do?"

I think of Marie-Josée coaxing me to share details with the girls about my experiences with the aristocracy. *Pay these girls some mind*, she said.

Not today, I think. Let them make up the worst stories they can about me—I don't care.

I turn to look at them and survey the faces: my colleagues are judging me. Some show pity, some contempt. I don't care about any of them, just Marie-Josée. I find her ruddy face and try to catch her eye. I'm looking for a sign of friendship. She doesn't avoid my gaze, but she meets my request for friendship with a blank stare. There is no familiar sparkle or warmth. I don't blame her. I treated her unforgivably.

There's a knock on the dressing room door. Laurent's handsome face appears, but today he looks serious, for once.

I know why he's here.

"Let me guess," I say. "Monsieur Durandeau would like to see me in his office?"

Laurent nods.

# Chapter 33

To my surprise, I am still an employee of the Durandeau Agency. February, cold and drab, has blown past. It's now March, marked by showers and occasional sun. Spring is coming, but my mood is still in winter. I am somber and listless. I take refuge in my room and watch the sunlight glimmer through a rain-soaked windowpane. Sometimes I stroll the streets, ending up by the banks of the Seine, which is as close an experience to the beach as I can find in the city.

As I stand with my colleagues in the salon for a client selection, I recall Durandeau's tirade of furious words.

"I knew you were trouble when you came in for the interview. Refusing the job in the first place, then coming back weeks later with your tail between your legs. Miserable waif, you would be nothing without this agency."

Durandeau used to intimidate me, but after the countess, I knew I'd faced my worst fears. He could shout and name-call all he wanted. I remained expressionless.

"You vile girl, treating the countess's patronage with such deviousness. Our most important client, and all you had to do was obey her instructions."

He punctuated this by waving a letter from the countess

in my face. It contained an exaggerated and misleading account of my sins. I felt numb. I said nothing. I knew that any utterance from me would be pounced on and would prolong the dressing-down. When was he going to get to the point and fire me?

"Do you know how much you've cost the agency in lost wages? When you secured the Dubern contract I made an estimate of how much revenue to expect. Now, due to your premature dismissal, the agency is hundreds of francs at a loss."

Here it comes.

"Mademoiselle Pichon, as much as it sickens me to do so, I shall keep you on, to earn out what you owe."

I couldn't believe it. His greed had gotten the better of his anger. As a fully trained repoussoir, I am still able to make money for the agency at a time when business is booming.

"Of course, you will only be permitted to work with lowertier clients: no aristocrats. With your low breeding and common manners, you've made it clear that you are unfit for such company."

So here I am, standing once again with the others, frozen like a statue while a client looks at the inventory. I keep my distance from the other girls now; I don't join in and chat like I used to. Cécile has been positively glowing whenever we cross paths.

But Marie-Josée is pained by my estrangement, I can tell. I'm sure if I were to approach her now with an apology, her uncharacteristic hardness would melt, but I am so ashamed of myself I cannot bear to speak to her. I feel that being shunned by the whole agency is what I deserve. When the girls gather in the dressing room, I sip my tea in the corner and keep quiet—holding a steaming cup in both hands is the closest to warmth and comfort I get these days.

After the client selection, it's time for lunch. I avoid the dining room and eat lunch away from the agency. As I walk down avenue de l'Opéra, I wonder how long I could support myself if I were to be fired, the threat of which hangs over me like a cloud. I don't know when Durandeau will consider my debt to the agency paid in full. After setting aside some money for the train fare home, the rest of my savings wouldn't keep me here beyond summer. Any day at the agency feels like it could be my last. I live in fear and secret anticipation—at least if I were fired the Paris experiment would be concluded. Will my father take me back? Will the whole town know I failed so spectacularly with my big dreams?

During the early days of working for the Duberns, I imagined I would leave the agency of my own accord and find work in service, as a maid, or maybe one of those fine shops would hire me, if I were to present myself as a well-dressed girl with letters of reference.

But now, I assume I am infamous across Paris as a con artist or petty thief, courtesy of the countess and her circle. I fear there could even be a police report on me if the countess decided to take her performance that far. I wouldn't be surprised. I can't escape reality—if I am let go from the agency, I will have no choice but to return to my father.

\* \* \*

I get to work early these days. This morning, it's just past eight o'clock when I enter the dressing room. I'm the only one here. I like to change quickly and find a quiet space to be alone before the workday begins. I am back to wearing traditional agency garb now, my beautiful wardrobe having long since been packed away and sent back to the countess. Leroux was delighted by that turn of events. Today I have finally brought back the fur mantle I stole; no doubt I'll be in even more trouble when I tell Girard what I did. I was going to sell it and keep the money, but I couldn't bear to profit from anything associated with the Countess Dubern. I hang it up next to my coat, and now when I touch the soft fur, I can only think of the poor beast that was sacrificed to make it.

I'm changing into an agency dress when I hear a step in the corridor and turn to see Marie-Josée arrive in the dressing room. My insides shrivel. I don't want to have to speak to her. She puts down her habitual white box of pastries from the bakery and takes off her coat and hat. I concentrate on doing the buttons of my dress so I don't have to look up.

I hear the box being opened and smell the waft of *pâtisseries*. I sneak a glance to see what treat she has today—freshly baked *pain au chocolat*.

She catches me looking. "You want some breakfast?"

I meet her gaze for what seems like the first time in weeks. I want to say how sorry I am, how awful I feel, how I wish I could undo my poor behavior. She was my first friend in Paris—a good friend. And I dumped her without regret. She holds out the pastry, a peace offering on a chipped plate.

"*Merci*, Marie-Josée." Thank you for being a true friend to me is what I want to say; Thank you for warning me about the Duberns, for trying to stop me from getting too close to the client. I take a seat and nibble at the pastry, but then put the plate down. I must speak.

"You were right, Marie-Josée."

She meets my shamed face with her kind one.

I go on, "You warned me and I didn't listen."

She approaches slowly and sits heavily on a chair next to me, placing her hand over mine and giving it a squeeze. "I expect it was easy to get caught up in all that glitter."

She forgives easily, and that breaks the seal on the tears, which have been welling behind my eyes. "Surviving in Paris was harder than I thought—less of a daydream and more of a nightmare. Then with the Duberns, I was scared and intimidated at first, but Isabelle made things fun, and I enjoyed my free time with her. I saw and experienced things I couldn't have dreamed of when I first stepped off the train at Gare Montparnasse. I got seduced by it all and I stopped thinking for myself."

"What went wrong?" she asks softly.

"I crossed the countess. I didn't want Isabelle married off to some cad. I spoke up, because that's what I thought a real friend should do. I didn't want to be her repoussoir—I wanted to be her friend."

"And after you did so, the witch decided to punish you by telling all?" she says with disgust.

"That's about the size of it." I don't feel as though I can go into any more detail or I will start crying again.

"But how did the girl react?" asks Marie-Josée. "Wasn't

she appalled at her mother? Didn't she see that none of it was your fault? It was her mother who hired you."

"I wasn't permitted to explain. I was basically separated from Isabelle and thrown out of the chateau immediately after." That walk through the snow was one of the loneliest times of my life. In remembering it the tears swell in my eyes again, but I fight them back.

Marie-Josée shakes her head. "If you ask me, you're best shot of the lot of them, the daughter included."

I sigh. "I know you don't approve, Marie-Josée, but Isabelle was a true friend to me."

She squeezes my hand. "I hope we are friends again, Maude."

"I said terrible things to you, and I'm truly ashamed," I say, meeting her eyes. I have a well of regret I can never fill. "Where would I be without you?"

She leans over and kisses me on the cheek. "People have said worse." It pains me to hear her say that. How could anyone treat her ill? Then I look down at my bootlaces, knowing I did.

"My, my, Durandeau is paying you too much."

I look up to see her staring at the mantle hanging next to my coat. "It belonged to the witch's wardrobe," I tell her, relieved to have an easier topic of conversation.

She gives me a knowing look. "It just happened to get mixed up with your own clothes, did it?" She laughs. "Well, let me try it on." She winks.

"Be my guest," I say, grateful we are friends again.

She throws it over her shoulders and struts around the dressing room. "Very nice indeed. I've a mind to borrow it for a night out on the town."

285

I'd do anything for Marie-Josée right now. "Go ahead. Keep it, for all I care. It's been ages since Leroux sent my wardrobe back to the Duberns, and no one's missed it."

Marie-Josée thrusts a hip forward in a pose. "Don't mind if I do."

The clock on the wall chimes the half hour. As if on cue the door opens and in comes the stream of girls arriving for work.

Pastries are shared, a pot of tea is made and the chatter swells. I sit next to Marie-Josée, and when the other girls notice the change in my status, my label of outsider is gone. Marie-Josée takes off the fur coat and fans herself with her hands. "It's stuffy in here. Open a window, someone."

I go over to the sash window, unclip the metal catch and slide it up, letting the sweet air blow in.

"Perhaps winter has finally taken itself off for another year?" Marie-Josée says.

I lean against the window frame and gaze out at the back alley and rooftops. The breeze strokes my cheek like a caress and I turn my head into its soothing hand; I close my eyes and inhale deeply. She's right: spring has arrived.

There's a knock on the dressing room door and Laurent calls out, "New client in ten minutes. Hurry up, ladies." The idle moments of chatter in the dressing room are over.

As we shuffle out of the little room and into the salon, I take my place next to Marie-Josée; we stand together, resigned and bored. The other girls are listless. With the whisper of warm weather, no one wants to be shut up in the agency salon for a client. But the moment Durandeau walks in, I let out a gasp. I could never have predicted who would be next to him. I nudge Marie-Josée with my elbow.

"What?" she whispers.

"It's her!" I say. "It's Isabelle Dubern."

# Chapter 34

I can feel Marie-Josée bristle at the name.

Isabelle stands next to Durandeau in front of the fireplace and scans the room until her eyes meet mine. Immediately I am back in the chateau watching her dissolve as the countess lashes out with all the revelations of our scheming and my helplessness to stop her. Why has she come here?

Durandeau is treating her like any other new client, and I have to guess that he doesn't know who she is. Isabelle meanders among the repoussoir statues, but all the while her eyes are fixed on me. I know which way she's heading, and I hold my breath, wondering what she's going to say. Durandeau makes his usual abhorrent suggestions as to which of us might best suit her. She ignores him and continues walking toward me.

"I didn't catch your name, mademoiselle," says Durandeau as he trots after her.

"I didn't give it," Isabelle says. "I like discretion." I can't help but smirk at her composure.

Durandeau is unusually flustered. "Why, of course. Naturally," he says, but I know he likes to be able to place who he's dealing with.

She stops before Marie-Josée and me. Durandeau immediately pounces on Marie-Josée. "Yes, a fine choice. This one's grotesque figure would complement your exquisite proportions."

Isabelle stares at me and I try to silently communicate with her. *It wasn't my fault. What are you doing here?*

Isabelle ignores Durandeau's suggestion. "I'll take this one," she says, pointing at me.

Durandeau tries to mask his surprise. "Very well, mademoiselle. We shall try to accommodate you."

"Is she available now? I should like her for an hour or two." She is curt with him, as if he's merely there to serve her desires.

His nostrils flare slightly. "Why, yes, that could be arranged. It's five francs an hour, as I said."

Isabelle pulls out a leather change purse. "I'll settle the account immediately."

Durandeau's chins quiver with enthusiasm. Money always placates him. "Excellent."

He takes the francs from Isabelle, then turns to me. "Maude, fetch your coat and hat. Go on." He prods me with his fat finger. "Don't just stand there, run!"

I obey and hurry out of the salon. By the time I return from the dressing room, Durandeau and Isabelle are standing in the hallway.

"I can tell you're a lady of refined taste," Durandeau says to Isabelle. He pulls his card out of his breast pocket. "I'd be happy to service your repoussoir needs again, and if you would care to refer our service to a friend—"

"*Merci.*" Isabelle cuts him off and turns away without

accepting the card. I follow her toward the stairs, leaving Durandeau standing in the hallway, perplexed.

Ever since the countess told Isabelle who I really am, I have imagined getting a chance to explain my story to her. A "what if" scenario has often run through my head, in which I run into her on the street or in a shop. But after the shock of seeing her at the agency and now walking with her down avenue de l'Opéra, my mind has gone blank.

"How does it work, then?" she says. "How do I best display my ugly accessory? I want my money's worth," she snarls.

I inhale deeply. I can't really blame her for wanting to exercise some revenge. I try to keep my tone even and controlled. "It's a bit early for high society. We could go to a café or something," I suggest.

She shrugs. "Fine, as long as I can show you off. I want to look my best."

We walk into a café on the corner and Isabelle chooses a table by the window. We both order a tisane but nothing to eat and we sip our tea quietly. I'm overwhelmed by all the things I've wanted to tell her since I was unmasked by her mother, but I don't know where to begin. Isabelle decides to break the silence.

"This is all there is to it? You just sit there and make me look good?"

I stare at the stray tea leaves swirling in my cup. "What did you expect?"

She slams down her cup, and I jump. "I thought I'd get

a show, a performance. Some made-up tales from my performing monkey, perhaps." She's ready for a fight.

"Is that why you came to the agency, Isabelle? To humiliate me?"

"Why didn't you tell me?" she asks. Now there is pain pushing through her temper. "How could you lie to me for so long?"

I'm not used to seeing Isabelle vulnerable, and it only makes me feel worse. "I'm sorry," I say. "I had no choice."

"Everyone has a choice, Maude." Her face is ashen, and her black-cherry eyes have lost their luster. "I trusted you. We were friends, but the whole time you were working for my mother?"

My guilt feels like a corset of iron, crushing the life out of me. "I wish I had told you from the beginning, but I needed this job desperately." My explanation sounds pathetic.

"Was everything a fabrication? Our friendship? All your conversation and opinions?" Her voice sounds composed, but her hands are trembling. "Did you make up a personality I would like?"

I'm horrified that she could think I would go to such lengths. "No, of course not. I spoke my mind with you. I didn't pretend." I reach out my hand to touch hers. "You're my friend, and I didn't want you to be sold off to that pig of a man. I could have tried to convince you to say yes to Xavier, but in the end I couldn't go through with it. I defied your mother, and her punishment was to reveal everything to you."

Silence descends on us again, and I wonder if the marriage is still taking place.

"It's ridiculous, this agency," says Isabelle eventually. Her face is stony. "Explain it to me."

I take a breath. It shouldn't sting for me to talk about it; I should be used to it by now. "Durandeau calls us foils, like the thin piece of metal placed under a jewel to make it shine brighter. Or you can think of us as ugly stepsisters for a client who wants to be Cinderella for a day."

"I don't understand." She looks at me intently, her brow creased as it is when she's studying.

"It's about the rule of comparisons," I say, feeling impatient. "My plainness augments your prettiness. Doesn't that make sense to your scientific brain?"

"It's outrageous." She folds her arms and sits back in her chair, as if she refuses to accept my explanation.

Is she angry at me or at the concept? I can't tell. "Do you know how much women are prepared to spend on beauty?" I ask. "Mother Nature is not democratic. Look at the orchid compared with the dandelion: one exotic and rare, the other a common weed." My throat is dry and I pause to take a sip of tea. "And so with beauty," I continue. "Some have an advantage, some a cross to bear. Some just fade into the background, forever plain and obscure—invisible, inconsequential."

"Such as you?" Isabelle asks.

Why must I explain what's so obvious? It's painful. "Yes, such as me," I whisper.

She picks up her tea and swirls the brew around. "I don't believe it. There is no empirical scale for beauty. Humans are more complex. By your reckoning, there is a formula of elements numbered like the periodic table, but there are other attributes to measure, aside from physical appearance, that can render one person more or less attractive than another."

How can she be so stubborn? I can't believe I have to argue a point that everyone else in the world accepts. "Such as what?" I ask, getting irritated. "In this city, physical beauty rules supreme."

"Intelligence, wit, kindness—in short, the quality of person you are. Then there's the other factor you haven't mentioned: the beholder of the gaze, yet another human complexity."

She puts her cup down on its saucer firmly, punctuating the end of her speech, a hint of triumph in her eyes.

I shake my head. "It's easy for you to argue your point," I say. "You are beautiful. I am not. You can afford to be charitable in your argument. It's like a rich person saying 'Money isn't everything.'"

She doesn't let up, because this is just the kind of mental challenge she relishes. "I'm not simply defending the repoussoirs," she says, leaning toward me. "I'm making the argument for myself. In my mother's eyes, I've never been beautiful or good enough in any way. I'm not a copy of her, not pretty enough or feminine enough to secure the right husband. Don't you see, Maude? The rule of comparisons is an endless circle, for there will always be greater and lesser people than yourself."

Her argument has silenced me. She's right.

Isabelle continues, "If only my mother could see that there is far more to me as a person than where my physical features depart from the perfection of hers. I have a mind, I have opinions, I have feeling and compassion for others. I have a heart, where she has a block of ice."

The waiter approaches. "*Quelque chose d'autre, mesdemoiselles?*" But our grave faces make him leave us alone. As he walks away, Isabelle continues.

"When you and I became friends, I got more confident. I felt galvanized by your faith in what I could do. I really believed in my Sorbonne dream. But when I found out the truth . . ." She trails off and shakes her head. "I felt the whole world was against me."

Knowing the consequences of my betrayal is worse than imagining them.

"What about this ridiculous job?" she asks. "Are you going to remain at this degrading agency? If it were up to me, that nasty fat man would be put out of business."

I laugh. "How on earth would you do that? Besides, it's not just me who depends on this job. The agency employs lots of girls." My tea is cold now. I push it aside. "I thought I'd quit after I saved some money. But I ended up blowing through my wages trying to emulate a real debutante. I bought myself new clothes and shoes. The truth is, if I lose my job, I risk destitution."

Isabelle doesn't argue; she just listens.

"Can you imagine how I came to work here in the first place?" I ask.

She shakes her head.

And then I tell Isabelle my story. I tell her about my father and his plans for me with the village butcher, about the excitement of running away, the grueling search for work, my garret room and the soul-crushing first visit to the agency. I can feel my eyes fill with tears. "I had to return to the agency. I had no choice."

Isabelle reaches out and touches my arm. "It's not right, Maude," she says softly.

"It's not your fault people are vain and cruel," I murmur.

A young couple takes a seat at the table next to us and I try to pull myself together, wiping my tears away.

We're both silent for some time. Isabelle stares down at her cup of tea. Then she breaks the silence with a sigh. "I have to get back home soon. Geneviève is waiting in the carriage. Mother thinks we're shopping for my trousseau. Why she would believe me, I don't know." But still, she doesn't make any move to leave.

"That means the wedding is still going ahead, then?" I ask. I hate to think of it.

She nods. "In July, supposedly."

"What about the Sorbonne?"

She shrugs. "Those dreams don't exist anymore." She sounds numb.

This makes me sadder than anything. After everything that happened, the countess wins. "There must be a way," I say. "Can't you sit the *baccalauréat* exam and just see what happens? All isn't lost, surely."

"The exams are next month. It's too late, Maude," she says, resigned.

She pushes her chair back. But before she gets up, she hesitates and says, "If you like, I could come and see you again. Durandeau doesn't know who I am, and I have money to spend." With those simple words, a sliver of hope is restored to my heart. Maybe there's a chance at rescuing something of our friendship.

"I'd like that," I say.

She nods. "Very well, then. The Durandeau Agency has a new regular client." Her smile is perfect mischievous Isabelle.

# Chapter 35

Life appears, on the outside, at least, to have returned to normal. I have been on some undemanding dates with a variety of midlevel clients, as well as weekly outings with Isabelle. I have persuaded her to sit the *baccalauréat* exams in May, to prove to herself, even if to no one else, that she is capable of attending university.

Our friendship strengthens a little more each time we see each other, but we both dread our uncertain futures: our lives are out of our control. Meanwhile, the countess is content that Isabelle is showing a newfound interest in shopping.

Paul is on my mind; he is the one person I have to speak to and try to make amends with. I just haven't been able to find the courage. He is swirling through my thoughts as I eat lunch in the agency dining room with Marie-Josée.

"Did you hear Laurent is leaving the agency?" Marie-Josée asks me. "He's going to manage a hotel in the South."

"Leaving? That's disappointing." I push away my plate. The boiled ham is tough and chewy. "I suppose that makes sense. He's good with people. But I don't like the idea of the agency without Laurent."

Marie-Josée nods. "He's been here since the beginning. One less friendly face, isn't it."

"Do you think it's a sign?" I ask. "Laurent is smart. You think he's leaving a sinking ship?"

"It's possible."

"Could the repoussoir thing be just a craze, a fashion that won't last?"

Girard suddenly looms at our table. "Maude, Marie-Josée, Monsieur Durandeau would like to speak with you both in his office."

"We're almost finished," says Marie-Josée, nodding toward her lunch.

Girard taps the table with her finger. "Now!"

I exchange a look with Marie-Josée as we push our chairs back and follow Girard out of the dining room, along the hall to Durandeau's private apartments. Since I lost the Dubern contract and he didn't fire me, Monsieur Durandeau scares me less. Right now, I'm not filled with the same sense of dread I used to feel when summoned by him.

When we arrive in his office, he is seated behind his desk wearing yet another new suit and fiddling with the rose in his buttonhole.

On the chaise longue that's positioned along the wall perpendicular to his desk, my eyes meet a curious sight—my belongings (boots, hat and coat) as well as Marie-Josée's are strewn across it.

Durandeau looks up and we stand at attention in front of the large desk, so vast and empty it reveals how little he has to do with his time. I doubt the inkwell has been opened in weeks. Girard stands just to the side and behind Durandeau to get a good view of whatever dressing-down we are about to receive.

"I'll put it simply," Durandeau begins. "One of you has committed a crime against the agency, and one of you shall pick up her belongings after this little chat, leave the establishment and never return."

I look across at Marie-Josée, trying to confirm that she's as shocked as I am. The familiar feeling of fear in the face of authority returns and swarms in my chest.

He turns to his second in command. "Madame Girard, if you would present the evidence."

Girard eagerly makes her way to the chaise longue, and from under Marie-Josée's shawl, she pulls out the countess's sable fur mantle and brandishes it as far as her arms will stretch. I glance at Marie-Josée. Why would she be so foolish as to bring it back to work? She looks at me apologetically.

"Madame Girard informed me some time ago, after doing a thorough inventory of the Countess Dubern's wardrobe, that this item was missing. Instead of jumping to the conclusion it was the fault of Mademoiselle Pichon, she encouraged me to wait until we had proof."

Girard chimes in, "Marie-Josée, I found this item among your belongings when I was doing my routine inspection of the dressing room this morning. Do you have anything to say to defend yourself?"

"It's not her fault," I begin, but Marie-Josée speaks over me.

"It was me. I took it from the special wardrobe weeks ago."

"No," I protest. My heart starts pounding. "Fire me, it's my fault."

"Mademoiselle Pichon," says Durandeau. "You are already in enough trouble, having to work off your debt to the agency for botching the Dubern job. I don't doubt you had a hand in it. But for simplicity's sake, Marie-Josée"—he points at her—"you are dismissed as of this moment. Mademoiselle Pichon, your debt to the agency increases with this second blight against your name."

I look in horror from Durandeau to Marie-Josée. She gives me a weak smile. There's no bravado or jokes. She doesn't throw a hand on her hip or deliver any comeback. She's suddenly vulnerable, and I can only watch in silence as she picks up her belongings and leaves the agency for good.

# Chapter 36

There is unease in the agency ranks since Marie-Josée was fired: tears, temper tantrums and general bickering. I hadn't realized until now that she was the linchpin holding us all together. Without her mother hen influence, the repoussoir spirit can only be crushed a certain amount before it is unable to reshape itself. The rumors of Laurent's departure have also been confirmed. The question everyone is too scared to ask: who will be the next to go?

Having Isabelle know the truth about the agency has reminded me of the humiliation and disgust I felt the first day of my interview. And now, with Marie-Josée gone, I feel encouraged to act. The seed of an idea popped into my head the day she was sacked, and it has grown into a fully formed plan. But first I must talk to my colleagues. Their jobs are at stake, so I won't go ahead unless we are all in agreement.

A client has pushed back her selection appointment by an hour, and most of the girls are gathered in the dressing room with time to kill. Now is the right moment, I think.

"Who loves her job?" My question is met with quizzical looks and a snort or two.

"Who genuinely takes pride in her job and feels good at

the end of each week, with the money she has earned?" I scan the somber faces looking back at me.

Silence. "No one?"

I am just getting started, but I can sense that my question has grabbed their attention. The other conversations have died down, and they're all looking at me. I feel self-conscious, but I decide to stand up. I might as well embrace everything I'm about to say.

"Does anyone have an alternative way of making a decent living?" I ask.

There's a moment of silence before Emilie says, "My uncle might be able to get me a factory job in Dijon."

All heads turn to her, which makes her look down at her lap and smooth her dress nervously. "I'll admit I don't think I can do *this* for another season." She looks up again and blinks guiltily; her big dark eyes are serious, after her confession.

"But the money is good here. How will you earn as much?" asks Cécile.

"I don't much care about money, as long as I can live. I'll have my self-respect. It won't be as hard to look at myself in the mirror every night."

Murmurs of surprise echo throughout the room.

"Ladies." I call for their attention again. I look at each of my colleagues, one at a time. "My question for all of you is: what are your dreams?"

They meet this question with puzzled looks.

I continue, "I don't know about the rest of you, but I feel that working this job has been holding me back, making me think less of myself and what I'm capable of."

I can see the flash of recognition when I say these words.

"What's your dream, then, Maude?" Cécile asks, trying to challenge me.

"To learn how to take pictures properly." The words that escape my lips are as much a surprise to me as anyone else. "Maybe get a job in a professional studio that takes portraits." I have never admitted this secret desire to myself, let alone another person.

"What about the rest of you? What are your dreams?" I ask again, looking around the room at each of them. For once, the girls can't find their voices.

"Come on. You want more than this, surely." I gesture to our surroundings. "Or do you think only beautiful people get to live life, pursue their dreams and fall in love?"

You could hear a pin drop, the room is so quiet. But there is a pulsing energy; I can feel it.

To everyone's surprise, Cécile answers first. "I want to be an actress," she says, almost in a whisper.

I look at the other girls, who are still silent. "Emilie? Is a factory job really your dream in life?"

"No." She shakes her head. "I want to be a writer. I like to watch people in the cafés and make up stories about them."

Hortense chimes in. "Think of the things we've learned— the manners, dress and elocution. We can use those skills for other jobs."

Cécile stands up and addresses the girls. "It's been two seasons I've done this job, and Durandeau and the clients just get worse every week that passes. I can't stomach it any longer. Yes, we've made some good money, but it's time to move on." She raises her hand. "I say we quit."

The chatter rises as the girls talk to their neighbors.

"If we are all in agreement . . . ," I say, fighting to be heard.

"Everyone listen to Maude." The girls obey Cécile and quiet down.

"I have a plan," I tell them. "We are going to bring down the agency."

# Chapter 37

Since the piano recital on New Year's Eve, I have dreaded running into Paul, and now, when I need to speak with him most, he is nowhere to be found. I've tried his apartment, Café Chez Emile and some other bars and cafés in our neighborhood, but it's Friday night and these places are full to bursting; it's not easy to tell one young bohemian from another. The last place I can think to try is the music hall on rue de la Gaîté.

When I walk in the band is playing, and I catch sight of him behind the piano. Now that I've found him, I feel like running away, but I must speak to him. As I fight my way through the crowd to the stage, I'm filled with doubt. How will he react? Is it a good idea to speak to him here?

I squeeze between two drunk women swaying by the stage. I'm glad he's playing; otherwise I worry that he would walk off before I have the chance to say a word. As soon as he lays eyes on me, surprise crosses his face. He quickly covers it with a hard contempt. The expression doesn't suit him.

"Paul, I have something to tell you," I blurt out over the music.

He shakes his head at me. "I'm working!" he shouts.

After the first song he immediately nods to the violinist and accordion player and the band starts playing another tune. I stand waiting by the edge of the stage. Everyone in the band is looking at me except for Paul. Over the din of the music he shouts, "More stories to tell me? I don't want to hear more lies."

"No!" I yell back, desperate to make him listen to me. "I want to tell you the truth. I've been looking for you all over Montparnasse for the past hour—for the past few weeks, if you must know. I want to make my peace with you, Paul. Can you at least hear me out?"

He doesn't respond, but once the song is finished, he gets up from the piano and calls out to the band. "*Pause, dix minutes!*"

Now that he's agreed to listen to me, I feel nervous in his company. We walk toward the bar. "Do you want a drink?" he asks.

I shake my head. "Can we talk outside? It's too noisy in here."

We muscle through the bottleneck of people at the entrance. Paul holds the door open for me and we step into the dark street. April is mild during the day, but the temperature cools at night; I welcome the chilly air, which clears my head and keeps me focused. We wander through the streets, the endless party of our artistic neighborhood. I'm glad of the crowds; their noise and banter breaks the painful silence between Paul and me.

"What do you have to tell me?" He speaks gruffly. He looks straight ahead, his hands in his pockets, as we walk side by side down the street.

I squeeze my eyes shut for a moment, then begin. "There is an agency in Paris. I doubt you've heard of it. It provides a unique service to its clients, who are wealthy women."

I see his eyes flit over to me. My story doesn't begin as he imagined—it doesn't sound like the pitiful excuse he was expecting. Just say it as directly and as simply as possible, I remind myself.

I continue, "The agency rents out ugly women to well-off clients, who use them as an accessory to make themselves look more beautiful by comparison."

Paul slows his pace as he listens.

Keep going, I tell myself. I've rehearsed it a thousand times; I know every word by heart. "In the way a metal foil is placed under a jewel to make it shine brighter, an ugly woman accentuates the beauty of an attractive client. I am one such foil." He glances at me, and I see his look of confusion betrayed by an ever-so-slight shake of his head.

I must credit Girard on her handy definition. It's proved useful when having to explain myself to everyone I've lied to. Paul still hasn't responded, so I finish my speech. "I was embarrassed and ashamed to tell you—to tell anyone, but especially you."

He stops walking and turns to look at me full in the face.

"Preposterous!" he bursts out. "How can you invent such a tale? You're not ugly."

I keep walking, and he follows beside me. I think back to my interview with Durandeau and how he described me to the countess.

"I am neither pretty nor ugly. The agency finds me

perfectly plain," I explain to him. "I am a light ornamentation of plainness, suitable for a debutante. My client was
the girl you saw me with at the recital; her uncle and a
prospective suitor were the men accompanying us. I am no
one's mistress. The fact that you might have thought—"

I can't bring myself to complete the sentence, because
if I do, the lump of shame in my throat will give me away,
and I don't want to cry in front of Paul.

We turn down a quieter side street, walking in silence
until we find a little courtyard framed by apartments. Even
though it's too chilly to sit outside, we take a seat on a
bench, under the yellow light of a streetlamp. Tree branches
shiver in the lamplight and make shadows of spring leaves
on Paul's coat.

He studies me, bemused. I didn't expect him to find my
tale funny. Again he shakes his head quizzically, as if trying
to find the right words. "Ugliness as a commodity for sale?
How perfectly abominable—what gross and indecent people
are these clients?"

"Oh, you'd be surprised." I laugh. "The cream of Paris
society. Renting a repoussoir has become quite the craze
this season."

He's silent for a few moments, staring at me intently.
"But they have it all backward." He reaches toward my face,
cupping my cheek in the palm of his hand. "You are lovelier
than any person I have met in this City of Light. You are
truth and honesty and imagination and, yes, beauty. And a
rich woman, dripping in jewels and silks with painted lips
and curled locks, is but a foil for your purity and strength
of character. *She* is the repoussoir, to your loveliness."

He keeps his hand on my face, draws me close to him and kisses me gently on the lips. I close my eyes and feel my stomach swirl and my heart leap, and I lean into him and kiss him back.

I have never been kissed before. After it happens, Paul's eyes study my face for what feels like a long time, and I want to hide. Despite his kind words, I'm not ready to be scrutinized. Thankfully he kisses me again and I learn my first lesson on the subject: it's easier to be kissed than to be looked at—kissing means your eyes are closed.

We walk back to the music hall hand in hand. I feel woken up from the last few months. I realize that I never did see myself as ugly until I became a repoussoir. Perhaps now I can see myself the way Paul sees me, the way I used to see myself, the old me, that true friend whose presence I haven't felt in so long. I squeeze Paul's hand, hoping that he has led me back to myself.

Later that night, after Paul has returned to work, after he has been yelled at by his band members and the manager, after he has finished his set and we are enjoying a quiet drink—it is then when I show him the photograph.

He studies the faces of my colleagues. "They're not the fairest faces I've seen," he admits. He smiles and I swat at his arm.

"You're going to help us."

He lifts his eyes from the photograph. "How?"

"Get in touch with Claude. Give him the photograph and tell him I have a story for his newspaper—a good story."

# Chapter 38

I sit on a terrace at a café near Montparnasse station. I open the newspaper on my lap to read the latest installment of *L'affaire Durandeau: l'agence des belles-soeurs*, as the press has named it. The agency has become the scandal of Paris. Claude's first article appeared on a Monday in *Le Figaro*. It caused a sensation with its cutting analysis of Durandeau and his operation. He followed it up with another the same week in which he blasted the whole of French society for helping to create a demand for such an abhorrent trade, declaring that society itself had descended beyond the shallow to the immoral.

By the end of that week the repoussoirs had become famous; the clients, infamous. Many a rich family was forced to combat a damaging reputation by trying to distance themselves from their association with the agency and its services. Unfortunately for them, the journalist's sources were detailed and extremely incriminating. I had provided Claude with a client roster containing names, addresses and even the details of each customer's physical preferences (all record of the Dubern family removed). The repoussoirs themselves have been sought for interviews, portraits and caricatures; many have even been offered new jobs by a host of different businesses hoping to cash in on their fame. The public sees them as heroic martyrs, trodden down by a morally bankrupt upper class.

Alongside that first article, an illustration was published above the caption *In Paris, is everything for sale?* It was made from the photograph I'd taken with such reluctance, using the last of the plates Isabelle had given me. She helped me develop the print I gave the newspaper. As the photographer, I was of course not in the picture, and I am happy to have been able to escape the attention of journalists and the public.

In this way, Isabelle's reputation, and that of her family, remains intact. Only Isabelle, her mother and Madame Vary know the truth about my role in the Paris season that winter.

"Sorry I'm late." I look up to see Isabelle out of breath and laden with a pile of books. She dumps them on the table. My coffee cup dances in its saucer. "You were right," she says. "That bookshop has amazing titles."

I fold my paper. "Do you want a coffee first?"

She shakes her head. "Let's get this over with."

I pick up the top half of the stack of books and Isabelle grabs the rest.

The Dubern carriage is waiting for us just around the corner, and the driver helps us with Isabelle's purchases.

Once the carriage door is shut, Isabelle looks at me. "Are you ready to face her?"

"As ready as you are." I smile.

I haven't seen the Countess Dubern since the night before I was banished from the duke's chateau. The carriage rolls along past the station toward the Right Bank.

"Is that today's paper?" Isabelle asks.

"Yes—still front-page news. Listen." I read the headline out loud to her.

## Durandeau's Name Is Mud— ## Agency Shuttered and Reputation Ruined

She smiles. "You did it, then."

I return her smile. "We all did it."

We have the carriage top down, and in the distance I can see a train winding its way out of Montparnasse station. The train I took to Paris last September soared through the French countryside, carried by winged horses, hidden in the swirls of steam outside my window. I watch as the train disappears into a tunnel. I'm never going back home.

When we arrive at the Duberns' cream-colored house, Isabelle puts her books on a table in the entrance hall and we walk up the curving staircase toward her mother's private sitting room. Again and again we have gone over what Isabelle will say.

The countess is taking afternoon tea and reading the fashion bulletins when we burst in. She freezes, a half-eaten chocolate in her mouth.

"*L'Affaire Durandeau.*" Isabelle flings the paper on her mother's chaise longue. "You do read the papers, don't you, Mother?"

"How dare you bring that *person* into our home, Isabelle!" says the countess, propping herself up on the couch and putting down her box of chocolates.

Isabelle ignores her mother's protest and continues, "It

would be social suicide for the family name to be mixed up in such a scandal. There are journalists hounding everyone who worked at the agency. Isn't that right, Maude?"

My pulse races as I nod.

Isabelle continues, "They're ravenous for details of the privileged classes run amok."

The countess folds her arms and flares her nostrils. She understands the power of her daughter's position immediately. "What does she want for her silence?" She looks directly at Isabelle, as though I'm not here. "Money, jewels?"

Isabelle reflects on this for a moment, enjoying having the upper hand. "Maude wants nothing from you." She throws her head back slightly as she gives her mother the ultimatum. "But I'm going to break off my engagement to Monsieur de Rochefort. You will have the announcement published in the society pages this week."

The countess raises an eyebrow.

"And . . . ," Isabelle continues.

"And?" the countess repeats.

"Mother, you will be delighted to hear that I passed my *baccalauréat* and have applied to the Sorbonne. I require your support, financial and otherwise, upon my acceptance."

The countess shakes her head. Her eyes narrow; her lips disappear into a tight frown.

"Well?" Isabelle asks. "Are we in agreement?"

Her mother shrugs, then holds her head up high, her nose in the air. "If you want to ruin your prospects and become a laughingstock, I suppose I am powerless to stop you."

Isabelle and I exchange a look of triumph. Before we turn to leave, I fire the parting shot in as grave a tone as I can manage. I lack Isabelle's air of defiance. She's better at this than I.

"Countess, should you take any action to contradict our agreement, I won't hesitate to sell my story of the inner workings of the Dubern marriage game to the journalist willing to pay most for it."

The warning has the required effect. "Get out," she snarls. "Both of you!"

We leave the room with smiles spreading across our faces. The queen has fallen.

# Chapter 39

In my childhood home, every commonplace item had a life and a personality of my invention. Some were friends—the kitchen table, the wooden stool, the fat kettle—and some were foes—the hat stand, tall and ominous, my parents' wardrobe, with its sharp corners and dark wood.

I write a real letter to my father, the first communication he's had from me since I left months ago. As I imagine him in the kitchen reading the letter, it is through the eyes of an adult that I take in these objects that make up the fabric of my childhood.

I review what I have written—just the essentials. I have a job at a photography studio. I am in good health and hope the same for him. There's no point in sharing more than that with my father. A decent wage, a respectable position is all that he cares about, not my experiences or my new passion for photography.

I enclose a portion of the money I owe him, which I've scraped together, as well as a photograph I took of a street scene in Paris—not a tourist attraction or a view, just people watching a street boy juggle. I don't know that he'll appreciate it. My mother would have. She would have enjoyed looking at the crowd's expressions as they watched the balls fly high in the air; she would have wondered about each of the people and imagined something about their lives. She had that curiosity about the world.

It changes you, losing someone so important as a child. I had no mirror of love telling me I was beautiful or special and could achieve anything. After my mother died, that mirror was gone. And I lived without that echo of love and confidence until I found it, once more, in Paris.

In my mind I walk along the beach as I used to. My simple pleasures and secret places seem immature and quaint to my Paris eyes. For what I know is possible has stretched too far to be able to fit back into the little nook of home.

# Chapter 40

As the aristocracy does, the bourgeoisie follow. People of means have left the heat of Paris for the ocean breeze or rolling hills of summer homes. But Paris isn't empty, as thousands of tourists have descended upon it for the Exposition Universelle. Claude, like many Parisians, has fled to escape the crowds, as well as the heat, and he has lent Paul his elegant townhouse in the 7th arrondissement for the duration of the summer.

My job at the photography studio is part-time, for now. At first I just served the customers and rang up their purchases. But since the owner discovered I know more than counting change and wrapping packages, once in a while he has let me loose in his darkroom to process customers' photographs, and he has begun to let me assist in the portrait sessions. Winning his trust is slow work, but I know I'm proving myself. Everything he shows me, I jot down in the notebook Isabelle gave me, and at night I reread my notes with a sense of delight and determination.

I visit Paul on my days off. I usually find him composing in Claude's sitting room, where there is a piano and space enough for his pacing. His fragments of composition, bars of music repeated, interrupted, then changed, are the accompaniment to my own acts of creation.

My mornings at Claude's are spent in the glass house and outside in the garden, where the light is brightest. After lunch, I develop my plates in the coal shed in complete darkness. Groping in the blackness seems an appropriate metaphor for the creative life. You are compelled to do this work but cannot know the end result; the truth of the moment you captured on the plate remains a mystery. You feel in the dark for the edge of the basin and the plate itself. I love this moment. The hope that I channel into each effort reaches its peak in those dark moments of mystery when the bow of the unseen connects with the taut string of my spine and sends a shiver the length of my back, not of fear, but of possibility. This time, I might have it. This time. This photograph.

I've been working on making prints of my former colleagues, each of them living a new life, which I have documented with a portrait. Marie-Josée and her sister opened a café with savings from the *Belles-Soeurs* interviews she did after the story broke. Marie-Josée is pleased as punch with the modest establishment and is already on first-name terms with the regulars. Paul helped Cécile get a position at the theater. She's not acting, she's selling programs, but with her force of character and lustful designs on the actors, I have a feeling she'll go far. And Emilie, with Claude's help, is working as a clerk at the newspaper.

In the afternoon, when the sun beats into the sitting room and disturbs Paul at the piano, he joins me in the garden. He lies in the sun and I sit in the shade. Sometimes we talk about our projects; mostly we think, each of us lost in our creative endeavors.

Today the sun is golden; the air is heavy and sweet as we doze in the garden after lunch. I watch a sparrow peck at crumbs on the warm flagstones and feel a sense of total contentment. My mind can't rest there long; it flits to the last photograph I took of Isabelle—standing in front of the science building of the Sorbonne. It was the day she received her letter of acceptance and was awarded a place, the only woman scholar in her year. I have one print and she has the other. In taking that photograph, I understood something I will never forget: how I wished to arrest all the beauty that came before me. Not the classical beauty of symmetry and exact proportions or the fancy of fashion, which is ever-changing with the seasons, but the beauty of a soul, that inner life that reveals itself so seldom, just for an instant, and only if you look closely and learn to see with an open heart.

Using the camera as my tool, I hope to find that elusive inner light in the subjects I photograph, both people and places, and to really see—see the truth and beauty of an instant. The fact that I myself am not considered beautiful is irrelevant. Or maybe it is necessary that I not be the object of flattery and homage. Because how would I have the capacity to observe and to see as an artist must, if I myself were to draw your eye? With photography, as with any art, you are given the gift of connection, when you can say to a stranger, "Look! I have something to tell you, I have something to say."

Perhaps one day my photograph will be taken, my

likeness painted or a word written about me by someone who can see into my soul and tell you something of it.

I look at Paul from the clarity of the shade. "We're going to go see it today," I tell him.

"I'm too lazy and it's too hot out." He keeps his eyes closed, and I notice the sun is turning his ears red.

I shake my head. "It will be cooler later on. I want to see it finished."

Eiffel's tower is complete. Its body is elegant yet strong, by day an iron giraffe, proud and soaring high above us, and at night a beacon of light. I hope when the novelty fades that the tower will remain standing. I want its unconventional beauty to endure.

The sun is almost setting when Paul and I are finally standing in line for one of the elevators hidden inside each of the hulking metal legs. My stomach lurches as we soar upward in the crush of people. There are many attractions at the Exposition Universelle: Edison's phonograph, the *galerie des machines* and even an exhibit of an Egyptian village. But it is Eiffel's tower that people line up for, visiting multiple times.

We step out of the elevator onto the platform of the second level. Only halfway up and we already have a bird's-eye view. The sky is marked with sorbet colors. And my heart stops as I draw breath. Paris: my city, with all of its beauty and possibility extending as far as I can see.

This is my time, my beautiful era, my *belle époque*.

# Author's Note

I was inspired to write *Belle Époque* after reading a short story called "*Les Repoussoirs*" by Emile Zola (1840–1902). First published in 1866, Zola's story describes a businessman named Durandeau opening a fictional agency of beauty foils. To me the concept seemed as relevant today as it was in Zola's time, and I couldn't help but imagine what it would be like to be one of those girls. Unable to get the idea out of my head, I eventually created my own characters and a story about one girl in particular, Maude Pichon.

I chose to set this story more than twenty years after "*Les Repoussoirs*" took place in the period of autumn 1888 to summer 1889. At this point France was a new republic and had undergone a period of change and upheaval—the fall of the Second Empire, the siege of Paris and a deadly uprising. By 1888 the city was preparing to host the Exposition Universelle, which would put Paris back on the map as a cultural and now technological center.

The Eiffel Tower was instrumental to the Exposition's success. As I researched its construction, I became intrigued by the fact that at the time—and for many years after—Eiffel's tower was decidedly unpopular with many Parisians, including some famous artists and architects. It's hard to believe now that they considered it ugly—a monstrosity, even. The building of this controversial tower, now the most recognizable symbol of the city, became the perfect historical event against which to set *Belle Époque*.

The art of the period was key to creating this Paris of my imagination. Henri de Toulouse-Lautrec was an artist and a contemporary of Zola. Depicting venues from the bars and music halls of Montmartre to the racetrack and the circus, Toulouse-Lautrec drew and painted popular life, its pleasures and its dark side. There is an unvarnished quality to his work, an immediacy that instantly transported me to the era. I found that in his exaggerated, caricature-like figures I could recognize the repoussoirs themselves. Themes of beauty and ugliness were likely central in his work because of his own physical deformities—a series of accidents as a child, combined with a genetic condition, left him a cripple. He told his friend and frequent subject, the famous singer Yvette Guilbert, that "Everywhere and always ugliness has its beautiful aspects; it is thrilling to discover them where nobody else has noticed them."

The 1880s was also an exciting time for photography. New techniques and innovations made it possible for amateurs to explore the medium. And although she was active decades earlier, the English photographer Julia Margaret Cameron influenced how I felt Maude would connect with this art form. "I longed to arrest all the beauty that came before me" is how Cameron described her passion for photography; her words directly inspired a line in the book. That she preferred to capture beauty rather than be considered a beauty herself was an important discovery for my main character and helped shape her story.

This brings me back to the theme of beauty, as coveted an attribute in 1880s Paris as it is today. What is considered beautiful has changed since those days, just as current tastes will change. What endures transcends fashion. For in every era it is the artists who show us, through their acts of creation and discovery, that beauty truly lives in the heart.

# Acknowledgments

I'd like to first thank my editor, the sensational Krista Marino—her talent, passion and guidance made this dream a reality. A huge thank-you to Beverly Horowitz, who, as a fellow Francophile, shared Krista's faith in this book. I am appreciative of the whole Delacorte Press team, including designer Stephanie Moss and copy editor Colleen Fellingham.

My agent, Brenda Bowen, is the classiest lady in publishing, and I'm so fortunate to have her vast experience and excellent taste guiding my career.

Beth Ann Bauman was an early champion of Maude's journey, and I benefited from her unparalleled knowledge of story and craft.

I owe an enormous debt to my critique group for their time and support. In particular, I'm grateful to Hilary Hattenbach and Lilliam Rivera, talented writers and treasured friends. Thanks to Paula Yoo for her inspiring class. I also want to thank the stellar organization SCBWI, especially Kim Turrisi, who helped my manuscript get into the right hands.

*Merci* to Laura Davies for her insider's guide to Paris during my research trip. Thank you to Jennifer Côté for the fabulous author photo.

Thank you to my family and friends, especially my parents. My father's passion for story, both in literature and film, and my mother's appreciation for language and all things French were invisible gifts I reaped without knowing.

Lastly, thank you to my husband, Shane . . . none of this would be possible without you.

# Elizabeth Ross

Elizabeth Ross grew up in Scotland where she studied French and Film Studies at the University of Glasgow. After graduation she worked in the film industry in Montreal for several years, becoming a film editor. That career path eventually led to Los Angeles where she now lives with her husband. BELLE ÉPOQUE is Elizabeth's debut novel, and she is currently at work on a new novel set in 1940s Los Angeles. Follow Elizabeth at: www.elizabethrossbooks.com or on Twitter: @RossElizabeth